THE INFINITE MOMENT OF US

Amulet Books
New York

Lauren Myracle

the infinite moment of us

PUBLISHER'S NOTE: This is a work of fiction. Names, characters, places, and incidents are either the product of the author's imagination or are used fictitiously, and any resemblance to actual persons, living or dead, business establishments, events, or locales is entirely coincidental.

Library of Congress Cataloging-in-Publication Data

Myracle, Lauren, 1969–
The infinite moment of us / by Lauren Myracle.
pages cm
Summary: As high school graduation nears, Wren Gray is surprised to connect with gentle Charlie Parker, a boy with a troubled past who has loved her for years, while she considers displeasing her parents for the first time and changing the plans for her future.
ISBN 978-1-4197-0793-3 (hardback)
[1. Dating (Social customs)—Fiction. 2. Love—Fiction. 3. Family life—Georgia—Fiction. 4. Assertiveness (Psychology)—Fiction. 5. Atlanta (Ga.)—Fiction.] I. Title.
PZ7.M9955Inf 2013
[Fic]—dc23
2013017135

Book design by Maria T. Middleton

Printed and bound in U.S.A.
10 9 8 7 6 5 4 3 2 1

115 West 18th Street
New York, NY 10011
www.amuletbooks.com

For Jerome and Ginger

CHAPTER ONE

It was all ending: high school.

It was all beginning: everything that came next.

This was true for every senior at Atlanta's Southview High School, not just Wren. And every senior would be setting off on his or her own path, and every senior's path would be different, so there were no earth-shattering surprises there, either. Still, Wren's situation was unusual, or at least she suspected it was.

She didn't always trust her own opinions, however, probably because her parents were so invested in doing her thinking for her. "Of course you like grapefruit juice," her mom said to her just this morning, drawing back in dismay after Wren said she'd prefer coffee, please. "You've always liked grapefruit juice. It's your favorite. I got it especially for you, fresh-squeezed, as a treat for the last day of school."

Wren drank the juice, ashamed of herself for complaining. Except Wren hadn't actually complained, had she? She'd just said, "No thanks. I don't really like grapefruit juice." Because she didn't—did she?

Her dad stayed out of the grapefruit juice discussion, but he had plenty to say on other topics, such as her plans for the future. Particularly her plans for the future. Wren's body felt heavy, and she wished that her friend Tessa, who was giving Wren a ride to school, would keep driving and never turn back.

But that was a fantasy. Tessa couldn't solve Wren's problems for her. If Wren wanted to change her life, then she was the one who'd have to make it happen.

Tessa pulled into the seniors' parking lot and turned off the engine. She finger-combed her long blond hair, swiped a coat of shiny lip gloss over her lips, and grinned at her reflection in the visor mirror. She slapped the visor shut.

"You ready?" she said to Wren.

"Sure," Wren said. Her gut clenched. "No—wait."

Tessa stopped smiling. She'd been Wren's best friend

since second grade, so she knew a bit about the ins and outs of Wren's home life. "What's up? Everything okay?"

"No, yeah, everything's fine," Wren said. "It's just . . . my mom made a special breakfast this morning. Bacon, eggs, and biscuits."

Tessa tilted her head.

"The biscuits were made from scratch. She used a heart-shaped cookie cutter."

"Ah," Tessa said.

"Oh, and grapefruit juice, because that's my favorite."

"What? You hate grapefruit juice."

"I know," Wren said, feeling a wash of relief.

Tessa searched Wren's expression. Occasionally, over the years, kids had teased Wren about what an "only" Wren was. Meaning an only child. Meaning that Wren, as an only child, seemed more sheltered than most kids. She was a people pleaser, a do-gooder, a worrier. She was too much of a watcher, not enough of a doer. Those were Wren's offenses.

Tessa had been to Wren's house, though. She knew Wren's mom and dad, so she knew that Wren's behavior was a product of more than being an only child.

"They think you're part of them," Tessa once said about Wren's parents. "Like a leg, or a spare arm. It's *weird*."

"I know," Wren said. "But they love me."

Tessa, who had two older brothers and lived with a

rush-about mom, had muttered, "A little too much, if you ask me."

Now, sitting in the high school parking lot, Tessa said, "You haven't told them?"

Wren shook her head. Way back in January, she'd been admitted early decision to Emory, the prestigious university where her mom worked. Then, in March, she found out she'd been awarded a merit scholarship. Her parents were over the moon.

"You can come home every weekend," her mom exclaimed. "Or we can come to you. Weekdays, too, if you feel like a home-cooked meal. Whatever you want, sweetheart."

But a week ago, Wren withdrew her acceptance agreement. She didn't know where she'd found the courage, but it felt good. Forget that, it felt great. Only, she kind of hadn't shared the news with her parents yet—the part about Emory or the bit about what she planned to do instead.

"My stomach hurts," Wren told Tessa. She frowned, trying to figure out what other emotions she might be feeling. "I *am* excited, though."

"About finally being free?" Tessa said. "You should be excited. God, you deserve to be." A friend of Tessa's rapped on the hood of Tessa's car, and Tessa waved. Kids streamed past them, laughing and talking. "Go with that, okay?"

"Okay," Wren said, glad when her voice stayed steady. "Thanks, Tesseract. Although you do know that there's no such thing as a tesseract."

Tessa laughed at Wren's slightly mangled version of the quote, which was from Wren's favorite novel, *A Wrinkle in Time*. A tesseract was a four-dimensional cube, which, by definition, couldn't exist in the three-dimensional world. In the novel, a tesseract was used as a shortcut through time, which, by definition, also couldn't exist in the real world.

Wren liked impossible things, though. Wren thought that Tessa, who flitted through life like a hummingbird, was an impossible thing. Tessa came across as go-go-go and all toe-bouncing high energy, but underneath her party-girl exterior, she had a wise and loyal heart. She came as close to knowing the real Wren as anyone ever had.

"No such thing as me?" Tessa said, gesturing like a game-show hostess at the physical proof of her existence. She looked adorable in a pink cami and cutoffs. "I think you're mistaken. So, shall we go greet our adoring fans?"

Wren smiled. "*Your* adoring fans? Let's do it."

They joined the throng of kids strolling toward the building. The warm spring air tickled Wren's legs, bare beneath her white skirt, which grazed the tops of her knees. The pressure in her lungs loosened.

"Can you believe it?" said Delaney, a drama club friend

who was off to New York in the fall. "Can you believe we're seriously done?!"

"Hells no," Tessa replied. "And yet here we are!"

Shaniqua Stewart bounded over and draped her arm over Wren's shoulders. "Hey, girl. You psyched about Emory?"

Wren smiled self-consciously. Shaniqua was one of her honors-track buddies. "Are you psyched about Princeton?" she shot back. "You're probably packed already, huh?"

Shaniqua laughed. To Tessa, she said, "And you. Don't go too crazy at Georgia—except, what am I saying? Of course you will."

Tessa blew her a kiss. At the end of August, Tessa would head to the University of Georgia with almost half their senior class.

"Tessa! Wren!" Owen Bussell shouted, making a megaphone out of his hands. Owen was the class valedictorian. On Saturday, at their graduation, he'd be giving a speech. "You're looking fine, ladies!"

"Right back atcha, O," Tessa called. "Don't bore us on Saturday!"

"I'll do my best," he said.

A group of girls spread the news about a party P.G. Barbee was hosting on Saturday night. "Y'all know P.G., right?" one of them said, and Tessa, with significant innuendo, replied, "Oh, we *know* P.G."

Wren rolled her eyes, because they didn't, really, and Wren had little interest in doing anything to change that. Right now Wren could see P.G. chatting up a freshman girl, who giggled at everything he said. The girl leaned against the wall of the main building, and P.G. stood in front of her, his forearms resting on either side of her like a cage.

P.G. was too slick for Wren's tastes, but he was Tessa's current crush, so it wasn't surprising when Tessa announced, "Hells yeah, we'll be there."

"Excellent," one of the party girls said. "It's going to be epic." She palmed Tessa's hand, and Tessa's feather earrings swayed.

While Tessa chatted with some of her cheerleader friends, Paige Johnson jogged over and said hi to Wren. Paige and Wren had been friends once, way back in elementary school, but they'd gone their own ways long ago. Paige gave Wren a bear hug and whispered, "I want to tell you something, but it might sound strange."

"What is it?" Wren said.

"It's just, I've always looked up to you," Paige said, pulling back and searching Wren's eyes. Her breath smelled like caramels. "Not in a stalker way. I just wanted to tell you that you've always been my role model, kind of."

"Your role model?" Wren said. "Why?"

Paige's eyes widened. "Um . . . you know. Because you have such a sense of purpose. You know yourself."

"I do?"

"You do, yes." *And the moon tugs on the earth, and that's how tides are formed*, her tone suggested. *The earth circles the sun, and that's why we have night and day, and, yes, you know yourself. Are you playing with me?*

Wren didn't understand. Paige was awkward but smart. In fifth grade, she and Wren had done an after-school activity together called Odyssey of the Mind, and for their final competition, they'd put on a skit. Something about pirates? Part of the skit had involved remote-controlled boats and cars, and one of the cars hit a tunnel, but Paige calmly repositioned it and tried again. Their team won first place. It was one of Wren's early tastes of how fun excelling could be.

"Oh," Wren said. "Um, thanks."

Paige pulled her long sleeves over her hands, nodding as she backed away. "Okay, well, I just wanted to tell you that. Anyway. Bye!"

Paige darted off, leaving Wren feeling like a phony. Once upon a time Wren might have been certain of herself, like maybe back in fifth grade, but now she went one way and then another when it came to what she wanted to do with her life. First she was going to go to Emory, then she decided not to go to Emory. She wanted to please her parents, but she was sick of pleasing her parents. She yearned to be her own person, not an extension of her mom and dad, and she longed to do something brave, something that mattered, something that helped others in an immediate and tangible way.

Her desire to escape her color-within-the-lines life *was* as strong as the pull of the moon, even if the lines themselves were muzzy. Was that what Paige saw as her sense of purpose?

She stood there, lost in her thoughts, until a boy from her AP biology class gave her a tentative half wave from across the parking lot, bringing her back to the here and now. A breeze batted at her skirt, flipping it high, and her cheeks grew hot as she clamped it down. Not only because the boy—his name was Charlie—had no doubt glimpsed more of Wren than either he or she expected, but because she realized that in her zoned-out state, she'd been randomly staring at him, possibly for quite a while.

Embarrassment coursed through her. Wren liked Charlie, but she didn't know him that well. He was in a couple of her honors classes. He had a lean, muscular frame, and Wren, on occasion, had caught herself enjoying the play of muscles beneath his shirt. His fingernails were often rimmed with oil, or maybe paint. He rarely talked, and some kids thought he was arrogant. But Wren had watched him interact with his small group of friends, and around them he seemed looser. More relaxed.

Once, Wren had spotted Charlie helping a freshman

with his locker. The freshman was scrawny, one of those unfortunate boys who wouldn't hit his growth spurt for another year or two, if ever. He'd looked close to tears. Charlie hadn't made eye contact with the kid but had twisted the combination lock with deft, sure movements, banged the metal door, and nodded with satisfaction when it sprang open.

Now, yards away in the senior parking lot, Charlie dropped his hand. Now he was the self-conscious one.

She waved back at him and smiled, and relief rippled across his features. Immediately he smoothed his expression, but she'd seen, for a second, what he really felt. She had the strangest urge to go to him and say, *No. Please. Sometimes the things we hide—aren't they the parts of us that matter most?*

Tessa called out to her, and Wren blinked. She started walking, slowly at first, and then faster. She reached Tessa, who hip-bumped her.

"I saw you wave at Charlie," Tessa teased. "Were you two having a moment, nudge-nudge, wink-wink?"

"Yeah, right," Wren said.

"Sweet!" Tessa said. "Is that a yes?"

Tessa had suggested on several occasions that Charlie had a thing for Wren, and she wondered if maybe he did. Her heart beat a little faster.

But no, she was being stupid. Wren was pretty sure

Charlie had a girlfriend, and plus . . . whatever. It was impossible, and not in the good sort of way.

"Let's talk about something more interesting," Wren said. "Don't you think you should go steal P.G. from that freshman—or save that freshman from P.G.?"

That did the trick. Tessa looked where Wren was indicating and scowled at P.G. and the freshman girl. Wren couldn't see P.G.'s face, just the back of his pale blue button-down. He leaned closer to the freshman—his cheek almost brushing hers—and said something that made her turn bright red.

"Really?" Tessa muttered.

The freshman squeaked out another giggle, and P.G. eased back. He turned and saw Tessa and Wren, and his face broke into a grin.

He strode toward them, owning the courtyard. Owning everything. Reeking of entitlement and cologne, which, thanks to his Facebook page, Wren knew was called Czar.

"Tessa Haviland," he said, stretching out her name. "You. Look. Hot."

"Why, thank you," Tessa said. She practically curtsied.

Wren snorted, and P.G. glanced at her. Whoops. He gave her a much quicker once-over than Tessa and nodded. "You look good, too. I approve."

"Oh," Wren said. "Then I guess I can die in peace?"

Tessa hip-bumped her. "*Wren*."

"And I'll leave you to it," Wren said, stepping back to let Tessa loop her arm through P.G.'s. They led the way toward the school, bantering easily, and Wren followed.

When they reached the set of double doors at the building's entrance, Wren paused to fish a Coke out of her backpack for Mr. Cameron, a math teacher who'd been stuck with foot-traffic control all semester. Mr. Cameron was a big guy, and he sweated profusely even when it was chilly out, so one day Wren offered him her drink. She'd planned on having it during her free period, but she could get another.

"Bless you, you are an angel, you have my permission to ditch your classes and go to the movies," Mr. Cameron had said, and a tradition had been born. Every morning, instead of skipping school, Wren tossed Mr. Cameron a Coke, and every morning, Mr. Cameron caught the can neatly and popped it open.

"Thanks," he said now. He took a swig. "I assume you'll swing by tomorrow and Friday? Keep your old buddy caffeinated?"

The underclassmen had to finish up the school week, but not the seniors. After today, the seniors wouldn't return until the graduation ceremony on Saturday.

"Ooh, sorry," Wren said, hating to disappoint him even though she knew he was teasing.

He clasped his free hand to his chest. "So this is it? This is how it ends?"

She winced. "Sorry!"

She was halfway through the doors when he called her name. She turned back.

"Hey," he said. "You're a great kid, Wren Gray. You're going to do great things with your life. Understood?"

There were so many people in the world. Some were jerks, but most were kind. Wren had to clear her throat before she could speak. "Understood."

Ahead of her in the crowded hallway, Tessa bounced from friend to friend. She truly was like a hummingbird, all bright flashes and quick movements. Wren moved to join her, then changed her mind and retreated, leaning against the glass-paned wall of the front office. She closed her eyes. She focused on breathing.

All kinds of big things waited for her right around the corner, all kinds of chances and risks and huge, crazy changes. She was supposed to let the thrill of it all sweep her away. But she was scared.

What happened with Charlie—what passed between them when their guards were down—that scared her, too. The idea of a person's hidden parts mattering most, when she was the one keeping a secret.

In AP English, she'd read a myth about the vastness of

the universe. In it, an old woman told her grandson that the world rested on the back of a giant turtle. "It does? Well, what does the turtle rest on?" the grandson asked, and Wren had read faster, naïvely hoping she was about to be given the answer to life.

But no. The old woman laughed and said, "That's the best part. It's turtles all the way down!"

CHAPTER TWO

When Gray was the most beautiful girl Charlie Parker had ever seen, and the most brilliant. She didn't seem to realize she was either, which was crazy. But Charlie had eyes. Charlie knew the truth.

When she smiled, Charlie wanted in on the joke. When she pushed her dark hair behind her ears, Charlie thought, Yes, that is how you do it. When she walked down the halls in her collared shirts and knee-length skirts, he saw with absolute clarity how much classier she was than the other girls in their tight jeans and peekaboo thongs. Charlie had had some experience with girls in tight jeans and peekaboo thongs, or with one particular girl in tight jeans and a thong. She hadn't left a great impression.

But Wren wasn't like that girl, or any girl, even though she was clearly and definitely a girl. Once, on the senior patio during lunch, she'd lifted her arm to call over her friend Tessa, and her blouse hugged her curves. He drank her in for as long as he decently could.

On Wednesday, Charlie drifted through the last day of classes as if he were in a fog. Everyone else was wired at the prospect of summer, but Charlie didn't want summer. He wanted Wren. But unless he manned up and took action—like exchanging more than half a dozen words with her—he was doomed. Wren would go her own way after Saturday's graduation ceremony, and Charlie might never see her again.

On Thursday, his first official day of no school, Charlie worked alongside his foster dad at the woodworking shop his foster dad owned. He clamped a slab of cream-colored birch onto the workbench and switched on the router, shaping the wood to fit an oddly shaped nook in a client's bathroom. His thoughts stayed on Wren as he rounded the corner of the plank. Her sweet smile. Her shiny hair. The way her brown eyes grew pensive when the end of her pen found its way to the corner of her mouth, suggesting that she was contemplating something important.

One day in AP biology, Wren had argued with Ms.

Atkinson about free will in the face of cellular determinism. It was at the beginning of the semester, but already most of the seniors were starting to tune out their teachers' lectures, and Charlie wondered if that was why Ms. Atkinson had tossed out the sensationally termed "parasite gene," a gene that supposedly triggered a propensity toward exploitive behavior in those who carried it. She encouraged the class to consider what the existence of such a gene might imply—"Is that what drives the president of a company to embezzle funds, or an addict to steal from a family member?"—and while Charlie drew into himself, Wren shook her head in frustration.

"Humans are too complicated to be explained by unraveling their DNA," Wren said. "Aren't they? Otherwise wouldn't our lives have no meaning?"

"Why do you say that?" Ms. Atkinson said.

"Because, okay, say a kid is born with the 'parasite gene,' if there is such a thing. Are you saying he has no choice but to grow up and mooch off others? He'll never contribute anything to society?"

"Nice job of assuming it's a guy," Thad Lundeen had said.

Wren had blushed. "Fine. Sorry. But what if a boy or a girl is born with . . . whatever. A fear-of-flying gene. Does that mean he or she can't grow up to be a pilot? No matter what, end of story?"

Different kids jumped in. The conversation grew loud

and off-track, and Charlie wondered if he was the only one to hear her last comment.

"And what about souls?" she said, bowing her head and addressing her desk. "Don't souls count for anything?"

Her downcast eyes, her pink cheeks—he saw them in his mind still. He held in his brain an entire store of the amazing things she'd done and said. He loved the whole package.

And then, yesterday, when she waved at him outside the school . . .

Something had passed between them. Something he couldn't explain, and it had made him forget that he didn't believe in souls. Anyway, who was he kidding? He didn't believe in love, either, but this he knew: He loved Wren Gray. He'd loved her forever, it seemed.

The router jumped beneath his hands. Ah, shit. He'd turned it up slightly, so that the bit was pointing toward the left rather than straight down, and the webbing between his left thumb and forefinger moved directly into it. *Shit.* Shit, shit, shit. He clamped his T-shirt over the wound, and his foster dad, Chris, glanced over.

"Wassup, Chahlie?" Chris said in his rough Boston accent. He took in the blood soaking through Charlie's T-shirt and put down his rag and can of varnish. He came over and gave Charlie's wound a close, careful look. He whistled. "C'mon, son. Let's get you stitched up."

∞

Grady Hospital was the largest hospital in Atlanta, as well as the fifth-largest public hospital in the United States. It smelled like shit, piss, and body odor. Patients on gurneys lined the ER hallway, since, with more than three hundred patients walking, stumbling, or rolling in each day, there were never enough rooms to go around.

"Just fill this out," a brown-skinned woman told the elderly white woman ahead of them in the long line.

"I'm fine," Charlie told Chris for the fiftieth time. He wasn't, but finances for Chris and Pamela were hard enough without adding on a couple hundred bucks for a drop-in visit to the emergency room. "Really. Let's go."

Chris ignored him, just as he'd ignored him the first forty-nine times.

Charlie sighed and searched fruitlessly for an escape route. At the next desk over, a girl tapped into a computer, head down, as a frizzy-haired woman standing before her complained about a crackling sound when she breathed.

"Don't worry," the girl said. "We'll get you taken care of." She looked up from the computer, and Charlie's blood froze in his veins. Not really; it oozed relentlessly through the towel Pamela, his foster mom, had given him, just as it had since he'd nearly sliced his thumb off. But it felt as if his blood froze, as well as his brain, his heart, and every last muscle in his body.

"Charlie?" Wren said, her expression registering equal shock.

Wren. Behind the desk. At the hospital. Why?

The frizzy-haired woman took her paperwork with a harrumph.

"Charlie," Wren said, beckoning him forward.

Chris approached the desk, relieved. "You know my boy?" he said. "Great, because Chahlie here got into a fight with a router, and if you've ever gotten into a fight with a router, you know who won."

Wren smiled uncertainly. "Ouch," she said. "Well, let me get you into the system. Can I see your driver's license and insurance card?"

Charlie had his license. That was no problem. But he had to look away as Chris patted his pockets and put on a show that they both knew would lead nowhere.

"Insurance card," Chris said. "Sure thing." He pulled out his wallet, a battered and bruised thing that was perhaps once made of leather. "Just give me a minute here . . ."

Wren watched. She bit her lip. She looked at the clock behind her and said, "Oh crap, Rhondelle's going to need her desk back. Her break's just about over." She stood up and came around to Charlie. "But, uh, come with me."

Chris frowned. "'Scuse me?"

Wren grabbed a clipboard. To Chris, she said, "Do you want to have a seat in the waiting room? I'll help Charlie with the forms, and I can come get you when we need you."

Charlie knew his face was a fiery red, but he followed Wren to a tucked-away corner of the reception area. He glanced over his shoulder. Chris looked confused, but he turned and walked toward the waiting room.

Wren sat on a cracked plastic chair and patted the empty chair next to her. Charlie sat.

"Thanks," he said. "Chris, he's not so good at . . . you know . . ." He sighed. He held his left hand, bundled and useless, close to his rib cage and stared at the floor, where a dead cockroach lay beside a vending machine.

"Why don't I fill this out for you," she said, sounding crisp and professional. He suspected she'd put some of the pieces together, such as the fact that Chris wasn't going to find that insurance card. He suspected she'd brought him over here as a way to let Chris off the hook.

"So, you have a job here?" Charlie blurted.

"Not exactly," she said. "I did it for my community-service hours." All Atlanta public school seniors had to complete seventy-five hours of community service. Charlie had fulfilled his through tutoring kids at his brother's middle school. "I finished in March, technically, but . . ."

"Working hard for free seemed like the best way to spend the first day of summer vacation?"

She looked at him strangely. He'd been trying to be funny. Had he sounded rude instead?

"They're always understaffed here," she said. "I like helping out. And it's better than fighting with . . . what's that thing you fought with?"

"A router. And, yes, working here *is* better. Better, smarter—you name it. I think it's cool that you help out just because."

"Oh. Um, thanks. What *is* a router?"

"It's a tool for making furniture. For cutting wood."

"And for cutting flesh?"

"Yeah, but only if you're a dumb-ass."

She smiled slightly, and they held each other's gaze. He still couldn't believe she was here, or that he was here. That they were here together.

Wren gave herself a shake and held the pen over the paper on the clipboard. "Right. So—oh my gosh, I don't know your last name. Crap. I am such a jerk. What's wrong with me?"

"Parker," he said. And nothing's wrong with you, not a single thing.

"Charlie Parker?" She sounded delighted. "Like the musician?"

"I don't know—which is to say no, I guess. Who's Charlie Parker?"

"Well, the *other* Charlie Parker"—she gave him a half smile—"was a famous jazz musician. Not that you should know who he is or anything. I just like jazz. Or, my dad does, and he's in charge of the stereo."

"I think my birth mom just liked the name Charles."

Charlie saw a subtle shift in Wren's expression, leading him to guess that "birth mom" wasn't a term she ran into often. She recovered swiftly. "And her last name was Parker."

"Still is, as far as I know." Except he didn't know and didn't want to know. "So. The other Charlie Parker. What instrument did he play?"

She opened her mouth, then shut it. Then she eyed him as if to say, *Yes, I really am about to do this*, before leaning close and singing a funny tune in a sweet, soft voice. "'Charlie Parker played be bop. Charlie Parker played alto saxophone. The music sounded like hip hop. Never leave your cat alone.'"

He grinned. She giggled. God, she was adorable.

"It's from a book my dad read me when I was little," she said.

"'Never leave your cat alone,' huh?"

"Words to live by."

Again, they gazed at each other. To Charlie, it felt like more than a coincidence that here they were, their thighs inches apart in their crappy plastic chairs, where, in any alternate universe, there was no way their paths would have collided like this.

She cleared her throat and sat up straight. Once more

poising her pen above the clipboard, she said, "Your hand. Can I see?"

He tried not to wince as he unwrapped his left hand, the towel sticking to the webbing between his thumb and forefinger. The gash was deep but not too deep. He felt self-conscious about his fingernails, which were dark around the nail beds from years of staining wood.

Wren gently lifted his hand, turning it this way and that. "I don't think you're going to lose your thumb." She glanced at him. "That was a joke. But you are going to need stitches."

Charlie had expected that. "Will it cost a lot?"

"Not if your dad—" She broke off, and Charlie could see the wheels turning in her head: how he'd called Chris "Chris," how he'd referred to his "birth mom." "Is the man who brought you in your dad?"

"Foster dad," Charlie said evenly.

"He doesn't have insurance?"

Charlie hesitated. "He makes cabinets. He owns his own shop. He has a workers' comp plan, but the insurance people aren't fans of power tools."

"Because in an accident, the power tools always win," Wren said. "And accident reports make the premium go up. Got it."

Actually, the problem was the high co-pays, but close enough. Charlie was surprised that she understood, but then he thought of the overcrowded emergency room and the cockroach on the floor.

Wren stood. "Stay here, okay?"

He tensed, because maybe he'd guessed wrong and she didn't understand. Maybe there were rules she knew about that he didn't. "What for?"

"So that I can . . . so I . . ." She looked at him. "Nothing bad's going to happen. But don't leave, because you *do* need stitches, or your thumb won't heal right. And you need that thumb, I assume? To keep making furniture or cabinets or whatever?"

He gave a terse nod.

She took the top sheet of paper out of the clipboard and folded it in half, then in half again. She put the clipboard on her seat. "Do you promise you'll stay?"

"I promise."

"Do you mean it?" she pressed.

He replied in his lowest, most serious voice: "I don't make promises I don't mean."

Twin spots of color rose on her cheeks, and, as was so often the case, Charlie had no idea what wrong or unusual thing he'd said this time.

She pulled herself together. "Um, good. Just stay here—I'll be right back."

She walked quickly toward what appeared to be a staff break room. When she returned, she carried a battered first aid kit. The first thing she did was very carefully clean his wound, and he winced at the sting of the antiseptic.

"Oh, I'm sorry!" she cried.

"No, please," Charlie said, chagrined that he'd made her doubt herself.

"Are you sure?"

"I'm sure."

She bit her lip.

"I'm sure," he repeated. "And thank you. Really."

Wren proceeded to stitch up Charlie's thumb herself. She cradled his hand in her lap and smoothed on a numbing cream first, and her touch was so gentle that Charlie knew he would gladly suffer a dozen injuries—a thousand—in exchange for this: the feel of her fingers on his, the tug of the thread, the slight pinch of the needle, the intoxicating scent of her as she leaned in close.

"Katya taught me," she told him. She pressed her knees together as she concentrated. When she shifted, the hem of her skirt rode up, revealing a finger's width of her skin. He wanted very much to look down her shirt, too, but he told himself not to. He almost succeeded.

"I think I know Katya," he said. "Russian? Wants to be a pediatrician?"

She glanced at him, baffled. "Yeah, that's her. But how do *you* know her?"

"I've met a lot of a nurses, that's all."

Now her expression was doubly baffled, and he felt like a fool. *I've met a lot of nurses*, as if he were bragging, as if he were some sort of player.

Speak, he told himself. Explain. *Now.*

"I've been here a lot, that's all. The pediatrics ward. That's how I know Katya."

"Why were you in pediatrics a lot?"

God, why had he brought this up? The last thing Charlie wanted was for Wren to be concerned about him. To see him as a charity case, or a charity case by proxy.

"Charlie?" Wren said.

"My little brother's in a wheelchair," Charlie said quickly. "He's fine, but stuff comes up. Like, we were here at the beginning of the year, because—"

He broke off abruptly. He picked back up with, "So, yeah. That's life. Who said life was easy, right?"

He forced a laugh. It was the stupidest laugh of all time. "Just shoot me," he said. "Do you have a tranquilizer-dart gun? A pill to make patients shut up?"

"You don't need to shut up," Wren said. She paused. "Why were you here at the beginning of the year? Does your brother have a chronic illness or something? You don't have to tell me if you don't want to, obviously."

But he did have to tell her. She sounded so worried. She was doing so much for him; he owed her an answer, even if he couldn't give the full answer.

"No chronic illness," he said. "Dev's paralyzed from the waist down, but not from a disease. He's eleven—did I tell you that? He's a sixth grader. He goes to Ridgemont. He's not, like, in some special school or anything. And in January, he . . . got burned. That's why we were here."

"I'm so sorry," Wren said. "How?"

Charlie went inside himself. How? Because two eighth graders cornered Dev in the bathroom of Dev's not-special school. They held a cigarette lighter to his leg. Dev couldn't feel it, but he could smell the burning. He could hear the laughter of the two eighth graders. Dev hadn't shared those details with Charlie, but Charlie had imagined the scene too many times.

"Charlie?" Wren said. She was waiting for him to answer.

"At school," he said. Then he closed himself off. He wanted to talk with Wren, but he didn't want her pity. He didn't want her to pity Dev, either.

She exhaled, then pushed the needle through the skin near the base of his thumb, knotted the thread, and clipped it off. "Now I have to do a row of stitches the opposite way." She peeked at him from beneath long lashes. "You doing okay?"

"I'm fine," he replied. "And Dev, he's doing better these days, too. He's a great kid."

"Is he your biological brother?"

"Nah. He was in the system, like me, until Chris and

Pamela said, sure, they had a spot for him. They're going to officially adopt him." They'd wanted to adopt Charlie, too, but Charlie, for reasons of his own that had little to do with Chris and Pamela, had said no.

"Pamela's your foster mom?" Wren said.

"Yep, she's Chris's wife."

"But you call them your foster parents. How come, when you call Dev your brother?"

"As opposed to foster brother?" Charlie said. He thought about it. It wasn't that he didn't love Chris and Pamela. He did. And they'd done so much for him. It was a debt impossible to repay.

But Dev was different. Though Dev was no more connected by blood to Charlie than Chris and Pamela were, he brought Charlie out of himself in a way that few people in the world ever had, possibly in a way that no one ever had.

"I don't know," he finally said. Dev was his brother. Period.

Wren nodded, seeming to absorb and accept this. "Cool. I think you guys are lucky to have each other." She tied off another stitch. "And in the name of fairness, I should tell you I'm an only. I'd hate to be accused of withholding dangerous intel."

An only? Oh. An only child. As for "dangerous intel," Charlie didn't get the joke. He knew enough to know it *was* a joke, or was meant to be, but he'd learned over time that normal kids spoke a language particular to normal life, the subtleties of which didn't make it into state-run facilities or foster families.

"So 'only' kids are dangerous?" he asked, keeping it light.

"Very," she said gravely. She looked at him, or rather into him, and he felt sure she was telegraphing something that mattered. Something she wanted to give a shape to. Something sad?

She ducked her head and gave a funny smile, and Charlie cursed himself for failing to decode her secret message.

"Oh my God, are you all right?" Wren said.

"What?"

"Your hand," she said, and he realized he must have flinched. Or maybe his fingers had tensed into a fist, or the start of one.

She lay her hand over his, above the area of his wound, and gave him a brief squeeze. Tender, and then gone. Warmth, then cold.

"All done," she said. "Keep it clean. The thread'll dissolve on its own, so you won't need to come back to have the stitches removed. Good news, right?"

Was it? He would have happily come back.

She was acting very polite now. She was packing up the needle, scissors, and gauze, but he wasn't ready to go.

"Wren. You didn't hurt me. You're going to be a really good doctor."

She gave him a startled glance.

"That's what you want to do, isn't it? Be a doctor? You told us in biology."

"I did?"

"Yeah. You applied early decision to Emory because of their pre-med program, and you got accepted, which is amazing. Not that you got accepted. Of course you got accepted. Any college would accept you. They'd be idiots not to."

Wren's eyes were huge, making Charlie wonder if he was the idiot in this situation.

"You should be really proud," he said. "Um, I'm sure you *are* really proud." Her deer-in-the-headlights expression didn't change, making him feel acutely aware of the muscles of his own face, which felt rubbery and no longer within his control. "Aren't you?"

She snapped out of her trance and busied herself with an antiseptic wipe. For a moment, Charlie felt relieved. She wasn't staring at him anymore. He could, and did, work out the kinks in his jaw.

But he doubted that the small square antiseptic package demanded all of Wren's attention, and before long, her reluctance to look at him forced him to open his big dumb mouth again. He didn't want to. He just couldn't help it. Her sad-shaped something had returned, and Charlie couldn't stand it.

"Did you *not* get into Emory?"

She made a sound that was perhaps supposed to be a laugh but didn't fool Charlie.

"Then, what?" Charlie said.

Wren stopped fooling with the antiseptic wipe. Keeping her head bowed, she said, "If I tell you, will you keep it to yourself?"

"Yeah. Of course."

"Do you promise?"

Was she serious? Charlie would promise her anything. The sun, the moon, the stars. "I promise."

Her lips parted. She seemed about to speak but then pulled back. "Oh my God, I'm being ridiculous. I mean, *God*, Charlie. For some reason it feels like I know you, but I don't, and—"

She covered her eyes and pushed on them.

He thought, You feel like you know me? You feel that? About me?

She opened her eyes and gave him a wobbly smile. "Okay, done now," she said. She even managed a laugh. "That was really weird. I am so sorry."

"Don't be," Charlie said, his heart pounding. He glanced at Chris, who appeared to have nodded off in the hard waiting-room chair, then back at Wren. "I know we don't know each other that well. That's what it is. But we *do* know each other."

He struggled to find the right words, and, failing that, he struggled to force out any words.

Charlie understood silence.

He embraced silence.

Silence in the face of sadness made sense to him. It was a survival strategy. But Wren's silence, which clearly wasn't making her happy, was something he could do something about.

"Whatever's going on, I wish you'd tell me," he said.

Wren looked at him. She held his gaze and *saw* him, or that's how it felt, and she whispered, "It's dumb."

"I doubt it."

"You'll think I'm being a baby."

"I won't."

She bowed her head, and a wisp of hair fell from her ponytail. He wanted to brush it back. He wanted desperately to graze her cheek with the back of his hand and swear to her that everything would be fine.

"Please don't tell my parents," she said.

"Okay."

"The only person I've told is Tessa. She's my best friend. She's not entirely thrilled, because she's worried I'll never come back, but she's happy I'm doing what's right for me for once. Well, I hope it's right. I think it is."

Charlie pulled his eyebrows together. He didn't know Wren's parents, and he knew Tessa Haviland only by sight.

And what did Wren mean by "never come back"?

Wren took a deep breath, then let it out in a whoosh. "I don't want to go straight to college. I know I'm supposed to, but I don't want to—not yet. I want to experience things and not just think and think and think about things. Does that make sense?"

Charlie wasn't sure what to say.

"Um, my dad," Wren said. "I love him. I do. But, like, when I showed him my college essay, he pulled my laptop out of my hands and fixed it for me." She looked nervous, as if she was worried she was being disloyal. "He rewrote the whole thing. Which was nice, I guess? But also . . ."

"Not cool," Charlie said.

"Not cool," she agreed. "It's like he wants to do his own life over, through me." She fell silent for a moment. Then she flashed him a smile that Charlie didn't quite believe. "So I applied to a program called Project Unity. And I got in."

"Wren, that's awesome," Charlie said.

"You know what Project Unity is?"

"Um. No. But I—whatever it is, I'm sure it's awesome." Dammit, he'd screwed up. She surely thought he was just saying whatever she wanted to hear, except he meant every word of it.

"What is it?" he said.

"It's like a starter version of the Peace Corps," she said.

"It's a government program for volunteer work, and it's for a year, and all my expenses will be paid. I'll even get a stipend. The volunteers get sent to Africa or Guatemala or Mexico, anywhere people need help. I put Guatemala as my first choice. I applied to teach English to little kids."

"Wow," Charlie said. "Like, with textbooks, or . . . ?"

"The people who run the program have all sorts of resources, but I thought maybe I could bring some picture books, too? Like ones I liked when I was little, and I could read those to the kids?"

She searched his face. "I might still be a doctor one day. But I want to do something now, not in eight years. I kind of feel like I *have* to, or I never will."

He wondered how much her desire to throw herself into Project Unity was tangled up with her need to get away from her parents.

"Did you ever want to go to Emory?" he asked.

She hesitated. "If I say no, will you be mad?"

Mad? Why would he be mad?

"Never mind," she said. "Ha. *I'm* the one who needs to be shot with a tranquilizer gun."

"No, you don't," Charlie said.

"I applied to Emory because that's where my mom works, and it's got a good reputation, and she and my dad were so proud when I got in," Wren said. "But there's just *so much pressure*. I'm sick of all the pressure. I'm sick of feeling like I'll ruin all their happiness if I don't do what they want me to do."

"Got it."

"Which I guess means . . . no, I didn't actually want to go. I feel bad saying that."

"Don't. It's your life, not theirs."

"Right," she said. She nodded. "It is, isn't it?"

Her determination, combined with her sweetness, disarmed him.

"And seriously, doesn't Project Unity sound awesome?" she said. "Tessa doesn't understand why I'd want to live in a developing country, but I'm excited. Going someplace totally new, where you can start fresh and do good things and be whoever you want—doesn't that sound amazing?"

Wren sounded amazing, talking about it. Wren *was* amazing.

Charlie's thoughts went to Starrla Pettit, who was the only other girl in his life, the only girl who served as a point of reference. Except Charlie didn't want Starrla to be his point of reference, and she wasn't in his life, not in that way. Except, she *was* Charlie's—what? What was Starrla to him, exactly?

Ah, shit. Charlie had no idea what he and Starrla were to each other.

But Starrla worked part-time at Rite Aid, and, starting next week, she was going to be bumped up to full-time, with benefits and a regular schedule. Charlie was glad for her. He hoped it worked out. He hoped she didn't screw it up.

Working at Rite Aid—hell, there was nothing wrong with that. If anything, he felt bad that Starrla didn't have the luxury of considering anything else, even if it was unlikely she ever would.

Wren wanted to do more, though. Wren wanted to save the world.

"Forget it," she said before he got around to responding. "You probably think putting off college is impractical, and that going to Guatemala is . . ." She sighed. "You think I'm crazy, huh?"

"No," Charlie said. "I think—" His voice sounded ragged. He shook his head, knowing he was trying too hard but unable to stop himself. "I think you're wonderful."

CHAPTER THREE

On Friday morning, Tessa invited Wren to go with her to a shooting range. To shoot things, with guns. With Tessa and her new crush, P.G. Barbee.

Wren's knee-jerk reaction was to tell Tessa absolutely not, because Wren hated guns. She hated their ugliness, and she hated what they did. Also, she didn't like P.G.

Then again, she'd said no to so many things over the years, often based on someone else's opinion. Wasn't she supposed to be experiencing new things and coming to her own conclusions? Wasn't that what signing up for Project Unity was all about?

"C'mon," Tessa wheedled over the phone. "Who knows? Maybe you'll meet a cute guy."

"At a shooting range?"

"Why not?"

Wren highly doubted she'd meet an appealing guy at a shooting range. Besides, she was already interested in a guy, although she wasn't ready to tell Tessa.

She thought about Charlie Parker, who'd showed up randomly—or perhaps not so randomly?—in the ER yesterday. She didn't think he'd cut his thumb on purpose, or even known he would see her at Grady. But his hand had been warm in hers as she stitched him up, and he'd smelled like pine trees, and being with him hadn't felt random at all.

His eyes were the same shade of auburn as his tousled hair. She'd lost herself in them, because who had auburn eyes?

"So?" Tessa demanded.

"Huh?"

"The shooting range. What do you say?"

"Oh. Um, sure."

"But it'll be so— Wait. What?"

"It's something new to try. I *want* to try new things. Unless you think that's dumb?"

"No!" Tessa said quickly. "Wren! Yay! We are going to have so much fun!"

Wren wasn't sure, but she was willing to give it a chance.

∞

"After you, ladies," P.G. said, using his body to hold open the door to the Sure Shot Shooting Range. In each hand he held a gun case. One contained multiple small pistols. The other case held a huge revolver, which took bullets bigger than Wren's thumb. Bigger than anyone's thumb.

The guns still made Wren feel queasy, but to P.G.'s credit, he'd spent hours teaching Wren and Tessa about gun safety before bringing them here. He took the task seriously, because it turned out that, when it came to guns, P.G. was very serious.

"You're kind of freaking me out," Tessa had said after P.G. explained, point by point, the differences between a handgun, a semiautomatic, and a revolver. "Are you ever going to smile?"

"I am smiling," he'd said without altering his expression. It was the closest thing to a joke he'd made all day.

Before the morning was over, Wren had learned what the different parts of a gun were called and how they worked. She'd learned where to put her trigger finger when holding a gun and where to point the barrel, and she'd learned that, with the exception of hunters, a gun owner's primary goal should be to prevent the loss of life.

"If you choose to bear arms, it should be so that you can defend yourself and those around you," P.G. had explained. "Are there gun nuts out there who do nothing but drink beer and shoot Bambi? Sure, but that's a stereotype. The majority of people who own firearms treat them with enormous respect."

Later, Tessa had waved one of the unloaded pistols around, pretending to be a bank robber, and P.G. had grabbed her wrist and gently but firmly guided her hand down.

"Watch it," he'd said.

"Sorry," Tessa had replied, crinkling her nose.

"Good," P.G. had said. "When you're dealing with weapons, there's no room for mistakes."

Tessa had uncrinkled her nose. "Okay," she'd said in a much smaller voice.

Wren, for one, had been impressed. She could tell that P.G. hadn't been trying to make Tessa feel bad. He'd just wanted her to know that she couldn't be silly if she had a gun in her hand. Oh, except P.G. didn't use the word *gun*. He preferred the term *weapon* or *firearm*.

At any rate, Wren felt surprisingly well-prepared as she followed Tessa into the shooting range. Then she made the mistake of looking around.

"Whoa, this is crazy," Tessa said.

"What you said," Wren replied. She took in the rows and racks and counters and shelves of guns, guns, and more guns before her. Also, ammunition. Also, gun safes, which looked like refrigerators. The safes had oversize price tags on them, which was how Wren knew what they were.

She flipped one of the tags over. HERE'S THE FIRE-RESISTANT GUN SAFE YOU'VE ALWAYS WANTED, AT A PATRIOT-SALE PRICE YOU CAN'T PASS UP! it read in thick black letters. HOLDS UP TO 24 LONG GUNS & PROTECTS THEM FROM FIRE FOR UP TO 30 MINUTES!

"Hey, I thought this was a shooting range," Tessa said, tugging on P.G.'s sleeve. She wasn't crinkling her nose, but she was back in flirty mode. "Is it a store, too? Do they sell shoes?" She grinned at P.G.'s consternation. "Kidding!"

Wren joined Tessa, who was standing by a glassed-in counter.

"Aw," Tessa said. She tapped on the glass. "Look, Wren, it's pink! It's a pink camouflage gun! I mean *weapon*! I mean *firearm*!"

"It's a Glock," P.G. said.

"It's so cute," Tessa cooed, and Wren caught P.G. giving the man behind the counter a look that said, "Sorry, dude." The man wore a bright orange vest and a bright orange hunting cap.

"It's pink," Wren said.

"Uh-huh," Tessa said.

"How can pink be camouflage?" Wren said.

"Well, look at it," Tessa said. "It is."

"Okay, yes. But *where* would pink be camouflage? At a baby shower?"

Tessa laughed. So did P.G. The man in the vest stayed impassive.

"This way," P.G. said, leading Tessa and Wren to another counter. This, it seemed, was where you rented a lane at the shooting range. It reminded Wren of bowling. So did the muffled but still-loud noise coming from behind a set of heavy doors.

"One lane, one hour," P.G. told the guy manning the register. Like the first man, he wore a bright orange vest and cap.

"They eighteen?" the guy in the hunting attire asked.

"Yep," P.G. said.

"They've had a safety class?"

"Yep," P.G. said. He handed the guy two twenties. "Thanks, bud. Have a good one." To Tessa and Wren, he said, "Grab a pair of safety glasses and ear protectors. Let's do this thing."

They had to go through a double-door system to get to the shooting lanes. The moment they passed through the second door, the sound of guns going off hit Wren hard. She flinched and put on her ear protectors.

P.G. said something else, but Wren couldn't make it out over the explosive bangs and pops.

"Huh?" Wren yelled.

He tapped his safety glasses, which he'd already put on,

and which looked far cooler than the nerd-wear loaners Wren clutched.

"Oh!" Wren yelled. "Right!"

"Quit yelling!" Tessa yelled.

"What?"

"You're yelling!"

"Huh? Speak up!"

"Sweet baby Jesus," P.G. might have said, and Tessa smiled a smile that was just for Wren.

Wren slipped on her safety glasses. The frames dug into the sides of her head. P.G. passed her one of his handguns and showed her where to position herself in the lane. She was still uncertain how she felt about this whole experience, but here she was, so she lined up the sight on the bull's-eye target five yards away, then pulled the trigger. Since she was the one controlling it, the *bang* the gun made didn't make her flinch. And she hit it! She hit the target! Nowhere near the center circle, but still!

"I hit it!" she yelled. "Did you see? Look!"

"Very nice!" P.G. yelled. "Especially for a rookie!"

"Way to go!" Tessa yelled, slapping her a high five.

Wren shot the five remaining bullets in the chamber, *bam, bam, bam, bam, bam*. Her reaction confused her. There was a thrill to shooting a gun—she had to admit it. If there'd been more rounds in the chamber, she would have fired them all off, every last one. But wasn't that what made guns scary? The fact that shooting them was fun?

She returned the gun to P.G., who reloaded the clip and jammed it into place with the heel of his palm. *Yes, he's hot*, Wren admitted to Tessa with her eyes. He handed the gun to Tessa this time. He stood behind her, resting his hand on the small of her back.

"Spread your legs," he commanded. "Wider base equals a steadier shot!"

Tessa spread her legs. She was wearing a short, flippy skirt, and she looked sexy.

Wren thought of Charlie. How she'd held his hand. Touched his skin. How they'd sat so close, their legs almost touched. A warm flush spread through her body, completely distracting her.

Focus, she told herself. Focus on your friend, because she is why you are here, and she has a gun in her hands. Watch her shoot things!

Tessa pulled the trigger. The bullet zinged past the target, missing it entirely.

"You anticipated the recoil!" P.G. yelled. "That's what threw you off!"

"Huh?" Tessa yelled. She handed the gun to him. "You do it!"

P.G. took the gun, and his body language told Wren he'd done this many times before. He shut his left eye and extended his right arm as he fired the round. It almost tore off the upper right corner of the target, and his next shots finished the job. He made it look easy.

"Dude!" Tessa crowed. "You did worse than Wren!"

Wren shook her head. The holes from her shots were scattered, and one of her bullets had missed the target completely. P.G.'s bullets had landed in almost exactly the same spot, all on top of each other.

"He wasn't aiming for the center," Wren told her.

"What?" Tessa yelled.

Wren raised her voice. "His aim was dead-on!"

"What?!"

P.G. grabbed his second gun case—the one carrying the big gun—and put it on the shelf in front of him.

Guys from other lanes looked over. Not at Tessa. Not at Wren. All their attention was on the weapon.

"Smith and Wesson 500?" yelled a guy wearing a tattered Halo shirt.

P.G. nodded, and the guy yelled, "Now, *that's* a fucking gun."

"Your face is a fucking gun!" the Halo guy's friend yelled.

The Halo guy ignored him, as did P.G. He loaded the firearm and offered it to Tessa.

"Try this," he told her. "You keep it steady, and I guarantee you'll knock out that bull's-eye."

"You'll knock out the fucking target!" Halo Guy yelled.

"Your face'll knock out the fucking target!" his friend echoed.

Tessa hesitated, toeing the floor. Wren couldn't believe it. Was Tessa playacting? No way. That wasn't Tessa's style.

It *was* a very big gun. A very big revolver, to be precise, with an enormous cylinder that P.G. had already loaded.

Oh, for heaven's sake, Wren thought.

"I'll shoot it," she yelled, stepping forward. She took the revolver, and it was so heavy, she swayed.

"Aw, Christ, no," Halo Guy yelled. "Dude, that's gonna knock her flat on her ass!"

"Your face is gonna knock her flat on her ass!" his friend yelled.

"She can handle it," P.G. responded.

He helped guide her right hand around the grip and her left hand over her right hand. He adjusted the position of her thumbs while she rested her right finger on the slide. She wasn't supposed to put her finger on the trigger until she was ready to shoot.

"It's going to kick like a mule," P.G. said directly into her ear. He probably wanted to avoid the inevitable "Your face kicks like a mule!" but his proximity was unnerving. Wren thought of Charlie again. She bet Charlie could shoot a gun if he had to—but only if he had to. She didn't see him as the gun-shooting type.

P.G. patted her shoulder and stepped back. "Do it, girl."

"Your face'll—" began Halo Guy's friend.

Wren pulled the trigger—she had to pull *hard*—and a sonic boom knocked her three steps backward. The front of the barrel, which she'd aimed at the target, now pointed at the ceiling, and her right shoulder stung. She wasn't foolish enough to say so, but she could have sworn she saw flames shoot out.

"Dude!" Halo Guy cheered.

"Nice!" his buddy yelled.

"Your face is nice!" Wren yelled, adrenaline coursing through her. She was sure she was grinning foolishly.

"Check it out," P.G. said, jerking his chin at the target.

The hole in the target was as big as a fist. The bull's-eye was gone.

Afterward, they sat at an outdoor table at El Elegante. P.G. ordered a pitcher of margaritas, and the waiter asked to see their IDs. When only P.G. produced one—fake, of course—the waiter said, "Sorry, señor. No pitcher for one person."

"You're killing my reputation," P.G. told the waiter, spreading his hands. "You know that, right?"

"Chips and salsa?" the waiter asked.

"Yeah, whatever, and a Corona for me," P.G. said. "No,

Cokes all around." He made a fist and stuck it into the middle of the table. "Solidarity. Righteous."

Wren and Tessa glanced at each other, amused, and added their fists to his.

"Righteous," Wren said, making Tessa laugh.

Tessa could have gotten them margaritas if she tried. She'd done so before. Once, when Wren and Tessa were juniors, they'd gone to a Mexican restaurant and Tessa had offered the waiter a kiss for a frozen strawberry margarita. When he agreed, she'd offered him a second kiss for another. "For my friend," Tessa had said.

Wren had been embarrassed that the waiter didn't ask for a kiss from Wren herself. On the other hand, she wouldn't have kissed him if he had. She also didn't drink her free margarita. She drank with Tessa at parties sometimes, but if she'd gotten caught drinking in public, at a restaurant, her parents would have killed her.

Wren wondered if Tessa was keeping her "kiss for a margarita" trick in her pocket since P.G. was with them. Wren was pretty sure Tessa would be kissing P.G. before the end of the day. It was clear Tessa liked him, and Wren realized that she liked him, too. Liked him *and* trusted him, despite her initial reservations.

She tried to pinpoint when her opinion of him had flipped. She'd been impressed with his gun-safety training, but the real turning point had been at the shooting range, when he put his hand on Tessa's back to steady her. There'd been protectiveness in that gesture that went beyond his everyday slickness.

Now, at the restaurant, P.G. slipped back into his macho, stud-boy persona, but it didn't bother Wren the way it used to. The day was warm. Her Coke, when it arrived, was cold. Tessa and P.G. were both amusing in different ways, and it was easy to relax and talk and laugh.

First, they discussed their shooting range experience. Wren said "no thanks" to the idea of going back—not because she hadn't had a good time, but because she had. She didn't feel like explaining—she suspected P.G. wouldn't understand—but her solution to gun violence would be to make all guns everywhere disappear.

Tessa, on the other hand, said she was definitely up for another trip to the shooting range, adding, "And I really do want that cute pink Glock. Was that what it was called? A Glock?"

"You don't want a Glock," Wren argued.

"I do want a Glock," Tessa said. "I really, really do." But she flitted to the next topic before Wren could decide if she was kidding, proclaiming with the same level of intensity that she could not wait for their graduation ceremony the next morning.

They talked about whether they were supposed to

show up in their robes or put their robes on at the school. They talked about P.G.'s graduation party the next evening, which P.G. assured them would indeed be epic. They gossiped about different kids in their graduating class, wondering who would become movie stars, who would be drug addicts, who would live in Atlanta forever, and who would move away as soon as they could.

Wren wondered about Charlie. She was curious about what his far-off future held, but she was more curious about his nearer future. Would he be at P.G.'s party?

She hoped so . . . unless he showed up with a girl, and the girl turned out to be his girlfriend. Did Charlie have a girlfriend? Might P.G. know?

"Hey, P.G.," she said. "Do you know a guy in our class named Charlie? Charlie Parker?"

Tessa's eyebrows shot up. She'd just grabbed a chip, and in her shock, she snapped it in half.

"Sure," P.G. said. "Why?"

"I don't know. I guess I'm kind of wondering if he's dating someone," Wren said.

"Oh my God," Tessa said. "Oh my *God*. This morning you told me you were up for new things. Is Charlie Parker one of those new things? Wren, this is huge!"

Wren tried to ignore her. "He hangs out a lot with this one girl, but maybe they're just friends. Her name's Destiny or Star or something like that. She's got long blond hair, and she, um, dresses kind of—"

"Skanky?" Tessa supplied. She clapped a hand over her mouth, then moved it to say, "Sorry, sorry. That was mean."

"Starrla Pettit," P.G. said, nodding. "Hangs out with the black kids."

Tessa whacked him. "Racist."

"What? She's talks black, too."

"Dude," Tessa said. "*Owen*, who happens to be our valedictorian, is black."

"And?" P.G. said.

"And *he* doesn't 'talk black,' does he?"

"Fine, Starrla talks ghetto," P.G. said. "Is that better?"

Tessa spoke loftily. "I don't know. And, plus, I would like to take this opportunity to point out that Starrla also hangs out with Charlie, who is *Caucasian*."

P.G. stretched out in his plastic patio chair, taking up space the way guys like P.G. did. "Starrla does hang out with Charlie. Yes. And I will take this opportunity to suggest, given her propensity to sit on Charlie's lap, that they're together, yeah."

"Oh," Wren said, disappointment plunging through her. Starrla sat on Charlie's lap? When? How often? *Why?*

"That doesn't mean they're a couple!" Tessa said.

"I've heard she's good in bed," P.G. said. He popped a chip into his mouth. "Just sayin'."

"Well, don't. Inappropriate and off topic," Tessa said.

"P.G., are you positive Charlie and Starrla are together, or do you just think they are?"

P.G. shrugged. *I've given you all I've got*, the gesture said.

"Well, did *Charlie* say she was good in bed?" Tessa pressed.

"Please," Wren said, and her voice came from somewhere far away. She felt sorry for herself in the most ridiculous of ways. She didn't even know Charlie, not really, and yet picturing him with Starrla, with Starrla on his lap . . .

P.G. considered. "I'm going to say no on that one. It's more just general knowledge."

"See?" Tessa exclaimed. "That means it's all stupid gossip, which I'm equally guilty of, I know. But, Wren. That means—maybe—that she's had multiple boyfriends, if *boyfriend* is even the right word, which means Starrla probably isn't with Charlie, at least not exclusively. Or maybe she was once, but they're not together anymore." She grabbed Wren's forearm. "Wren, this is so exciting!"

Wren pried Tessa off and said, "Let's drop it. I was just curious."

"No, because you don't do 'curious,'" Tessa said. "Not when it comes to guys." Tessa turned to P.G. "Wren's never had a boyfriend. Her parents didn't let her. Well, there was this one guy in middle school, but that lasted all of—what, a month? So believe me, her asking about Charlie is exciting."

"Whoa, back up," P.G. said. He looked at Wren. "Your parents don't let you date?"

Wren quietly died.

Tessa winced and mouthed "sorry" and then launched into an explanation that only made things worse.

"No, it's not that," Tessa told P.G. "Well, it is, kind of, but also Wren decided when she was a freshman that she didn't want to get distracted by all that. Right, Wren?"

Wren pressed her fingers to her temples. Phrases from Tessa's monologue made their way into her consciousness: ". . . because she's brilliant . . . actually studies, unlike the rest of us . . . and her parents said that if she stayed single, basically, and didn't have sex during all of high school, then they'd—"

"Okay, that's enough," Wren said, cutting her off. Yes, Wren's parents had made a deal with her when she was a freshman, but it wasn't as dramatic as Tessa liked to make it seem. Or maybe it was. Wren had a hard time seeing things clearly when it came to her parents. But she hated to imagine what P.G. was thinking about all of this.

At any rate, she'd promised her parents she wouldn't get hung up on guys when she should be focusing on her grades, but the decision had been about showing good sense. It wasn't a virginity pledge.

P.G. popped a chip into his mouth. He didn't seem too concerned about Wren's love life one way or another. "So you haven't found the right guy," he said to Wren. "No big."

"That's what I say!" Tessa exclaimed. "But when she does, it'll be great. *He'll* be great—the guy—and she'll be great with him." She turned to Wren. "You are awesome, Wren. And when you finally fall for someone, it will *mean* something. Right?"

Tessa had a dab of guacamole in her hair. Just a dab at the bottom of one long strand. Wren frowned.

"Wren?" Tessa said, a note of alarm creeping in.

"I hope so," Wren replied. She made herself change expressions. "I mean, sure. Yes. Whatever you say."

Their waiter swung by and refilled P.G.'s Coke.

"Thanks, man," P.G. said.

Tessa immediately claimed his big plastic cup, found the straw with her mouth, and took a long sip, even though her own cup was still nearly full.

"Hey," P.G. protested.

Tessa kept sucking. She smiled from around the straw and batted her eyelashes, and P.G. raked a hand through his hair.

Wren knew the feeling. Tessa could be annoying and lovable at the same time. She was kind of like a Muppet.

"Don't worry," Wren told P.G. "You'll get used to it."

The tips of P.G.'s ears turned red. He tried, visibly, to reclaim his slick veneer, then gave up and laughed.

Wren laughed, too.

"What?" Tessa said. She glanced from Wren to P.G. "What's so funny?"

"Oh, Tessa, I'm going to miss you," Wren said.

"I'm going to miss you, too, you big dummy." She flicked Wren's arm. "But we have the whole summer ahead of us."

"You're right," Wren said.

"Anyway, sure, we're going our separate ways"—she didn't mention Guatemala in front of P.G.—"but none of us will be gone *forever*," she said. She put her hands on the table. "*This* is our home."

"El Elegante?" Wren said.

"Ha-ha. Atlanta's our home, because we grew up here, and that will never change."

"Do you really think that?" Wren said. She wasn't trying to mess with Tessa. She was honestly trying to figure out what she thought. What did *home* really mean, especially if a person chose, on purpose, to leave it? "You think that wherever you grow up, that's your home, by default?"

"Of course I think that," Tessa said. "Don't you?"

"I don't know."

Tessa stuck out her tongue, and Wren had a small epiphany. Tessa, who had always been there for Wren, needed Wren to be there for her, too. Maybe all that confidence Wren assumed Tessa had was a little bit of an act. Maybe, with graduation a day away, Tessa wanted the world to be big enough to move around in but not big enough to get lost in. Wren, on the other hand, secretly *wanted* to get lost, or was already lost, or something.

"Home is where the heart is," P.G. said expansively.

"Damn straight," Tessa replied. "Go big or go home."

"Home is where you can pee with the door open," P.G. added. He lifted a finger. "Wait, wait . . . die like a hero going home."

"Home wasn't built in a day," Tessa countered, and P.G. high-fived her.

Wren racked her brain for a *home* quote. "Oh!" she said. "There's no place like home?"

"Exactly!" Tessa said. She clapped. "Oh my God, I love that movie, and, yes, that's ex*act*ly what I'm trying to say. So let's click our ruby slippers and say it together." She held out her hands. Wren took one and P.G. took the other, but only P.G., looking amused, chanted along: "There's no place like home. There's no place like home. There's no place like home."

CHAPTER FOUR

Getting Dev's wheelchair into Chris and Pamela's converted Dodge Caravan wasn't easy. Dev bore the process without complaining, but Charlie knew Dev hated it. Hated that it had to be done with the garage door open, so that anyone walking by could see. Hated Chris's grim determination as he muscled the wheelchair up the ramp and through the not-quite-wide-enough side door. Most of all, Charlie knew how much Dev hated Pamela's concern.

No. What Dev hated was being the cause of Pamela's concern, even if it wasn't his fault. He hadn't chosen to be paralyzed.

Charlie understood completely.

"Careful!" she exclaimed. "Honey, don't—" She craned and fluttered. "Honey, you're going to scrape his arm!"

"Mom, chill," Dev said. Unlike Charlie, he did call their foster parents Mom and Dad. Maybe because he was younger? Chris and Pamela wanted both boys to call them Mom and Dad. Charlie just couldn't.

With Charlie's help, Chris got the wheelchair into the van and oriented it so that Dev was facing forward.

"Safe and sound," Dev told Pamela. "See?"

Charlie secured the straps that kept Dev's wheelchair in place. His hand hurt where his stitches were, but he pushed past the pain and worked quickly, knowing Dev hated this part, too. He straightened up, one knee on the floor of the van and his other foot planted by Dev's chair.

"Give me some skin," he said to make Dev laugh.

Dev skimmed his hand over Charlie's, a smooth-as-silk slide.

"Nice, my brother," Charlie said.

"Nice, *my* brother," Dev replied. He grinned. "Hey. What do you call a brownie with nuts?"

Charlie knew the answer, but he played along. "I guess I'd call it . . . a brownie with nuts."

"A Boy Scout!" Dev crowed. He slapped his knee. "I'm so awesome. I know."

"Uh-huh. Is that why the ladies love you?"

Dev gave him a point and wink. "They do love me, my brother, and I love them. Wanna know why? Because I'm—"

"So awesome?"

"You better believe it," Dev said.

Charlie did.

"Dev? Charlie? Everyone ready?" Pamela asked, peeking into the van. She wore heels and her nicest dress.

"All set," Charlie said, and Pamela looked at him with such pride that Charlie's heart constricted.

"My sweet boy," she told him. "A high school graduate!"

"*Almost* a high school graduate," Dev pointed out. "Hell, they might give him the boot at the last second."

"Oh, they will not, and, Dev, watch your mouth," Pamela scolded. "And, Charlie, you *are* allowed to smile, you know. You look so serious!"

For Pamela's sake, Charlie smiled, and Pamela's face lit up. She leaned into the van and gestured for him to come closer. Physical affection was hard for him, but for Pamela, Charlie would do almost anything. He hugged her awkwardly and steeled himself for the big wet kiss he knew was coming.

The seniors congregated by the main building while their families and friends and parents and guardians got settled in the chairs set up on the lawn to watch the ceremony. *To be signed by your parent or guardian*, forms always said, and they said that for Charlie. Charlie was the kid with the guardians instead of the parents. Whatever.

You have family out there just like everyone else, he told himself, thinking especially of Dev. Family is how *you* define it.

"Du-u-ude," said Ammon, Charlie's best friend. He came toward Charlie at half speed, his strides and the pumping of his arms exaggerated. He was pretending, Charlie could only assume, to be a track star whose triumphant passage across the finish line was being rebroadcast. "Supah slo-mo, yo?"

Ammon held up his hand, still moving through molasses, for a high five. Charlie slapped his palm, and Ammon, mercifully, returned to normal mode, or what counted as normal for him. Ammon had a baby-smooth face and a skinny frame. To compensate, he wore the most jacked-up shoes on the planet. Today's pair, jutting from beneath his black gown, were red DC high-tops, puffy and enormous.

"Oh yeah," Ammon said, grinning and bouncing from foot to foot. "We *did* it, uh-*hu-uh*, we *did* it, uh-*hu-uh*."

"We haven't done it yet," Charlie said. "If you're talking about graduating, that is."

"Details, details," Ammon said. "But very soon we will be bona fide high school graduates, my friend. And you know what that means."

"Do I?"

"Girls love a bona fide high school graduate."

Charlie arched one eyebrow. "Do they?"

"Oh, they do, believe me," Ammon assured him. "And speaking of, there's a big party tonight. Big, big, big. It's at P.G. Barbee's house, and, news flash, we will both be attending. *Both* of us. So repeat after me: 'Yes, Ammon. I will be there, Ammon.'"

"P.G. Barbee?" Charlie said skeptically. The Barbees were rich. So rich, they bought a new boat as soon as the old one got wet—that's how Chris put it. Mr. Barbee had hired Chris to do some cabinetwork for them not long ago, and Chris had returned from his on-site visit with tales of gleaming hardwood floors, chandeliers bigger than tricycles, and lawn jockeys that may or may not have been ironic. Charlie didn't ask, because Chris would have found the question puzzling. "Ironic?" he'd have said. "Whaddaya mean *ironic*, Chahlie? They were, you know, those thingies. On the lawn. Little black kids playing polo or sumpin'."

"You're not getting out of this one," Ammon said. "It's a graduation party. *Our* graduation party, and it's going to be epic."

"Epic."

"Yes, epic, which means we should dress sharp to make ourselves stand out, yo?"

Charlie marveled, not for the first time, at the unlikeliness of their friendship. Ammon danced, snapped, and wore shoes the size of small islands. Endless streams of words flowed from his mouth. He said things like "yo," and not ironically. But Ammon was a loyal friend, and kind. He wanted good things for Charlie, even when Charlie resisted.

Ammon pointed at Charlie. "So, eight o'clock? You and me? Yeah? Yeah?"

Charlie was giving legitimate thought to responding when Ammon's features twisted and flattened. Charlie knew without looking who was approaching.

"Hey, babe," Starrla said, draping her arm over his shoulders. She molded her body to his and traced his jaw with a bright red fingernail. "You lookin' good."

Charlie peeled Starrla off him. She was still in her regular clothes, which today consisted of a tube top and a skirt—though was it a skirt if it barely covered her ass? Charlie hated himself for noticing. He didn't know how not to notice, and he hated himself for that as well.

"Ain't my boy lookin' good, Ammon?" Starrla asked.

Ammon didn't answer. He didn't like Starrla, and Starrla didn't like him.

"I'm not your boy, Starrla," Charlie said. "Don't you need to go put on your robe?"

Starrla pouted. "Too hot for a damn robe. Too hot for this damn ceremony. I says we just get out of here. Wanna?"

"You're supposed to put your robe on, Starrla," Charlie

said. "You're supposed to put your robe on and go over there." He gestured toward the other end of the building. "That's where the girls are. See?" Without making a conscious decision to do so, he searched for Wren, spotting her next to a large terra-cotta planter. She was up on tiptoe, using the planter for balance as she turned her head one way and then another.

Her eyes met his. They widened. She smiled, and Charlie smiled back, foolishly and happily.

Starrla laughed.

Cursing himself, Charlie wrenched away his gaze. Wren's face fell, but he couldn't think about that right now. Right now his biggest concern was Starrla, because although Starrla didn't want Charlie (not the way Charlie wanted to be wanted), she didn't want other girls to want him, either. She certainly didn't want him wanting any other girl.

"Oh, sugar," Starrla said. Her voice was a purr, but her eyes were feral. "That girl you were staring at? No, sir. That girl ain't done one wrong thing in her life, and she ain't gonna start with you. Ain't I right, Ammon?"

Ammon shifted. He glanced at Charlie.

"It'd take a crowbar to pry that girl's legs apart," Starrla went on. "She think she better than us, that's why."

She is, Charlie thought, his heart aching.

But before Starrla had ruined things, before *he'd* ruined

things, Wren had looked at Charlie from across the crowd. It had happened. It was true, and for that brief moment, Charlie had felt seen.

"All right, everyone, line up," the vice principal said. He whistled through his fingers. He was wearing a suit. "Guys over here, girls over there, and remember to *walk slowly*."

"I likes it slow," Starrla murmured. "I also likes it fast."

"Miss Pettit?" the vice principal said. "Miss Pettit, go get your gown on. *Now*."

"I'm going, I'm going," she said, dropping her gangsta-speak. "Have a cow, why don't you?"

Her high heel caught in a crack in the sidewalk. Charlie grabbed her elbow, saving her from tripping, and she said, "See? My hero."

The seniors, once they were seated in the plastic chairs that wobbled on the lawn, formed a semicircle in front of the makeshift stage and podium. The boys were on the right. The girls were on the left. Charlie had a clear view of Wren, when he gave himself permission to take it. The sunlight, dappled by overhead leaves, brought out every shade of brown imaginable in her hair. Unlike Charlie, she seemed to be paying attention to the parade of speakers, but Charlie couldn't tell what she was thinking. Was she amused? Moved? Melancholy at the end of things, or eager for a new beginning?

He could stare at Wren all day, but he didn't want her to catch him. Also, his side of the lawn had no tree cover. His black gown was stifling. His tasseled mortarboard was a black square on top of his head, absorbing every ray of the bright Georgia sun, and the heat made his thoughts wander.

This kind of heat, this stifling, smothering heat, had bad associations for Charlie. It brought up memories of his mother, his biological mother. She was young when she'd had him. Young and scared and desperate. Two jobs but never enough money, and certainly none for child care.

"I expect you to be quiet and behave," Charlie heard her telling him, and he pictured a skinny little kid—him—being pried off the faceless woman's leg and pushed firmly into a cramped garage. Maybe she said it once more before yanking down the garage door, staring hard at her three-year-old son. "Stay here and be quiet for Mommy."

Garage doors were heavy, and they could be closed with some amount of speed, but surely Charlie could have ducked beneath it and tried to get to her. He hadn't. "*Stay*," his mother had said, and like a good dog—or if not a *good* dog, a dog who'd learned about cause and effect—he'd obeyed.

He was in there for a long time, day after day. August, in Atlanta, was brutal.

He must have cried out eventually, or hit his small fist

against the door, because they found him, didn't they? A neighbor discovered that it was a "who" and not a "what" making such a racket in the garage behind the apartment units, and after that, Charlie was placed in the care of Atlanta's Child Protective Services.

For several years, he lived in a facility called Saint Joseph's with other unwanted kids. Once, a social worker brought him jelly beans and gave him a thick and wonderful book called *The Boys' Guide to Automobiles*.

Another social worker, a flat-eyed man named Dave, sat with the kids in the "family" room. Dave didn't make the kids do their homework like he was supposed to. Instead, he let them watch movies. He jammed DVDs from his personal collection into the crappy DVD player connected to the even crappier TV. He sat back, grunting occasionally during scenes of men shooting. Men shouting. Men hurting women in ways Charlie didn't understand.

Charlie swore to himself that he would never be like that.

Then came a series of foster families. Some placements worked out better than others. But none of them was forever. And he was lonely. He tried not to be. He tried to be strong and self-reliant. If he could figure out how to stop needing anything (or anyone), then his loneliness would go away—that was his hope. But it never quite worked out that way.

He got better at being alone, but the loneliness stayed.

He got better at hiding his loneliness, or so he imagined. For long stretches of time, he'd be convinced he was pulling it off, that finally he'd gotten it down, but invariably some kid would look at him funny, or get up and move to another table in the cafeteria, and he'd think, Do I stink? Is my hair greasy? What am I doing wrong?

Once, a girl smiled at him, and her friends immediately closed ranks, shutting him out with glares.

"What?" he heard the girl say from within their small circle. "I feel sorry for him. Don't y'all?"

Shame nearly drowned him.

In seventh grade, Charlie was placed with Chris and Pamela.

In eighth grade, Charlie met Starrla, when the two of them, along with half a dozen other misfits, were shuffled once a week to a mandatory support group for kids from troubled homes. Starrla sniffed out his neediness and was drawn to it. Her attention was a drug. Charlie couldn't get enough.

One day, sitting in a secluded spot behind the middle school, Charlie hunched his shoulders and ripped apart clumps of grass and forced himself to tell Starrla about his past. Just a little to start with. Even so, he felt as if he might throw up. But she'd given him the most private parts of herself—back then, he'd believed that sex meant the same thing to her that it meant to him—and if he were any kind of a man, he should do the same.

"Ew," she said when he finished talking.

Startled, he glanced up at her.

She scrunched her nose. "What did you do when you needed to take a dump?" she asked. This was before she'd taken up her forced bad grammar. "Did your mom leave a pail in there, or what? Who had to empty it? Did you?"

Charlie lost all words.

When Starrla registered his response, she rolled her eyes. "For fuck's sake. Was I supposed to go all mushy? *Walk into your pain, Charlie. I'll be right here, holding your hand.* Is that what you wanted me to say?"

She was mocking their guidance counselor.

Charlie felt numb.

"Go on, then. Walk into your fucking sob story." She shoved his shoulder. "Will there be a unicorn on the other side and nothing bad will *ever* happen *ever* again? Because, oh boy, I want to go to that land!"

Charlie moved to stand up. Starrla sighed and pulled him back. She seemed so angry, and yet she reached over, grabbed his hand, and shoved it under her shirt. "There. Is that better? Jesus, Charlie."

She scooched closer. Her skin was warm, and she held

his hand against her. In a low, tight voice, she said, "I won't tell anyone about any of that. The garage, and your mom. All right?"

After that, but only when she was drunk, Starrla whispered stories to Charlie. Her stories were about men who were violent, men like the ones on Dave's DVDs, and they made Charlie want to punch walls. But Charlie couldn't save her. No one could. So Starrla moved on to other warm bodies.

She always came back to Charlie, but as eighth grade turned into ninth, and ninth into tenth, he began to wish she wouldn't. He tried to put distance between them. She wiggled her way back in, like the time she showed up at Dev's Science Olympiad competition in a too-tight shirt, cheering loudly and making Dev blush with eleven-year-old pride. Starrla made Dev look good in front of his buddies—because Starrla was pretty despite the clothes and makeup she hid behind—and so what if she was actually there for Charlie and not Dev? Charlie would never say anything, and Starrla knew it.

Or Starrla would compliment Chris on the beveled legs of a chair he was working on ("That looks so hard, Mr. DeLucco. You're so talented"). Or she'd bring Pamela a Toffee Nut Iced Latte (Pamela's favorite) from Starbucks and comment on how tiring it must be for Pamela to run her at-home day care business while at the same time raising two boys.

"She's a sweet girl," Pamela said to Charlie after one such coffee delivery.

"Uh-huh," Charlie replied. He didn't say, "Sure, Pamela, only, after she gave you your coffee, she gave me a blow job behind the workshop. And, afterward, she said, 'Oh, Charlie, just think how disappointed Pamela would be if she knew. Should we confess? What do you think?'"

Charlie shifted on the plastic chair. The graduation ceremony went on and on, full of words like *hope* and *promise*, and Charlie felt ashamed. His relationship with Starrla hadn't held either of those, and finally, last year, he called it off for real.

She laughed. "You're breaking up with me?" she said when he finished his stilted, overly rehearsed speech. She reached to stroke his hair. He grabbed her wrist to stop her, and she laughed again, because she'd made him do that. Grab her.

"Charlie," she said, regarding him as if he were a child who would never, ever grow up. "You can't break up with me. We were never together."

Exactly, Charlie thought.

She tilted her head and touched her lower lip. "There's another reason you can't break up with me. You want to know why? Because I will always be here for you. *Always*. Do you hear me, Charlie?"

Charlie felt uneasy. That was an alarmingly intimate thing for Starrla to say, never mind that it was in direct contradiction to her earlier proclamation. Still, he held his ground and took nothing back.

"Hmm," she said. Then she made two kissy sounds, winked at him, and sashayed off. Her parting words were bright and cruel. "Just remember—we're the same, you and me!"

They weren't, though. Charlie was not like Starrla. He tugged at his shirt collar beneath his gown and glanced at his watch. The ceremony had to be almost over, didn't it?

As the speaker droned on, Charlie told himself not to look at Wren—don't, don't, don't, not with Starrla still on your mind—but his eyes sought her out of their own accord, and the sight of her made him feel calmer. She was in a white gown like the other girls—the boys wore black; the girls wore white—and her hair spilled in waves over her shoulders. She looked beautiful. And, unlike the girl next to her, who was yawning but trying to hide it, she looked . . . hopeful.

No. That wasn't it. Well, *yes*, hopeful, but . . .

Alive.

Except that wasn't it, either. Of course she looked alive. How else would she look?

Her lips were slightly parted. Her chin was raised. Earlier he couldn't read her expression, but now it seemed she was interested in what the speaker was saying, which made Charlie wonder if maybe the speaker was saying something interesting after all. Not as interesting as Wren, but surely more interesting than the endless loop of crap playing in his own mind.

He would go with Ammon to the graduation party, he decided. He'd go to the party at P.G.'s house, and if Wren was there, he would approach her. Talk to her. Something. He swore to himself that he would.

He had a past with Starrla. He regretted it, but the past was the past.

Imagining a future with Wren, on the other hand . . .

No. Stop, he told himself firmly.

But he could spend time with Wren, maybe. Was there any reason he couldn't stand next to her at P.G.'s party? Share a laugh, offer to get her a drink? His pulse grew stronger.

There was rustling, and excited energy wafted off his classmates as they stood and formed a line. It was time to receive their diplomas, or rather their fake diplomas. They'd get their real ones after the ceremony, pressed flat in commemorative leather folders that cost twenty dollars apiece.

Charlie joined his classmates, but as he walked across

the makeshift stage, he didn't think about the end of high school, or graduating, or diplomas, genuine or fake. His thoughts were occupied by the one real thing he knew: Wren.

CHAPTER FIVE

Wren's graduation luncheon was a chaotic swirl of photos with family, photos with friends, and hugs and hugs—so many hugs. Wren's parents bragged about Wren to other parents, and it made Wren uncomfortable, but at least it took the burden of conversation off her. She still hadn't broken the news about Project Unity. She needed to, and she would, but not yet. Not with so many people around.

Wren's father put his arm around her as he talked with Bob Hammond, her friend Delaney's dad, about colleges and financial-aid packages. Two feet away, her mom listened patiently as another mom went on and on about thank-you notes and where to buy the best-quality embossed envelopes. She glanced over, and Wren saw her share a private smile with Wren's dad.

Wren's parents weren't perfect, but she told herself that no one's were. Anyway, she loved them, and she wouldn't be here without them, and one thing she was proud of was how solid they were. She thought it sweet how they always checked in with each other at events like this, whether through a quick glance or a light brushing together of their fingertips.

A few years back, a slew of her parents' friends had split up—four or five divorces, all in a row—and Wren's parents had talked with her about how much work relationships required.

"Oh, Wren, just wait till you're in your thirties before you even consider getting married, will you?" her mom had said.

"Forget marriage," her dad added. "How about you wait till you're thirty before you have a boyfriend."

"*Dad*," Wren said. She was fourteen at the time, a freshman, and thirty seemed impossibly far away. Being a senior seemed impossibly far away.

"I mean it," her dad said. "If you wait to have a boyfriend until after high school, we'll get you a car when you graduate. How does that sound?"

Wren wanted to think he was joking, but she wasn't sure. Just by saying something, just by throwing out an expectation, her father and her mother both had an amazing ability to make Wren shift around her own expectations.

Later, her mom came to her room and said, "Honey, just so you know, we're not trying to *bribe* you. We just hope you'll show good judgment."

So Wren had focused on her schoolwork instead of boys. Her parents' approval felt so very good—and not only good, but necessary. As a child, Wren had felt vaguely like a toy that was paraded out in front of her parents' friends, there to be shown off. At the graduation luncheon, standing beneath the weight of her father's arm, she wondered how far she'd come. She felt young all of a sudden, and lonely.

Her dad squeezed her shoulders. "Isn't that right, Wren?" he said.

Both he and Bob Hammond gazed at her expectantly. Past them, the entire Cherokee Club ballroom, where Wren and her set of friends were celebrating, was filled with boys in suits and girls in white dresses. Her mom held up her slender hand, waving a "no thanks" at the platter of bacon-wrapped dates a caterer offered.

"Yes?" Wren said. She had no idea what she was agreeing to, but certain habits were deeply ingrained.

Bob Hammond laughed and gestured at the caterer.

"Well, that's fine," he said, "and I'll take one of those." He put three on a cocktail napkin. "John? Wren? They're good. Want one?"

"Yes," Wren said more firmly. "I mean, please. Yes, please."

She filled her mouth so she could go back to not talking.

You're no longer the same innocent fourteen-year-old you once were, she told herself.

How sad it would be if she were.

How sad it was that she wasn't.

After the luncheon, Wren and her parents headed home. When they were within a few blocks of their house, her parents told Wren to close her eyes.

"And keep them closed until we say so," her mom said.

Oh dear, Wren thought. What now?

The car slowed. There was a small bump, and Wren knew her dad had pulled into their driveway. He cut the motor. Her mom helped Wren out of the car, and, for good measure, she placed her own hand over Wren's eyes.

She guided Wren a few feet forward.

"Is it time?" her mom said, presumably to her dad.

"I think so," her dad replied.

She removed her hand, and Wren opened her eyes. Before her was a white Toyota Prius.

"Well?" her mom exclaimed, practically humming with

delight. "Go see. Don't you want to go see?"

Oh shit, Wren thought. The car. For good grades and no boys. They really meant it, and oh shit, oh shit, oh shit.

She walked to the Prius. She placed her palm on its side, which was warm from the sun. She looked back at her parents.

"It has a moonroof," her dad said.

"And we picked white because white cars are the least likely to be involved in accidents," her mom said. "White and silver."

"Safe drivers are even less likely to be involved in accidents," her dad said in a dad-tone.

"Wren is already a very safe driver," her mom said.

"Of course she is," her dad replied.

Wren's throat tightened. She felt insanely guilty. Her parents were giving her a car when she was about to disappoint them more than she ever had. She also felt confused. Her parents had actually given her a car as a reward for good behavior. It felt icky for some reason.

"I—I love it," she told them.

"How about that moonroof?" her dad said.

"I love the moonroof. Thank you so much."

"Check the glove compartment," her dad said.

"The glove compartment?" Wren said. She didn't want to check the glove compartment. "Why?"

"You'll see."

Wren went to the driver's side door, opened it, and slid into the seat. She peeked at her parents, who stood with their arms around each other. Then she leaned over the console and opened the glove compartment. An envelope lay on top of a thick booklet that was probably the owner's manual. Her fingers hovered over it.

"There should be a letter," her dad called. "Read it."

It was a notice, printed on Emory University letterhead, stating that Wren had been granted the privilege of having a car on campus. A parking permit would arrive with her orientation materials, and the Provost's Office as well as the College of Liberal Arts would happily address any questions or concerns Wren might have. They looked forward to Wren becoming part of the Emory family.

Her mom and dad came up to the car door.

"We'll still drive you to your dorm and help you unpack," her dad said. "We'll take two cars."

"I pulled some big strings for you," her mom said. "Most freshmen won't have cars. You're going to be pretty popular, I imagine—not that you wouldn't be anyway."

"Wow," Wren said.

Her dad leaned over the open door. "Hey. You lived up to your end of the deal; we lived up to ours. And we couldn't very well give you a car and then make you leave it here, could we?"

Wren's mom took in Wren's expression and frowned.

"Sweetheart, what on earth is wrong?"

Wren put the letter from Emory back inside the glove compartment, climbed out of the car, and carefully shut the door. "Can we go inside?" she asked her parents. "I sort of need to tell you something."

In the family room, Wren sat balled up on one side of the corner sofa. Her parents sat across from her. They didn't yell. Her parents weren't yellers. They didn't respond the way Charlie had, though.

He'd said she was wonderful.

Her parents said nothing about "wonderful."

"You made a commitment," her dad said. "You applied for early admission. You got in. By agreeing to attend, you took away a slot that could have gone to some other student."

"There's a wait list," Wren said. Her mouth was dry. "The spot will go to someone."

"But what about *your* spot?" her mom asked. "And what will I tell everyone? I work with these people, Wren. I see them every day!"

"Um, I asked if I could defer?"

"And?"

"And . . . they said it will probably work out."

Her mom shook her head. "'Probably'? You didn't give up your spot, did you? You would *never* do something that foolish, Wren."

But I did, Wren thought. "It just, um, feels like the right thing for me."

"For myself," her dad said.

Wren looked at him.

His jaw was tense. "'It feels like the right thing for *myself*.'"

"You're correcting my grammar?"

"I'll always correct your grammar, just as I'll always love you," he said, managing to make it sound like a threat.

But *myself*, the way you used it, isn't correct, Wren was tempted to say. She stuffed her hands under her legs.

"You're being very selfish, Wren," he went on. "You're showing extremely poor judgment."

Wren pulled her hands from beneath her and drew her shins toward her chest.

"Please be still and stop wriggling," he said.

She lowered her legs.

"We put down a five-hundred-dollar deposit when you accepted," Wren's mom said. She swiped beneath her eyes. "Wren, sweetheart, you withdrew all your other applications because you knew what you wanted, and what you wanted was to go to Emory."

"I'll pay back the money."

Her mom held out her hands. "When we visited the campus—when I brought you in to meet everyone—you loved it. What changed?"

I changed, she thought. But that wasn't an acceptable answer.

Selfish. Foolish. Bad judgment.

"Nothing changed," Wren said to her knees. "I don't know. I don't *know*."

"Use your words," her dad said.

She shook her head. "You took me to that TED Talk, remember?"

"The talk Professor Tremblay told us about?" her dad said. "Professor Tremblay, who wrote a letter of reference for you?"

Yes, that Professor Tremblay, whom her mom knew from her job at Emory, and, yes, Wren felt guilty. He'd gone to so much trouble. Everyone had gone to so much trouble. She was so much trouble.

Charlie, Charlie, Charlie, she thought, and miraculously, it gave her strength.

"What talk?" her mom said.

"It was called 'The Road Not Taken,'" Wren said. "All these people talked about their lives, and how they chose unconventional paths, and how that made all the difference. Like in the Robert Frost poem."

"Yes? And?" her mom said. "You don't even like that poem."

"Mom, I do," Wren said. How in the world would her mother know what poems she liked? "I guess it made me think about things. Like, one woman was a lawyer, but she gave up her job to go help people in developing countries have clean water. Another guy was in an accident and ended up in a coma, and when he came out of it, he could suddenly play the piano, and he became a concert pianist."

"So your plan is to fall into a coma and wake up a musical prodigy," her dad said. "Terrific."

Wren pressed her lips together. She loved her dad, but right now, she hated him.

Her mom cleared her throat. "I wonder, Wren, if maybe you don't know enough yet to make this decision. You can always do . . . something like this . . . after you get your college degree, can't you? You don't know what you're throwing away."

Wren dug her fingernails into her palms.

"I'm sorry you're upset," she said. Her voice quavered. "And maybe it wasn't the talk, and even if it was, that wasn't the only thing. And you're right that I don't know enough. I kind of think I need to rethink everything."

"Like being a doctor?" her dad said. "Wren. You've wanted to be a doctor since you were ten."

No. When she was ten, Wren had wanted to work with animals. She'd had a book about a hospital for cats, and she'd carried it around everywhere until it mysteriously disappeared. When Wren asked about it, her father had said, "What book? Wren, I have no idea what you're carrying on about, but for the record, you can do better than becoming a veterinarian."

But she didn't go there. She said—and it was awful, because disagreeing with him felt like saying she didn't love him—"I kind of think I need to figure out if being a doctor is my plan or yours."

"And I think you need to figure out why you made such an impulsive decision without consulting us," her dad said. "I don't just *kind of think* it, either. I know it."

Wren made herself smaller.

"This isn't like you, Wren," he went on. "Am I to understand from the half answer you gave your mother that Emory was unable to guarantee deferred admission?"

"They said it would most likely work out," Wren whispered. "But it will depend on next fall's numbers."

"So they were unable to guarantee deferred admission," he said.

"Yes, Dad. Yes! God!" She didn't want to cry, but it was happening anyway. She sniffled and dragged a hand under her nose. "And maybe it *was* a mistake, but maybe I need to not be perfect for once!"

"We never needed you to be perfect!" her dad said in a raised voice, while at the same time her mom cried, "But you *are* perfect!"

The three of them fell silent. Wren gulped. She blinked back her tears.

"Wren," her mom said. "You know we love you."

"And I love you." She refused to make eye contact with either of them. "But you need to know . . . I'm doing this."

Her dad stood abruptly. He left the room.

Her mom stayed but didn't speak. Wren wrapped her arms around her legs and rested her chin on her knees.

"I'm sad, Mom," Wren said at last.

"I am, too," her mom said.

But later, when Tessa beeped her horn from Wren's driveway, Wren strode out of her house and didn't look back. She needed out, and she was getting out. She'd done the horrible, awful thing, and yes, her parents were disappointed in her, and yes, it was terrible. It was also terribly liberating, especially with dusk coming on and a party right around the corner.

Thank goodness her parents had always approved of Tessa, and thank goodness Wren had told them about the party—with Tessa standing next to her—earlier in the day. Her parents, and especially her mom, had always thought it was important that Wren "be a part of things" socially. If the other kids in her class were going to a party, then Wren's mom wanted Wren to go, too.

"Whoa," Tessa said when she saw Wren's outfit. She let out a wolf whistle.

"Don't say a word," Wren begged her, climbing into the

passenger seat. "I'm self-conscious enough already."

"But—"

"No."

"But, Wren, you look—"

"No! Shh!" Wren put her hands over her ears and hummed.

For three blocks, Tessa kept her mouth shut, but she kept sneaking appreciative peeks at Wren. It was absurd, since Tessa, in her black skirt and silver tank top, was the one who looked fancy. Wren had taken the opposite approach, pairing a T-shirt with low-slung jeans as soft as butter. The jeans came from Tessa; she'd given them to Wren a month or so ago, claiming she'd found them on sale. "Just try them on," Tessa had pleaded, making praying hands.

Wren never did, because Wren was a "preppy J.Crew girl," according to Tessa. Wren wasn't sure about the "preppy" and "J.Crew" parts, but she'd never been much of a jeans girl. Or maybe it was her mom who wasn't much of a jeans girl? In elementary school and halfway through junior high, her mom had picked out Wren's outfit each morning. By eighth grade, Wren had convinced her mom that she could actually pick out her own clothes, and her mom had capitulated with surprisingly little resistance. Maybe, in retrospect, because Wren's own choices had so closely mirrored her mother's.

Tonight, she'd decided *not* to think. Not about her parents or Guatemala or her new car, and not about what kind of girl she was, jeans-wearing or otherwise.

"Hey, Wren?" Tessa said. She tapped Wren's shoulder. "Can I say one teeny-tiny thing?" She tapped Wren's shoulder again. "Please? Pretty please? Just one teensy-weensy little thing?"

"What?" Wren said.

"You look really hot."

"Really?"

"Really."

Wren wasn't convinced, but she hoped so. "Well . . . thanks. And *you* look amazing."

"Why, thank you," Tessa said with a happy grin.

"And, Tessa?"

"Yes, Wren?"

She started to tell Tessa about her afternoon, and how she wept in her bedroom after the big talk with her parents, and how she wasn't positive her parents would ever love her again.

Except of course they would. Of course they *did*. Didn't they?

Why was Wren always trying to convince herself of things? Her brain was like a gerbil on a wheel, spinning and spinning in its ceaseless gerbil way. For a moment, everything locked up and she felt paralyzed. Then she thought, What the hell. Let it all go.

“Let’s do anything we want tonight,” she said to Tessa. “What do you think?”

“Absolutely,” Tessa said.

She cranked up the music and sang along, and Wren, catching her hair in a ponytail with her hand, turned toward the open window and closed her eyes. She let herself be swept away.

CHAPTER SIX

"Dude, can I grow up to be rich one day?" Ammon said, finding Charlie by the open front door to P.G.'s mansion. Neither boy had entered the house. It looked like a movie set inside—the arched front door opening into a well-lit foyer, the guests milling about, smiles and laughter and the clink of ice against glass. Just past the foyer, Charlie spotted caterers serving flutes of what appeared to be either champagne or sparkling apple juice. Charlie put his money on champagne.

"Just tell me where to sign, and I'll do it," Ammon said.

"I don't think it works that way," Charlie said.

"It might. It could. The Barbees could adopt me."

Charlie's mouth twitched. "You want to be P.G.'s little brother?"

Ammon, in his oversize shirt, flung out his arms. "Twin brother, yo. And it could happen. You know why? Because this is a time of no rules. Everything's changing, and no one cares anymore about social standing, or who's cool and who's not." He stepped directly into Charlie's line of vision, his face half a foot away from Charlie's. "The playing field's been leveled, Charlie. Do you appreciate what I'm saying?"

"Yeah, sure," Charlie said, moving to one side. He continued to scan the party guests, and—*whoa*. There she was, just past the foyer, laughing with her friend Tessa. She was gorgeous. When he'd seen Wren at school, he'd thought she looked great in her never-wrinkled blouses and skirts. He'd thought her style of dressing was better than the other girls' jeans and T-shirts.

Charlie now realized he'd missed out on one key factor. A girl in jeans and a T-shirt looked amazing, if the girl was Wren Gray. Even if the shirt said *Speedster!* across the front and sported a picture of a girl on a motorcycle. *Especially* if the shirt said *Speedster!* and sported a picture of a girl on a motorcycle.

Her curves made him hard.

"—even listening, Charlie?" Ammon said. He lightly

slapped Charlie's cheek. "Dude, you still with me?"

"Huh?"

"Something's up with you, buddy. I noticed it this morning at the ceremony, too." He slung his arm around Charlie, rising up slightly in his puffy high-tops to do so. "Tell your old pal about it. Go on."

Charlie wrenched his attention from Wren. He moved so that Ammon's arm fell off him, but he looked at Ammon, blinked, and said, "I'm going to ask out Wren Gray."

"Pardon?"

"On a date. I'm going to ask her if she wants to do something."

"To do something," Ammon repeated. "Like what? Bowling?"

"Anything, as long as it's with me."

"With you."

"With me. Yes."

Ammon opened his mouth to speak, then closed it.

"What?" Charlie said.

"I said everything's changing. I fully own up to that, and I fully hold that it's still mainly true. *Mainly*." He puffed his cheeks with air, then exhaled. "But, Charlie, some laws stay laws even when all the others fall away. Like . . . gravity. Like the movement of the planets. I mean, the sun still revolves around the earth, right?"

Charlie raised his eyebrows. "Does it?"

"It does. Yes."

Charlie had to laugh. "The earth revolves around the sun, Ammon."

"Whatever. You know what I'm saying."

"That Wren's out of my league?"

"No. No way. I'm saying she's out of everyone's league, because she's not in a league. She's, like, in a league of her own."

Charlie nodded. He would agree with that.

Ammon looked pained. "I'm just keeping it real, bro."

"No worries," Charlie said. He cocked his head at P.G.'s house. "I'm going in."

Ammon's voice went up a pitch. "In there? Where all the people are?"

"Yep. I'm going to ask Wren out." He clapped Ammon on the back. "Just keeping it real, bro."

When Charlie first spotted Wren, she'd been in one of the front rooms, standing by an antique sideboard. By the time he angled his way through the crowd of milling, happy seniors, and people from other grades, too—people from other schools, too, from the looks of it—she was gone.

He went into the dining room, glanced around, and scratched the back of his neck. He checked the living room, the TV room, and a room he assumed was a library, based on the shelves and shelves of books. P.G.'s house was huge. The party was huge. Wren could be anywhere.

He came to a room that he didn't know what to call, or what purpose it served. No shelves, no tables, not much in the way of furniture at all. Just a tiled floor, a ceiling fan, and two overstuffed armchairs. Huh. No people in this odd side room, either, so Charlie turned to go.

"Hey, wait, can you give me a hand?" a guy called.

Charlie turned back with a start. P.G. Barbee, the guy who lived in this huge, crazy house, was kneeling by a large oak liquor cabinet. Broken glass glittered around him. He dropped a large shard into a dustpan full of other large fragments, then gestured at a broom propped against the liquor cabinet and the wall. He flexed his fingers impatiently. "You think you could . . . ?"

"Right. Sorry." Charlie stepped carefully over the glass, grabbed the broom, and thrust it at P.G.

"Some ass-hat dropped a bottle of my dad's bourbon," P.G. said. He didn't take the broom but shifted his weight to his heels. "Would you just sweep the glass in? There's tons of tiny pieces, like glass dust. Shit. But, hey, keep your eye out for the stopper. It's got this, like, horse guy on it. What do you call those horse guys? You know, those guys who ride racehorses?"

"A jockey?" Charlie answered, trying to keep his tone neutral. Was P.G. making fun of him in some complicated way? The Barbees had lawn jockeys in their front yard. Did

P.G. call the lawn jockeys "horse guys"?

"Yeah. That." P.G. grinned. "Man, I've wanted that jockey since I was—shit. Ten? Twelve? It's taken my dad this long to finish the damn bottle, and hell if I'm going to throw it away now."

P.G.'s dad hadn't finished the bottle, not if someone broke it. Charlie wondered if P.G.'s father would be pissed. He wondered if P.G.'s father was even here, or his mother, for that matter. Charlie had seen plenty of caterers but no other grown-ups.

He didn't ask. He swept glass into the dustpan. With his third reach of the broom, he pulled out a cork stopper with a metal base with a tiny statue of a racehorse and a jockey fixed to it. He grabbed it and offered it to P.G.

"Here," he said.

"Sweet!" P.G. exclaimed. He grinned at Charlie, and Charlie grinned back before realizing it.

"See how he's leaning way over the horse?" P.G. said. "Means he's almost to the finish line."

"Cool," Charlie said.

P.G. propped one knee beneath him, evening out his weight. "Thanks, man. You're Charlie, right? Charlie Parker?"

Charlie nodded.

"I'm P.G. This is my place."

"Yep," Charlie said. "Uh, great party."

"Thanks. Hey, that Starrla chick you're always with. Is she your girl?"

Charlie was more than surprised. "Is she . . . ?" He raised his eyebrows, then pulled them together. He couldn't find words.

"She's smokin'—I'll give you that," P.G. said.

"She's not my girl, no," Charlie finally said. He grew suspicious. Was P.G. interested in her? He shouldn't be. If he was, it was for the wrong reasons. "Why?"

"Relax, man. I'm asking for a friend. For my girlfriend's friend." P.G. considered. "*Maybe* my girlfriend. On the way to being my girlfriend, at least, I hope."

Charlie was baffled. P.G. was asking about Starrla on behalf of his maybe-girlfriend's friend? Who was P.G.'s maybe-girlfriend, and who was her friend?

"Who is this guy?" he asked, because Starrla wasn't his girl, but he would still look out for her if he could.

"Huh? What guy?"

"The guy who's . . . after Starrla. Interested in her. Whatever."

"Huh? You lost me, dude. What are you talking about?"

"What are *you* talking about?"

P.G. regarded him. "Tessa Haviland. That's who I'm talking about, not some guy. Tessa's awesome. Her best friend's Wren Gray. Awesome girl, too. She was asking about you."

Charlie couldn't process this. "She . . . Wren Gray . . . in the motorcycle shirt . . ."

P.G. chuckled. "You know who she is, then. And, yeah, amazing body. I agree."

What? Charlie hadn't said anything about Wren's body. He didn't like P.G. discussing it, either, amazing though it was.

"She's interested in you, man. If you're interested back—and I'm getting the feeling you are—well, she's with Tessa in the sunroom."

Charlie rubbed his temple, his fingers going to the scar along the side of his right eyebrow. He dropped his arm when he realized what he was doing.

"Go back through the living room and hang a right," P.G. said. He lifted the dustpan. "I'll be there in a sec."

Charlie propped the broom against the wall. Dazed, he headed out of the liquor-cabinet room. He tried to remember where the dining room was.

"Thanks for your help, man," P.G. called. "And thanks for finding the horse guy!"

Wren wasn't in the sunroom. Neither was Tessa. Maybe because, even with P.G.'s directions, it took Charlie far too long to find it—and when he did, he wasn't even sure it was the sunroom. The rooms in this house needed labels.

He finally found Wren and Tessa by wide French doors

overlooking an outdoor pool. Wren spotted Charlie, and her eyes widened. She smiled.

He worked his way through the crowd to get to her.

". . . sure I do," Tessa was saying. "Anyway, you're too sensitive. Anyway—Charlie!" Her laser beam gaze brought Charlie to a dead stop. "Wren! It's Charlie!" She grabbed his arm and pulled him toward them, wobbling a little. "The real live Charlie Parker, from El Elegante! Remember?"

Wren's cheeks turned red. "Oh my God. Tessa?"

"El Elegante?" Charlie said. "Uh, what's El Elegante?"

Tessa tugged on her skirt. "Frick. I. Am. *So* hot. Jesus Christ. Is it burning up in here, or is it me?"

"It's you," Wren said. To Charlie, she said, "Ignore her. She's had too much champagne."

"I have," Tessa agreed. She fanned herself. "El Elegante is a Mexican restaurant. Wren and I ate lunch there yesterday with P.G." She glanced around the room. "Where'd that boy go? P.G.! Where are you, P.G.?"

"He's coming," Charlie said. "Someone broke something. He was—we were—cleaning it up."

"Awww, you helped him," Tessa said. "That was nice." She whispered, very loudly, "Holy pickles, Wren, he's *totally* cute. Not as cute as P.G., but yes. Totally cute."

She gave Wren a thumb's-up, and Wren whacked her.

"Owwie," Tessa said, stumbling a little but grinning. "And, Charlie, guess what?"

"*Tessa*—"

"When we were at El Elegante, guess who Wren kept going on and on about? Want me to tell you?"

"No," Wren said. "Oh my God." She took Charlie's arm. "Will you come with me? Please?"

Charlie let Wren pull him away, but he heard Tessa raise her voice and say, "She was going on and on about *you*! And how wonderful she thinks you are! And cute! And wonderful! Right, Wren?"

Wren walked faster. Charlie wanted to comfort her, to tell her everything was fine. No big deal. But *cute* and *wonderful* were helicoptering madly in his brain, and a fizzy feeling pushed against his ribs. He realized he was grinning, and he clamped down to make his grin go away.

It came back.

They passed P.G. as they pushed through the French doors.

"Hey, hey," P.G. said to Charlie. "You don't waste time, do you?"

"Do *not* let Tessa drive," Wren told him. "I'll take her home, okay? But she's drunk, and . . ." She shook her head. "Can you go to her? And take care of her?"

"On my way," P.G. said, slipping past them.

Wren led Charlie a little farther, not toward the pool but toward a courtyard sort of space. Japanese lanterns hung from the trees, and strings of Christmas lights made the lush ivy twinkle in the dusk as if lit by a thousand fireflies. It gave the backyard a magical feeling.

Or maybe that was Wren.

A cluster of stoner-druggie kids sat about ten feet away, sprawled over one another and laughing.

"Your shirt! It's breathing!" one of them sputtered, ratcheting up their laughter another notch.

Charlie didn't care about them. He cared about Wren.

She let go of him, and he missed her touch. She turned her back to him and stared up at the sky. Night had fallen, and the first stars had winked their way into existence, twinkling against a palette of inky purples, deep reds, and one last slice of pearly, light-infused blue. It was a blue that reminded Charlie of the ocean, or of pictures of the ocean. He'd never been. He wondered what Wren saw.

He stepped forward. Their shoulders barely touched.

"Tessa . . ." Wren began. She kept her eyes on the sky. "She's great. I love her. She's my best friend."

"Okay," Charlie said.

"But she's so big. She's just so big." She hugged her arms around herself. "Her personality, I mean."

Charlie didn't know Tessa well, but he could see that.

"And El Elegante. Yes, it's a restaurant. But Tessa—oh, I don't know. I am so sorry. Could she not tell how much she was embarrassing me?"

"You have nothing to be sorry for," Charlie said, adding silently, *And absolutely nothing to feel embarrassed about. Nothing.*

She dropped her gaze and toed the ground. The stoners were loud, and their conversation filled the silence. Bats. They'd moved from breathing shirts to something about bats.

"—not the way, man. Totally won't work," a guy with greasy hair said.

"No," stated a girl with a squeaky voice. "If you let the bat sit long enough—"

"But you can't cure something by just letting it sit there," said a second girl. "Not even a bat."

"To properly cure a bat, the first thing you have to do is eviscerate it," pronounced a pale, lanky boy wearing a Bob Marley T-shirt and, for some reason, a lei.

"The first thing you have to do is kill it," the greasy-haired boy said.

"Ugh," Wren whispered. Her eyes, wide and alarmed, met Charlie's.

The lanky boy continued with his lecture, and Wren started a slow, backward retreat from the group. At any moment, she would turn and go back into the house. Bright lights and crowded rooms. Tessa. A different set of conversations, none of which Charlie was interested in.

"I know a park nearby," he blurted. He gestured toward the street. "I've got my car. We could go there and talk, if you want."

Wren bit her lip. She was startled, Charlie could tell, and he mentally kicked himself for being so unsmooth. *I know a park nearby.* Why would Wren want to go to a park with him?

She looked over her shoulder at P.G.'s mansion. Voices and boisterous laughter spilled out, competing with the dead-animal debate the stoners were vehemently engaged in.

Charlie opened his mouth to say, "Never mind, crazy idea," but Wren spoke first.

"Sure," she said. She tilted her head and gave him a beautiful smile. "That sounds nice."

CHAPTER SEVEN

The park, when they arrived, was inhabited by drunk college kids—Wren assumed they were college kids because of their Georgia Tech T-shirts, and because they looked old in a way that even Tessa and P.G. couldn't yet pull off—and they were as loud as the bat killers back at the graduation party had been, if not louder.

There could be no talking here. No nice boy to unsadden her. Her heart felt heavy, and after a Frisbee flew at her out of the darkness, making her duck, she exhaled and said, "We should go."

"Already?" Charlie said. "We just got here."

"Yeah, but . . ." She gestured at the partiers by the swing set.

One of them cupped his hands over his mouth and called, "Yo! Frisbee! Sorry 'bout that!"

Charlie knelt, grabbed the Frisbee, and threw it deftly back at the group. To Wren, he said, "One second." He started for his car, then stopped. Came back for Wren and took her hand. "Actually, come with me."

Wren's tummy turned over. Charlie was . . . why was Charlie holding her hand? She'd held his arm earlier, but that was to get him away from Tessa, and she hadn't thought about it first. She'd just done it. But unless she was mistaken, he was holding her hand on purpose.

She looked at their linked hands as if the answer lay there. She noticed the stitches on his thumb from his visit to Grady Hospital two days ago. She took in, again, how strong and capable his fingers were. With his hand curled protectively around hers, she felt safe—only, as soon as she recognized the feeling, she tugged her hand free. Or tried to. He tightened his grip, striding across the grass.

"What about Starrla?" she said.

Charlie stopped. She bumped into him.

"Ow," she said, rubbing her nose with her free hand.

"Why are you asking about Starrla?" he said. He held her hand tightly.

"Uh, because you two are going out?" Wren said. A guy

wasn't supposed to hold another girl's hand when he had a girlfriend. Even if he was handsome. Even if he smelled like pine needles. Even if he looked dismayed at the very thought of . . . well, whatever he was thinking of.

"I'm not going out with Starrla," he said. "I thought . . . well, no, I guess he couldn't have."

"Huh?"

Charlie's shoulders relaxed. "Nothing."

"Well, good," Wren said. "I mean—"

Hush, she told herself. She was glad, very, that Charlie wasn't claiming Starrla, even if she was fairly certain Starrla still claimed Charlie. This morning, before the graduation ceremony, Starrla had caught Wren looking at Charlie and narrowed her eyes. *Back off*, Starrla's expression had said. Her lips, curving into a smile, had added, *Don't even. You are weak, and I am strong.*

But Charlie was with her, holding her hand, and Wren had her own brand of strength, brought to the surface by the dim glow of the streetlight and the whisper of night air on her skin. It was new to her. Her heart beat with a low, thrumming exhilaration.

"Starrla and I did . . . date," Charlie said. "Once. A long time ago. But now we're just friends."

"Oh," Wren said. "Um, thanks. For explaining."

The moon was full, lighting up Charlie's face. He looked as if he wanted to say something more, perhaps to make sure she truly knew they weren't together anymore. Then he furrowed his brow adorably—he *was* adorable—and squashed the thought, whatever it might have been. He fished in his pocket for his car keys and popped the trunk, all the while not letting go of Wren's hand.

What am I doing? she wondered. What is happening?

Go with it, she told herself. For heaven's sake, stop *thinking* for once.

With a coarse army blanket tucked under his arm, Charlie shut and locked the trunk. "This way," he said, and Wren allowed herself to be led across the far corner of the park and into the bordering grove of trees. Cautions from her mother burbled through her—never, ever go to an isolated spot with a stranger, you don't do that, Wren—but Charlie wasn't a stranger. Also, Wren wasn't her mother.

"You carry a blanket with you everywhere?" she asked. She was trying to tease him, as in, Just how many girls do you take into the woods once the sun sets?

He looked puzzled, and Wren felt dumb. She wasn't her mother, but she wasn't Tessa or some other flirty girl, either. She needed to just be Wren.

"One of my . . . um, at one of the houses I was in, the dad was a scoutmaster," he explained. "'Always be prepared.' That was his motto."

"Oh. That's cool." To try to normalize things, she added, "Was he a nice guy? That dad?"

"No," Charlie said.

"Why not?"

He was quiet, and she wished she hadn't asked.

They were thick in the woods behind the park now, and she had to watch her footing. Then the ground sloped down, and the trees thinned out. They reached a small ditch—maybe a ravine that had been eroded by running water? Behind them were trees, and on the other side of them were trees, but the ditch itself was clear and dry. There were leaves and a few sticks and a mat of prickly grass, but once Charlie let go of Wren's hand and spread out the blanket, none of that was a problem.

He had climbed to the bottom of the hollow on his own, and now he held out his hand. Wren accepted it, grasping him as she slid-hopped down. Following Charlie's lead, she sat on the blanket. Gingerly, she leaned all the way back, her body at an incline on the ditch's banked slope.

"Oh," she said, enthralled. Through the gap in the trees she could see the sky. The moon, luminous and huge, peeked through the leafy branches. "Beautiful."

They lay next to each other, not speaking. Wren could feel the heat radiating from Charlie's body. Tiny hairs on her neck and on her forearms seemed to prickle awake and stand alert. Wren felt very strongly that, since he had brought her here, to this secret place, it was her job to keep the conversation going. Just not by talking about foster families. At first she thought, Guatemala, but she realized she didn't want to talk about Guatemala, either.

Guatemala would work itself out. She'd bought her plane ticket the very day she got her Project Unity acceptance letter—and yes, she probably should have used her savings to pay back the money her parents had spent on college fees, but she didn't—and either her parents would get used to the idea of her leaving or they wouldn't. She hoped they would.

But she didn't want to think about Guatemala, or leaving for Guatemala, right now. Right now, amazingly, she was exactly where she wanted to be.

"Your thumb seems better," she said.

Charlie held out his hand, examining it in the pale moonlight. His fingers, splayed against the stars, seemed . . . more than. More than fingers. More than a part, or parts, of a whole. Just as one plus one is more than two, she thought, not knowing where the idea sprang from, or why.

"Good as ever," he said. He turned his head toward hers just enough so that she could make out his grin. "Better."

She smiled back. She felt her pulse in the hollow of her throat, and she felt the night air on her throat as well. She didn't think she'd ever noticed that sensation in that specific location.

"Bodies are funny, aren't they?" she said.

"How so?" Charlie asked.

She stared at the sky. She was nervous. She didn't want him to laugh. "Just . . . are they us? Are we them?"

Charlie was silent long enough for Wren to regret her words. Then he said, "Do we have souls, you mean?"

Relief pressed her deeper into the scratchy wool blanket. "Yeah. I guess. Or are we just, you know, chemicals? Brain cells talking to brain cells, talking to lung cells and spine cells and thumb cells?"

"Like when Ms. Atkinson compared us to computers with organic hard drives?" Charlie said. "A blow to the head can create a system failure? A disease, like Alzheimer's, is a computer virus?"

Wren nodded. She didn't like that concept, because if it were true—if a human was a highly specialized computer, but a computer nonetheless—where did that leave the "human" part?

"My dad's an atheist," she said. He wanted Wren to share his beliefs, but she didn't.

"My foster mom teaches Sunday school," Charlie replied. "And during the church service, when it's time for 'A Moment with the Kids,' she plays 'Jesus Loves Me.'"

"'A Moment with the Kids'?"

"When the youth minister calls up all the kids and tells them a story that has to do with the day's Scripture."

"Didn't know," Wren said. She rolled onto her side to face him. "So, you go to church?"

She bent her knees slightly to get more comfortable, and her thigh touched Charlie's. She inhaled sharply. Charlie didn't move his leg. Neither did she.

What passed between them, even through the fabric of their jeans—it felt like way more than computer circuitry.

"Sometimes," Charlie said. "Pamela likes it when we do, me and my brother. But Chris usually stays home and works. When I can, I like to stay and help out."

"In the wood shop?"

"The cabinet shop, yeah." He raised his arms and clasped his hands beneath his head, and she saw the hard slope of his biceps. The expanse of skin stretching from his bicep to his shoulder, paler than his forearm and more vulnerable, disappearing into the shadow of his sleeve. Not an entirely private place, but not a part of this boy—*Charlie*—that everyone had seen, either.

And, again, not just a part. More than.

"I think souls are real," Wren said in a burst. "Maybe they're not things you can measure or hold or feel—"

"You can feel them," Charlie said in a low voice. He turned his head, and she saw his cheek meet his upper arm.

I would like to feel that arm, Wren thought. I would like to touch that cheek.

She swallowed. "What about trees?"

His lips quirked. "Trees?"

"Do they have souls?" she asked, because at that moment

they seemed to. Leaves rustled, saying *shushhhh, shushhh*. Branches formed a canopy high over their heads. Add in the matted grass below them, and Wren and Charlie were nestled in . . . a set of parentheses. They were in a moment outside of time. Just the two of them. Their eyes locked. Their bodies, as Charlie rolled onto his side, forming parentheses within the parentheses, and within the parentheses, their souls reached out. Like roots. Like fingers. Like wisps of clouds and slivers of radiant moonlight.

Wren shivered.

"They probably don't," she said. "That's just in fairy tales, right? Druids and dryads and alternate worlds?" She was babbling, but her heart was fluttering, and she was helpless to stop her string of words from issuing forth. "Anyway, I'm a scientist. Or will be, probably, since doctors are scientists. I know that's silly—trees with souls—but I just . . . I guess I just . . ."

She waited for Charlie to jump in and rescue her from her stupidity. He didn't, and when Wren checked his expression, when she let herself truly see his expression instead of hiding from it, she realized he was waiting for her to finish. Not because he was enjoying watching her make a fool out of herself, but because he cared about her thoughts and was interested in hearing them.

His auburn eyes weren't auburn in the dark ditch. They were dark and liquid. A well to fall into. The ocean.

"I guess I think the world is more connected than people realize," she said, choosing her words carefully. You're allowed to have thoughts, she reminded herself. Just because others might scoff, that doesn't mean Charlie will.

She tried to steady her breath. "I think . . . sometimes . . . that scientists . . . *some* scientists . . . want to package things up into neat little boxes. Explain, explain, explain, until there aren't any mysteries left."

"I think you're probably right," Charlie said.

"Well . . . I like the mysteries," she said. Her skin tingled. Those little hairs stood up again, all over her. It wasn't as if she were undressing in front of him, and yet that's how it felt. And she wanted to keep on going, even so. What had this boy done to her?

"I want to understand them, or try to," she said, "but I don't want to put them away in boxes. And if there doesn't seem to be an explanation for something, I don't want that to scare me away. I don't want to force an explanation to fit or throw my hands in the air and give up. You know?"

He nodded. A faint shadow of stubble ran from his hairline down and along his strong jaw.

She swallowed. "Does that make any sense?"

He pulled his eyebrows together endearingly, like a little boy trying to act grown up. "You're saying the mysteries are worth examining, even if they're too big to be understood. That maybe they're bound to be too big to understand, but that doesn't take anything away from them, and in fact just adds to their beauty. Is that close?"

"That's it exactly," she said. He put it into words so beautifully: Marvel and wonder all you want. There will always be more. She laughed, and the surprised smile she got from Charlie was a pure gift.

Then he grew serious. He pulled his eyebrows together again, but this time he didn't look like a little boy at all.

"Hey," he said. He propped himself up on one elbow. With his other hand, he reached out and lightly, lightly stroked her cheek.

Wren's chest rose and fell. She almost felt as if she were out of her body, except she was very much in her body, and her body knew what it wanted.

Charlie leaned in, and she leaned to meet him. His mouth found hers, and her thoughts flew through her, as loud and raucous as magpies. My first kiss. I am eighteen, and this is my first kiss, unless I count Jake What's-His-Name in eighth grade, which I don't. Because this is . . . different. So different.

And then her thoughts dissolved into lips. Breath. A soft sigh, a shifting thigh. She gave herself over to Charlie and the night and the world, full of mysteries. She allowed herself to just be.

More than.

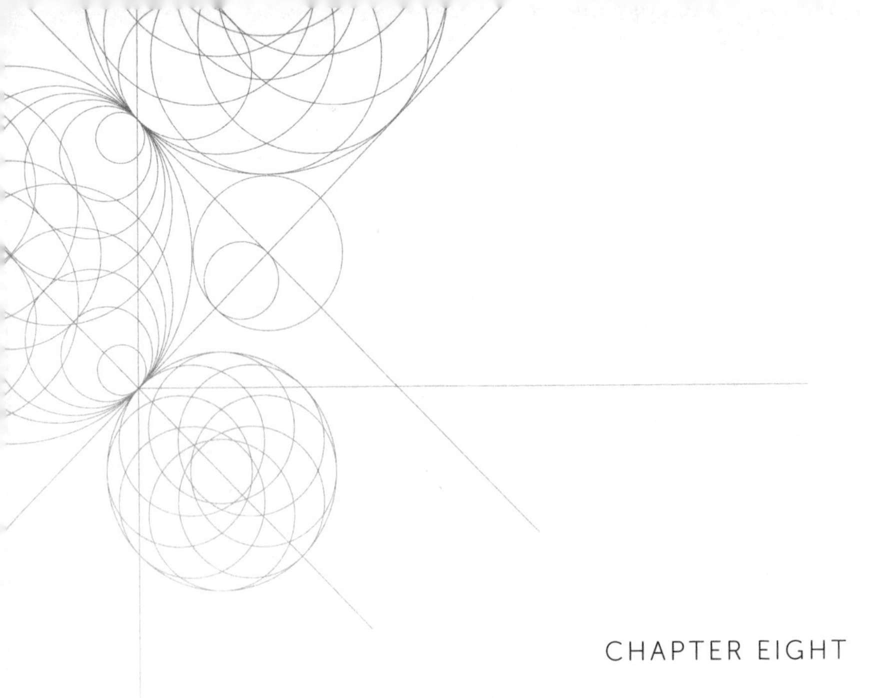

CHAPTER EIGHT

Charlie wanted to see Wren again. She was all he could think about—kissing her, touching her, being with her—and he wanted to do it again. Right away.

He called her the morning after P.G.'s party.

"Charlie?" she said when she answered, and his heart jumped.

"Hey," he said.

"Hey."

"How are you?"

"I'm good. How are you?"

"I'm good," he said. His conversation skills sucked. He

couldn't talk worth a damn, but last night he kissed her, and she kissed him back. So, yeah. He was very, very good.

"I was wondering if you'd like to do something," he said abruptly. "I'd like to see you."

"Today?"

"I could grab some sandwiches if you want. I could come pick you up. I was thinking we could go on a picnic, if that sounded like something you might like. Is that . . . something you might like?"

"Um, sure," she said.

"Great. Awesome. *Great*."

She giggled. "What time?"

"Now," he pronounced, and she giggled again. He was too thrilled to be embarrassed. "I'll be at your house in fifteen minutes. Hey—are you afraid of heights?"

"Of heights? Why?"

"No reason. See you soon."

He took her to a spot along the Chattahoochee River where the sky was wide and blue. Trees lined the bank, and birds sang as they flitted from branch to branch. The water was brown, but it glinted and turned to gold when it splashed over the moss-covered rocks.

Charlie drove here when he needed to think. Until today, he'd always come alone.

"It's beautiful," Wren said after climbing out of the car.

She was wearing a sundress, or some sort of dress, and it swished against her thighs. She had on cowboy boots, and her hair was pulled into a ponytail. *She* was beautiful.

"Come on," he said, almost reaching for her hand. He didn't, and he cursed himself.

He headed up the trail. She followed.

"Do you go hiking a lot?" she asked.

"Um, what do you mean by hiking? You mean like what we're doing now?"

"I guess," she said. "Being outside—is that something you like?"

"Oh," he said. "Yeah. When I was a kid, I was inside a lot, so yeah, I'd rather be outside if I can." He glanced back at her. Her skin was smooth and creamy. When she stepped over a log, he caught a glimpse of the paler skin of her inner thigh. There, and then gone.

Take her hand, he told himself, and this time he did.

"And you?" he said. They started back up the trail. "Do you like being outside?"

"Mmm-hmm," she said. "Especially the ocean. Oh my gosh, I *love* the ocean. I love catching waves and getting all salty, and hungry—I get so hungry after swimming in the ocean—and then flopping down all wet on my towel and letting the sun soak in."

She made a small sound that was almost a moan, and Charlie's cock stirred. Wet and warm and salty? Damn.

Everything she said, she said so innocently, and yet she drove him crazy. She drove him more crazy because she was so innocent.

Discreetly, he tugged at his jeans. "I've never been."

"To the ocean? You've never been to the ocean?"

He shook his head. "One day."

"Oh, Charlie, you have to," she told him. "If you like being outside—wow. You will love the ocean. It makes you feel so . . . I don't know. Small, but not in a bad way. Small because you realize you're part of something bigger. It gets you out of your head, if that makes sense."

She almost tripped on a root. Charlie caught her.

"You all right?" he said.

"Yeah, thanks," she said, looking embarrassed. She let go of his hand. He wished she hadn't. Then, after a moment's hesitation, she looped her arm through his, and he was elated. Her breast brushed against him. She brought her other hand across her body and rested it on his biceps, above their linked elbows.

She smiled shyly up at him. "Is that okay? I'm not making it hard for you to walk or anything?"

She was, but not in the way she meant. Yes, it was okay.

"Do you think that life has patterns in it?" she asked.

"Patterns? Like what?"

She exhaled in a sweet way. "Like, in a non-random way. Like, do things happen for a reason?"

"Hmm," Charlie said. Science and math were subjects he did well at, and in general, he was more comfortable with ideas that could be expressed in formulas than ideas that couldn't fully be explained. Then again, scientific theories started with the seed of an unexplained idea. Mathematical formulas often described phenomena that couldn't be physically verified.

"I'm not sure," he said. "I'm certainly not willing to discount it."

"Me either," she said. "And, okay, this is going to sound silly, but when you called me this morning . . ."

"Yeah?"

"Well, when I heard your voice, I felt . . ."

He waited.

She blushed and squeezed his arm, and he realized that she wasn't going to answer. But he thought that if the world was layered with meaning, then she was the evidence, right here. She was the mystery and the explanation, both.

They reached the place in the trail Charlie had been waiting for, and he gestured with his chin at what lay ahead.

"Hey," he said. "Take a look."

She caught her lower lip between her teeth. "Whoa."

"Yeah," Charlie said.

"How did I not know this was here?" Wren said. "How have I never been here before?"

"Let's go up," Charlie said, leading her toward the embankment. Above them stood a decaying railroad bridge that was built probably a hundred years ago. The wooden support beams stretched like a row of giant As into the clouds. The steel rails that trains once rode on were long gone, but the underlying tracks remained.

At first, Wren kept her arm linked in his as they climbed. Then the dirt grew loose, and she had to use her hands for balance and to clutch at branches. Charlie, behind her, glimpsed the curve of her ass and a flash of panties.

He took several big steps to pass her. From the top of the rise, he extended his hand.

"Oh wow," she said, breathing hard. "We're as high as the treetops."

"Let's go out," he said. He squeezed her hand. "You want to go out?"

"To the middle of the bridge?"

"Yeah, come on."

Two rotting wooden tracks, each approximately three feet wide, stretched across the gulley below. They were sturdy enough to walk on—Charlie would never put Wren in danger—but the ground dipped steeply away several yards past the top of the embankment. Walking along them was like walking along a wide balance beam, only much higher off the ground. Charlie went first and kept Wren's hand in his.

"Crap," Wren said when they reached the center. The

trail they'd hiked up was now fifty or sixty feet below them. "O-o-okay, this is far enough for me."

"Let's sit," Charlie said. "Wait, hold on."

He let go of her hand and dropped to one knee. He brushed sawdust and decaying leaves from the track, and a musty, earthy smell rose up. He took her hand again, and then her forearm, steadying her as she lowered herself down. Then he sat beside her and let his feet hang over the bridge. After checking his expression, she gingerly scooched her legs to the side and did the same. Her cowboy boots dangled in the air. She was so cute. And last night—her lips, and the moonlight, and the way she pressed up against him. He hadn't imagined that, had he?

No. Of course not.

She shifted to arrange her skirt, and her leg touched his. "We're on top of the world," she said.

"We are," he replied.

A breeze lifted her ponytail, and he smelled her citrus shampoo. He smoothed the hairs by her face.

"You are so beautiful," he told her. "I'm going to kiss you now, okay?"

Her eyes widened. She opened her mouth, possibly to answer, but he actually hadn't been asking for permission.

Later, they sat on the hood of his Volvo and ate the sandwiches he'd packed. He'd brought a two-liter bottle of Dr

Pepper, which for some reason she found funny, and they passed it back and forth. Their legs touched, her bare skin against his jeans.

She smiled as they talked, and leaned against him, and once she reached up and pushed his hair behind his ear, which nearly undid him. She also scarfed down her entire sandwich, a bag of chips, and at least three of Pamela's homemade cookies.

"I'm starving," she marveled. "I don't know why, but I am seriously *starving*."

"We walked a pretty long way," he said. "And that hill, to get to the bridge, it's pretty steep."

"I guess," she said. She seemed happy, which made him happy. Happy and proud. "Charlie?"

"Hmm?"

"Earlier, I was going to say . . . well, I'm glad you called me."

"Of course I called you. Why wouldn't I call you?"

She ducked her head. "I don't know. I'm glad you did, that's all."

He lifted her chin with his finger and gazed into her eyes, which were brown with flecks of green. He leaned in and kissed her, because now that he knew he could, he planned on kissing her every chance he got.

CHAPTER NINE

By the time Charlie took Wren home, it was nearly seven. Wren knew her parents would be waiting for her to come eat dinner. They were probably peeking out the window of the front room and checking on her, though they would pretend not to be when she walked in. They were acting very stiff around her. It hurt her feelings, but one good thing came of it. Since they were pretending not to care what she did, she could do whatever she wanted.

Like go on a picnic with Charlie, and when the picnic was over, sit with him in his car in her driveway. Hold his hand. Talk. Hopefully kiss him again—and be kissed again and again—before they finally said good-bye.

She asked him to name five places in the world he'd like to live. Quick, no overthinking.

"Hmm," he said. "Well, Italy. Brazil . . ."

"Brazil?"

"Really cool waterfall. Really cool *big* waterfall. Iguazu Falls? Second biggest in the world after Niagara."

"I didn't know you were a waterfall guy."

"Huh," he said. "Guess I am." He folded his arms over his chest, which was hard and strong. She didn't want to stare, or rather she didn't want to be caught staring, so she filed away a mental image that she could return to later.

"And Italy?" she asked.

"Pasta."

"Ha. Okay, three more."

He took a moment to think, and she said, "What about Paris? Aren't you going to say Paris?"

"Paris," he said.

She laughed again. "Omigosh. All right, why Paris?"

"Because maybe you'll go there with me?"

She shoved him. He grinned and put his arm around her shoulders, and she scooted closer.

"Two more," she said.

"Give me a second. I haven't traveled that much, you know."

"I haven't either," she said. She'd gone on a couple of

trips with her parents over the course of various spring breaks and summer vacations—Florida, to check out Disney World; Colorado, to go skiing; and South Carolina, which was where she and her parents went to the beach—but that was it. She'd applied for her passport at the beginning of the month, though. It felt like a good, if scary, step.

"All right, how about Santa Barbara, because it's on the coast," he said. He played with the hairs at the nape of her neck. "I've heard the ocean is pretty awesome."

"Ah. I've heard that, too. I've only swum in the Atlantic, but I'm sure the Pacific Ocean is nice."

"And for my last place . . . Singapore."

This surprised her, and she liked it.

"Why Singapore?"

"Because it's in Asia. It's an entirely different continent, an entirely different culture. Singapore is the crossroads of the East, right?"

"Is it?"

"I think it would be cool." He leaned over and brushed her lips with his. "And you? Where would you want to live?"

Back into your arms, she thought. She tried to focus. "Um . . . Paris."

"Why?"

"I guess because of the movie *An American in Paris*." She

felt sad for a moment, thinking of how she'd watched that movie with her parents. She'd watched so many movies with her parents. Often on Saturday nights, when Tessa was out on a date, Wren had eaten popcorn with her mom and dad, and they'd taken turns choosing which classic film to introduce her to.

She wasn't with her parents now. She turned toward Charlie. "It's good. Have you seen it?"

"I haven't. I'd like to."

"Okay," she said.

"Where else?"

"Um . . . Guatemala."

"Right. Okay, how come Guatemala?"

She thought about the question deliberately and was surprised by what floated into her mind. "Sarah Shields."

"Who's Sarah Shields?"

"Wow. I haven't thought of her for ages. She was a neighbor of ours when I was little. She always wore long skirts, down to her ankles, and kept her hair in a bun. I think she was super religious?"

She shifted her body. "But her husband—he was a big guy with a baby face—he always, like, barked at her. 'Why hasn't the car been washed?' 'Why haven't you done the laundry?' Stuff like that."

"Sounds like a jerk."

"Yeah, I didn't like him. I thought Sarah was great,

though. She talked to me whenever she saw me, and she always smiled, and she gave me cookies whenever she baked a batch, although they weren't all that good, because she put flaxseed in them."

Charlie traced the line of her neck. "Flaxseed?"

She laughed. "It's weird what your brain stores away."

"What does she have to do with Guatemala?"

Her laughter trickled off. "Um . . . one day I came home from school, and my mom told me Sarah was gone. She'd moved to Guatemala to do mission work."

I guess she got out, Wren's mom had said, and it must have meant something to Wren, for her to have remembered it all these years later.

"So are you going to visit her when you're there?" Charlie asked.

"Visit who?"

"Sarah. In Guatemala."

"Oh. I doubt it."

Charlie rubbed his eyebrow. Wren wondered what else about her own life she wasn't aware of.

"Okay," Charlie said. "Well, Paris and Guatemala—that's two places. You get to name three more."

"That's all for now," Wren said. "There's tons of places I want to go, but for now, that's enough." She bit her lip. "Will you kiss me?"

He took her chin and guided her mouth toward his.

∞

On Monday night, at 11:58, Charlie sent Wren a text that said, I miss you. Is that weird?

They'd talked and texted during the day, but they hadn't gotten to see each other, and Wren missed him, too.

Not weird! Wren typed back. No more long days at Chris's shop!

Agreed, Charlie texted. Can I call you tmorrw?

tmorrw? Wren typed, smiling at his typo.

*Tomorrow. Sorry, crap phone. Can I?

Absolutely, Wren typed back.

Good. Are your parents awake?

??? she typed.

You might turn your ringer off, that's all, he texted.

Her phone rang. Oh. Ha. It was tomorrow already.

She hit ACCEPT and brought her phone to her ear.

"Hi," she said.

"Hi," he said. "Did I wake you?"

"Yes, because I was asleep. That wasn't me just texting you. It was my doppelgänger."

"Your doppelgänger is pretty cute."

She drew her knees to her chest and pressed the phone to her ear. She was wearing a thin T-shirt and the soft cotton shorts she slept in. She was sitting on her bed, with her comforter half-turned down and her pillow propped beneath her. A sock monkey sat beside her, a sweet little sock monkey with bunny rabbit ears. Sometimes she still held it while she slept.

Her bunny rabbit sock monkey sat beside her, and her parents were right down the hall, and Charlie Parker was talking to her from his house. She asked about his day, and as she listened to his reply, she thought about how much she liked his voice. It was low and gentle, and he articulated his words in a deliberate way. He said *At-lan-ta* with both *t*s enunciated, for example. Most people, Wren included, said it more like *Atlannuh*.

She wondered what his room was like. She wondered what he was wearing. She wondered if he thought about her, and all the ins and outs of her existence, as much as she thought about him.

"So, yeah, it felt good to get it all done," he said, wrapping up his story about an order he'd been working on. "What about you? You had that thing with Tessa, right?"

He meant the mom-and-daughters luncheon she'd gone to.

"Totally fine, totally unexciting," she said. "They served chicken salad. It had too much mayonnaise."

"I'm sorry to hear that."

"Yes. Alas. Oh, and my dad . . ." She broke off, not sure she wanted to follow up on that thought.

"Your dad doesn't like chicken salad, either?"

"No, he does. I think. I was going to tell you something else completely . . . but never mind."

"Why never mind? Does it have to do with your parents and Guatemala?"

Wren had told him about her conversation with them after graduation, when she broke the news about Project Unity. She was touched that he grasped how much it mattered.

"Well, yeah, I guess," she said. She rested her chin on her knees. "My dad gave me a guilt trip about the car he and my mom gave me, that's all. I don't know. It had to do with Guatemala, but it didn't have to do with Guatemala. I guess it made me a little sad. But it's no big deal."

"It *is* a big deal if you felt sad. What happened?"

Tears welled in her eyes. He was just being nice, but how nice that he was nice!

Oh, Charlie, she thought. Her body softened. She turned her head and rested her cheek on her knees.

"First of all, they gave me a *car*," Wren said. "I have nothing to complain about, right? I'm so, so, so, so, so thankful . . . mainly. And I only say 'mainly' because I don't actually need a car. But whatever. Maybe I just feel guilty?"

"What happened?"

"Um, this afternoon I did a grocery store run for my mom, and I drove my car, and my dad made a comment about how he was glad I was getting *some* use out of it since

I wouldn't be using it this fall. By 'some use,' he meant not enough. Meaning, why did he buy it in the first place."

She sighed. "But that's all that happened, just that one passive-aggressive remark to make sure I knew what a bad daughter I am. So seriously, it isn't that big of a deal."

"I'm sorry," Charlie said. "Sounds like he let you down."

Wren was startled. She'd expected him to accept her dismissal of the whole thing. "What do you mean?"

"There's no way you're a bad daughter. I know you, and that's impossible."

She gripped her phone. *Did* he know her? She hoped so. And she didn't think she was a bad daughter, either. Not truly.

"As for your dad, it sounds like he's struggling with letting you go," Charlie went on. "It's sounds to me like . . ." He paused. "Um, I don't want to overstep."

"You're not," Wren said.

"Will you tell me if I do?"

"Yeah, absolutely, but I want to hear what you're thinking."

"It sounds to me like you want him to support your choices."

"I do."

"And you feel bad for not choosing the path that would make him happy, but you want him to want *you* to be happy."

"I do. Yes!"

"Instead, he's saying he wouldn't have gotten you a car if he'd known you weren't going to go to college next year."

"He didn't actually say that, but yeah. And not just college. Emory. And I guess it's more like he's *confused* about why he got me a car, since I'm not holding up my end of the bargain."

"Did you have a bargain?"

"N-n-nooo, not about what would happen after high school. He assumed he knew what would happen, maybe? I think we all did. I just changed my mind."

"Which you're allowed to do," Charlie said.

"Huh."

"He's your dad," Charlie said in his measured way. "It would be great if he could say, 'Okay, this is what you want, so I'm here for you. I want to support you in whatever way I can.'"

"It would, wouldn't it?" Wren said. She shifted onto her side and propped her weight on her forearm. She ran her finger along a line of stitching on her bedspread. "Now I'm the one who doesn't want to overstep, but . . . do you have a relationship or whatever with your dad? Your real dad?"

"My biological dad? No."

"Biological. Sorry."

"He took off before I was born."

"Oh." She felt out of her element. Charlie had said to her, just now, *Hey, you're a good person. I care about what you're going through*. He hadn't used those words, but she wanted him to know she felt the same way.

"What about your mom?" she asked tentatively. "Your biological mom. Do you ever see her?"

"She's an addict. She gave up visitation rights a long time ago."

"Oh. I'm so sorry."

"Thanks, but you don't need to be." His tone wasn't sharp, exactly, but there was an edge to it.

Wren twisted a lock of her hair. On the other end of the line, Charlie breathed out.

"I was six the last time I saw her," he said. "The family I was with—not Chris and Pamela—took me to her every so often. They'd tell me to get in the car, and we'd go to McDonald's, or a park, or sometimes this weird room in the basement of a church. They'd say, 'You're going to see your mom,' and I'd get excited, because I was little."

"And because she's your mom," Wren said.

"Mmm," he said noncommittally. "Half the time, she didn't show up. I guess I must have cried, because that couple—I know they got mad."

Wren didn't know what to say.

"Shit," Charlie said. "I shouldn't have told you that, huh? Wren, shit. I'm sorry."

"Charlie, please," she said. "I just complained about my father, who bought me a car. You just told me about . . ."

She pressed her lips together. "Please. Charlie."

"I didn't mean to mess things up," he said, low and fast. "I don't know why I even—"

"Because I asked, and so you told me, and . . . thank you."

"For what?"

A lump formed in her throat. "For trusting me."

He fell silent. She rolled onto her stomach, bending her knees and pressing the toes of one foot into the sole of the other.

"You're welcome," he finally said. He sounded embarrassed, and Wren wanted to wrap her arms around him and hold him.

They spoke at the same time.

Wren said, "Do you want to . . . ?"

Charlie said, "Is it all right if we change the subject?"

"Whatever you want," Wren said, although the question she'd started to ask was, *Do you want to talk about it?*

Apparently not, and that was his choice. She meant it when she said thank you, though. She felt different now than she'd felt twenty minutes ago. She felt honored that Charlie had shared the story about his mom with her, even though it was sad.

"So," he said. "Chicken salad. Not a fan?"

She attempted to giggle. "Not a fan."

"Is it the mayonnaise?"

"Yep. I hate mayonnaise. My mom doesn't understand that, but I do. I like mustard, but only honey mustard or spicy mustard. Not yellow mustard."

"So you don't have a strong opinion about it," Charlie said. "That's what I hear you saying."

"Exactly. And you?"

"Are you kidding? Mayonnaise all the way. I *live* for mayonnaise. Bread is just a vehicle."

"So you don't have a strong opinion, either."

"The hell I don't."

Her laughter came more easily.

They chatted for a few more minutes about other this-or-thats: dogs versus cats (Charlie liked both, Wren preferred cats), mornings versus nights (Charlie was a night person, Wren liked getting up early), and snooze versus no snooze (they both chose no snooze, agreeing that they got more real sleep that way).

"I should let you go," Charlie said reluctantly. "You probably need to go to bed, huh? Given that you're a mustard-eating morning person?"

"I guess," Wren said.

"All right. But I miss you."

"Me, too," Wren said. And all at once the thought of *not* missing him—and not knowing him, since she had to know him in order to miss him—seemed impossible.

They breathed together for several long moments.

"I wish I could kiss you good night," Charlie said.

"I wish that, too."

"Imagine I am," he said.

Her breath hitched. "Okay."

"I'm sending you kisses, baby."

Her skin tingled. He called her baby, and he sent her kisses, and everything hard turned good.

Everything good was new.

CHAPTER TEN

June flew by, and Charlie fell deeper and deeper in love. He walked hand in hand with Wren along trails by the river in the Chattahoochee Nature Center. Sometimes they returned to the railroad bridge, but they explored new trails, too. Or they sat on the floor of Chris and Pamela's house and leaned against each other as they watched movies on Wren's iPad. Once, Charlie had dinner with Wren and Wren's parents, who were nice, if overbearing. Wren's dad told Wren to lower her voice when she was talking—not the volume of her voice, but the pitch—because apparently Wren's dad thought women shouldn't be shrill.

Wren wasn't shrill. Wren was perfect. Charlie put his hand on her thigh under the table. Wren slipped her hand under the table, too, and squeezed his fingers.

Sometimes Wren packed a lunch and brought it to Chris's shop so that she and Charlie could eat and talk and laugh before Charlie returned to work. Sometimes she baked cookies, and she always left him with a Ziploc bag of extras for later. Always he walked her to her car. Always he kissed her before she left, slipping his hand to the small of her back and pulling her closer.

When Charlie couldn't be with her, he ached from missing her. When he was with her, he felt as if all was well with the world. He smiled without meaning to. Stroked her hair. Talked with her about friends and movies and books, and talked about how lucky they felt to have found each other.

He told her, when she asked, that, yes, he'd felt something pass between them on the last day of school. She'd brought it up shyly, as if worried he might think she was being silly, but he never thought the things she had to say were silly.

"It was before first period," he said. "We were outside the main building. You had on a blue shirt, and you looked beautiful, as always."

She blushed and nuzzled his shoulder. He kissed the top of her head, which was warm from the sun.

"You were with Tessa," he continued. "I was with Ammon. He was telling me about a new computer game he'd bought, but I wasn't paying attention. A breeze made your skirt fly up—did you know that?"

"Are you saying I flashed you?" She hid by pressing her cheek against his collarbone. "Great."

"It *was* great. Yes. And then I waved at you, because you were staring at me."

"Oh my gosh."

"But you didn't wave back. You were kind of in a fog or something. Finally you snapped out of it, and you *did* wave, and everything got—I don't know—sharper. Because—"

A lump rose in his throat. Because she'd seen him, he'd almost said. Really seen him.

Wren pulled back and searched his face. "Charlie?"

"Sorry. Don't know what happened there."

"It's okay," she said.

He gave himself a shake. "So, yeah, you came out of your fog and waved at me, and everything else fell away."

She took his hand and squeezed it. "I think our souls touched," she said.

He squeezed back. "I felt it."

He loved talking to Wren. He also loved touching her. The back of her neck. The skin of her wrist, so pale that he could trace the blue veins beneath. Her lower lip. Once, he ran his finger over the swell of her lower lip, and she surprised him by parting her lips and capturing his finger between her top and bottom teeth. She sucked on him, circling the tip of his finger with her tongue, and he got hard. She had no idea. At least, he thought she had no idea, although when she let his finger go, she smiled impishly.

At moments like those, she could have asked him to do anything—scale a mountain, push down trees, bring her a single wild strawberry from a secret patch—and he would have done it.

But what they were doing, and what was happening between them, was all new for Wren, and Charlie needed to remember that. Well, it was new for Charlie, too, though. If not physically, then emotionally. One day, when Charlie was worn out after hours of work, Wren told him to stretch out on their blanket. She lay behind him, hiked up his T-shirt, and scratched his back, using her fingernails to draw loops and spirals on his skin. It brought tears to his eyes. He didn't know why.

Then he realized it was because she was taking care of him, because she *wanted* to take care of him. It was a gesture more tender than sexual, and yet it felt more intimate than sex ever had.

More intimate than sex with Starrla, he meant. Starrla was the only girl he'd slept with.

He wanted to have sex with Wren. God, he wanted to, and he hoped she eventually would, too.

As for Starrla, she had a new boyfriend herself, but her having a boyfriend in no way made it okay for Charlie to have a girlfriend. Starrla had strong opinions about Wren, and she shared them frequently and creatively.

One afternoon, after a picnic with Wren in what they now called "their ditch," Charlie's beat-up flip phone chirped as he and Wren were walking back to their cars. Sometimes when they got together—which was most days—Wren asked Charlie to pick her up in his Volvo. More often, she drove herself. It made more sense, she said. Charlie put in so many hours at Chris's shop, and she had her volunteer work at Grady. Also, even though Wren's parents continued to lay a guilt trip about having bought her a car she never asked for, Wren seemed to think it helped her case, a little, to drive it as often as she could before fall.

Charlie's phone chirped again. When he didn't answer it, Wren cocked her head.

"Your ghetto phone is calling you," she said. She called it that because it was old. No apps, no voice activation, no Internet access.

It chirped again.

"Aren't you going to answer?"

"If it's important, they'll leave a message," he said, slipping his arm around her waist. He slipped his other hand into his pocket and switched off his phone's ringer. "Right now I'm with you."

She liked that answer, he could tell, because when they reached her Prius, she leaned back against the front door and put both arms around him, pulling him in for a long, slow kiss. He felt the length of her against him as she rose onto her tiptoes.

He couldn't believe she'd never had a boyfriend, but damn, he was glad she hadn't. *He* was her boyfriend now. "My Charlie," she whispered once when they lay, entwined, on the blanket in their ditch. He hadn't replied, because he sensed he wasn't supposed to have heard. He just held her tighter.

In the parking lot, still leaning against her Prius, Wren pulled out of their kiss. "Wait," she said. "What if it was Dev? If it was Dev calling you . . ."

If it was Dev calling, or Chris or Pamela calling about Dev, then Charlie would go to him. Wren knew this because more than once he'd had to push back their date or even cancel on her—which killed him—due to a minor Dev emergency. A urinary tract infection. A pressure sore on Dev's leg that Pamela feared might be a blood clot. Joint problems that Dev couldn't feel but that couldn't be ignored.

It wasn't always Dev or Chris or Pamela, though.

"I'll check," Charlie said. He pulled out his phone, flipped it open, and flipped it shut again. He shoved it back into his pocket.

Wren lifted her eyebrows.

"Ammon," Charlie said. "I'll call him later."

"Okay," Wren said. "Tell him hi from me."

"He still can't believe we're going out," Charlie said. "Wait, let me rephrase. He can't believe a girl like you would be willing to go out with a guy like me."

"Well, he's nuts," Wren said.

"I can't believe it, either."

Wren groaned. She didn't like it when Charlie made comments like that. "Well, I can't believe you'd be willing to go out with me," she said, "except yes I can, because here we are. I think we're both lucky to have found each other. I think we're equally lucky. All right?"

"You're right. I agree."

"Thank you. That's better." She reached up and tugged on the hairs at the nape of his neck. Charlie loved how she did that, twining her fingers and locking on. "I guess I should go home, but I don't want to."

The tiniest furrow formed in her brow, and Charlie suspected she was thinking about her parents. They'd accepted her choice to put off college, but in a pursed-lipped, disapproving way that forbade Wren from feeling good about it, or so it seemed.

"I suppose we don't need to buy anything for your dorm room after all," her mother might say while Charlie was standing by. "I was so looking forward to helping you decorate it. Well, next year."

Or, from her father: "You realize this means an additional year before you can practice medicine." And then, like from his wife, a sigh.

Charlie wanted to like Wren's parents, but he wanted to jump in and protect her from them, too.

Last week, Wren had hooked her computer up to the TV and used the TV as a monitor so that she could show Charlie and her parents a slide show she'd put together. It was about Project Unity. It was a peace offering, to try and help her parents understand.

"Why Guatemala?" they said. "Why now?"

Wren didn't bring up that neighbor she'd told Charlie about, Sarah something. Instead, she knelt on the rug by her computer and clicked through pictures of young adults wearing T-shirts, shorts, and ball caps posing with brown-eyed, brown-skinned people from Guatemala. Blue skies, lush green forests, explosions of colorful flowers. Lots of white teeth. Lots of smiles.

"I'll probably travel between three or four towns," Wren told them. "I'll spend the mornings working at summer camps—"

"Summer camps?" her dad said.

"Not summer camps. Um, summer schools. Summer language schools. And in the afternoons, all the volunteers do other service projects, like help repair houses and stuff."

"So you'll be doing construction," her dad said.

"John," Wren's mom said.

"Dad, listen," Wren said earnestly. "I want to be part of something bigger. I just . . . I want . . . it doesn't *have* to be Guatemala, but—"

"If it doesn't have to be Guatemala, then why not Atlanta?" her dad interrupted.

"John!" Wren's mom said, but then she turned to Wren and added, "Yes, Wren. Why?"

Wren grew flustered. "Because I know Spanish. Because the people are supposedly really nice, and they need our help, and it's warm, and the food's good—"

"The *food's* good?" her dad said.

"Dad," Wren said, her breath hitching. "Please."

Charlie wanted to go to her and put his arm around her. The only reason he didn't was because he sensed that Wren needed to plow through this on her own.

"I want to make a difference in the world, and change people's lives, and . . . yeah," she said.

"Becoming a doctor will change people's lives," her dad said. "Your volunteer work at Grady changes lives. If you can't explain why this grand plan of yours has to happen in a foreign country, then I don't see how you have much of a leg to stand on."

She doesn't have a leg to stand on because you keep knocking her down, Charlie thought. She wants to go to a foreign country because maybe, if she's a thousand miles away, you won't be able to.

"Dad, I already signed the Project Unity acceptance letter—"

"Just like you signed your acceptance letter to Emory," her dad said. He snorted. "How do you expect that to convince me?"

Her tone was imploring. "I've been given so much—by y'all, by my teachers, by my friends. I want to give something back. Does that make sense?"

"No, Wren, it doesn't," her father said. "This plan of yours, though I can hardly call it a plan, is foolish and fanciful, and I'm sorry to disappoint you, but nothing you've told us has changed my mind." He splayed his fingers and exhaled, his nostrils flaring. "Do you want to know why your mother and I are letting you follow through with it?"

Wren's lips parted.

"We decided to let you fail," he said, clipping his words. "If you won't listen to reason, what other choice do we have?"

Wren's cheeks went blotchy, and Charlie tightened his jaw. He'd tried to give Wren's dad the benefit of the doubt, but he was a bastard. Couldn't he see that he was hurting his daughter? Making her want to run farther and faster?

Charlie didn't want Wren to go to Guatemala any more than her parents did, but it was her decision, and he wasn't about to tell her what to do. He hugged her instead, leaping up and joining her the minute her parents left the room.

"It's okay," he told her when she clutched him. "You're okay. And you're not going to fail."

"I might," she said dismally.

He kissed her forehead. "Never."

Now, in the parking lot, Charlie kissed her forehead again. "Hey. If you don't want to leave yet, don't. Let's hang out a little longer."

"I thought you needed to get to the shop," Wren said.

He did, but he said, "Not yet. We're good. Want to sit in the back of your car?"

A particular smile lit up Wren's face, one Charlie knew and adored.

"Yes, please!" she said. She unlocked her car, climbed into the backseat, and pulled him in behind her. The back of her Prius was another of their favorite spots, and their backseat activities had a rhythm all their own.

First she locked the doors and tossed the keys into the driver's seat. Next she kicked off her flip-flops. Then, utilizing the full length of the backseat, she scooched down and stretched out as best she could. He propped his weight on his elbows and stretched out on top of her. He bore part of his weight with one foot, which he wedged against the car's floor, and kissed her nose.

"Mmm," she said, and she arched her back. In some

ways they'd moved fast physically, which Charlie was 100 percent fine with, although there were certain things they hadn't done that he wished they would. She'd touched his arms, his abs, his chest—she seemed to adore running her hands over his chest, which made him happy—but she had yet to touch his dick, for example.

Was she shy? Nervous? Worried he wouldn't like it?

He would love it. Christ.

He kissed her for real, and she looped her arms around his neck and her legs around his hips. Skin. Warmth. Sweat and breath and Wren's perfume, all of it intoxicating.

"God, you drive me crazy," he said. He kissed her neck. Ran his hand over the curve of her breast, and then down along her side. Down farther, pulling her close. She was wearing a skirt today, and he found the hem and slipped his hand underneath. Her thigh, her ass. Silk panties with soft lace around the edges.

He ran his fingers below the lace, and Wren made a small sound. Wren tried to be quiet when they were together like this. It embarrassed her, she said, that she made noises. But Charlie loved it. His cock strained against his jeans. He pulled back slightly and used his forearm to push her legs apart. He slid his hand beneath her panties again and found the spot he was looking for—heat and wetness and skin softer than any silk or lace—and slipped two fingers inside her.

"Oh," Wren said. She was breathing hard. Charlie drew away from their kiss, but kept on with his fingers, watching her. Her eyes were closed. Her lips were parted. She lifted her hips, and when Charlie leaned in and kissed her again, the universe opened up and swallowed him whole, and Charlie brought Wren with him. This, the two of them together, was how it should be.

They stopped, eventually and reluctantly. They were still in the backseat of Wren's car. It was still a bright June day. They heard kids shrieking on the play structure, which was far away but not far enough away.

Wren sat up and wriggled out from under him. Charlie sat up, too. As always, he wished her hand would go to him, but he didn't want to push her.

He pressed his hands onto his quads. He knew he'd have to let off steam soon.

"Hi," she whispered.

"Hi," he whispered back.

"You have amazing eyes," she said. She nestled up close, tucked her legs beneath her, and rested her head on his shoulder. With one hand, she played with his hair. Her other hand drifted down his chest, stopping at the waistband of his jeans. She put her hand under his shirt and found his belly, tracing lazy circles. It amazed her that he wasn't ticklish. She'd told him so. For a while, she'd tried to prove him wrong. Now she seemed to simply enjoy running her fingers over his skin.

She sighed happily and hugged him, a warm kitten snuggled against his side.

"I'm glad it wasn't Dev who called," she said.

"Me, too."

"I mean, I'm glad he's okay."

"Mmm," Charlie said.

"Can I ask you something?"

Tension coiled in his stomach. "Sure."

"What happened to him? Was he born with his legs paralyzed?"

Charlie, as a matter of principle, didn't talk about Dev that way. Dev's story was Dev's to tell, not Charlie's.

Charlie knew Wren would keep it to herself, though. Anyway, he couldn't say no to Wren if he tried.

He exhaled. "When he was a baby, his father punched him in the gut."

"What?" Wren said. "When he was a *baby?*"

"He got a blood clot in his spine, and a week later he was paralyzed from the waist down."

"Poor Dev," Wren said. "And then—social services . . . ?"

Charlie nodded tersely. A baby. Who punched a baby?

"I'm glad he found Pamela and Chris," Wren said. "Or that they found him. Either way."

"Me, too," Charlie said. Dev came to them when he was eight, and having him there was good for everyone. One night, early on, Charlie had helped Dev into a pair of soft pj's, because Dev asked him to. When Charlie wheeled Dev out to the TV room, Pamela looked at Dev and said, "Aw, honey. You look so cuddly."

"I *am* cuddly," Dev said. "Right, Charlie?"

"Sure," Charlie said, and when Charlie sat down, Dev found a way to put his head on Charlie's shoulder. That was it. Sold. Charlie had loved him fiercely and protectively from that moment on.

"I'm glad *you* found Pamela and Chris," she said. "Or they found you. Either way."

"Me, too," he said. "Dev and I are lucky."

"Pamela and Chris are just as lucky," she said.

"That's what they say. That, and stuff like how we should never feel like guests, and how their house really is our house." He rubbed Wren's arm. "You know what's amazing? I think they really mean it."

"Of course they do," Wren said. "You guys make their house a home." She groaned. "Ugh. Corny."

"I don't mind corny. Not from you."

She sat up straight. "We were talking about 'home' recently, P.G. and Tessa and I. Tessa was being mopey about everyone splitting up, and she was like, 'But Atlanta will always be our home! We'll always come back to Atlanta!'"

"I hope she's right," Charlie said.

Wren shot him a look. "Maybe. I'm just not sure a person's home is determined by where he or she lives. I think home is more than that."

Charlie mentally cataloged all the places he'd lived. "Okay."

"That's it? Just 'okay'?"

He nodded. "Okay."

"You say 'okay' to the strangest things."

"Do I?"

"You do."

"Okay," he said, and then he glanced at his watch and realized it really was time for him to go. He told Wren good-bye and gave her one last kiss. He missed her even before he pulled out of the parking lot.

At a stoplight, he fished his phone out of his pocket and flipped it open. Starrla had left not just one voice mail but four, and he grimaced. He was glad he'd turned his ringer off.

CHAPTER ELEVEN

"You two are going like gangbusters, so when are you going to *do it* already?" Tessa asked, loading the term *do it* with every ounce of cheesy intonation she could muster. Tessa's mom was out and about, and Tessa and Wren were sharing Tessa's backyard hammock, Tessa's head by Wren's bare feet and vice versa. Tessa wanted girl time with Wren. Demanded girl time with Wren, since soon—too soon—Wren would be gone.

Leaving would mean being separated from Tessa, and that would be hard. It would also mean being separated from Charlie, and that would be awful. Wren was reluctant to admit this to Tessa, and she would never admit it to her parents, but the thought had crossed her mind that maybe she didn't want to go so far away after all.

It wasn't as if she wanted to go to Emory instead. She just wanted to be with Charlie. It felt like an unsolvable dilemma, because if she stayed in Atlanta, she'd "fail," to quote her father. She'd fail to stand up for herself, fail to help the kids she'd committed to helping, fail to escape her parents' control.

But if she went to Guatemala, she'd fail, too, because she'd have left behind the boy she loved.

Tessa touched Wren's chin with her big toe. "Tickle, tickle," she cooed.

"*Tessa*," Wren said, pushing Tessa's foot away.

"Then answer my question. Do you *want* to?"

Did Wren want to have sex with Charlie? Definitely. It was hard to talk about, that's all. Tessa had had sex for the first time when she was sixteen, and since then she'd had sex with two other boyfriends before P.G. And, yes, Tessa and P.G. were now having sex ("And it is soooooo good," Tessa raved), which brought Tessa's count up to four.

That was a lot of sex, Wren thought.

"Have you at least touched his dick yet?" Tessa said.

Wren squeezed shut her eyes. "Tessa!"

"Oh my God, Wren. That poor guy must have the worst case of blue balls ever."

"Not helping, Tesseract," Wren said. She peeked at Tessa through half-opened lids. "I *want* to. I want to do everything. I just . . . don't know how."

"Dude. Lady. You just *do* it!" Tessa said. She handed Wren a water bottle full of "special" lemonade. Enough lemonade to make it taste good, but definitely lots of "special."

"Here," she said. "Drink."

Wren obeyed. The late-afternoon sun felt wonderful on her skin. The sun, plus the vodka in the lemonade, plus Tessa's questions . . .

She thought of Charlie's strong chest. His forearms. His kind auburn eyes. She felt tingly, and she draped one foot off the hammock and pushed against the ground.

"Sex is a basic human drive, Wren," Tessa said. "And you know what else? It's fun, especially with the right guy, and P.G. is definitely my right guy. Sex with P.G. . . . oh man." She softened her tone. "It's incredible. I had no idea."

"That's awesome," Wren said, and she meant it. It scared her, too, though. If—or more likely, when—Charlie and Wren had sex, Charlie would be Wren's first. Would Wren be Charlie's first? She was pretty sure the answer was no, though she hated thinking about that. What if Wren wasn't good at sex? What if Charlie was disappointed? What if he couldn't help but compare her to . . . ?

Forget that.

Back to the question of the day: Did Wren want to have sex with Charlie?

She took another swig of lemonade for courage. "Yes, I want to have sex with Charlie. I even"—she stopped breathing—"went on the pill?"

"Are you serious?" Tessa exclaimed. "*You?* Went on the *pill?*"

"I did." She winced. "Is that bad?"

"Are you kidding? Wren! Yay!" Tessa said. She wiggled her fingers for the lemonade, and Wren passed it to her. "To you and Charlie!" she exclaimed, downing a long sip. "This is huge!"

Wren's heart felt jumpy. She smiled.

"I really like him, you know," Tessa confided. "Charlie, I mean."

"Yeah?"

"P.G. does, too. P.G. says he's a good guy."

"He *is* a good guy," Wren said. "So is P.G."

Tessa propped herself up, not an easy task on a hammock. "Do you mean that, Wren? About P.G.?"

Wren was surprised at Tessa's sudden intensity. Then she felt dumb. Tessa's approval mattered to Wren; didn't it make sense that Wren's approval would matter to Tessa?

P.G. had continued to grow on Wren over the course of the hot, lazy summer. She appreciated how outgoing he was. She liked his easy grin, and his ability to act like an arrogant ass-hat while somehow letting everyone know that he was fully aware that he was acting like an arrogant ass-hat, which made it funny instead of annoying.

More importantly, P.G. saw the real Tessa, Wren thought. Possibly because he was like her in so many ways.

P.G. was Tessa's "more than."

"P.G.'s great," Wren said, and Tessa flopped back onto the hammock, making it bounce.

"Yeah, I love him," she replied. "Or, I think I do. Do you love Charlie?"

"*Tessa*," Wren said.

"What? Why is that not an okay question to ask?"

Wren tilted her head and gazed at the sky. The sun was sending up its last orange rays of the day. Charlie would be finishing work before long.

"I don't know," she said. "Why do you only *think* you love P.G.?"

"I didn't say *only*. Even if I think I do . . ." Tessa pushed Wren's rib with her bare foot. "Love's a big deal."

"You think?"

"I know. And here's something else I know: I've got kind of a big personality, if you haven't noticed."

"Ah."

"Yes, you're making fun of me. All right. But I wonder if sometimes you forget that I'm putting on a show.

I'm almost always putting on a show. Do you know that, Wren?"

"Are you putting on a show now?"

"I'm not, which is why what I'm saying matters. I think I love P.G."

"That's huge," Wren said.

"I know." Tessa's foot lay against Wren's side. It was the same foot from when Tessa was younger. It would be the same foot when she was ninety-nine.

"When I'm sad, do you know what P.G. does?" Tessa asked.

"Why are you sad?"

"Wren. Everyone's sad sometimes."

Right, Wren thought. Now *she* felt young. "What does he do?"

"He brings me frozen yogurt. He picks out a movie for us, one he thinks I'll like. And he holds me."

"That's sweet," Wren said.

"And for the rest of the night, or whenever, he's just . . . extra nice. Like, I can tell that he cares. It *is* sweet."

"And you're not pretending."

"I'm not pretending."

"Got it," Wren said. She hesitated. "Well, Charlie, he's wonderful. He's so *good*, as in a good, good person."

"Tell me more," Tessa said, her voice shifting to a less serious mood. Still serious enough, but more back to fun-

and-games Tessa. "Don't get me wrong. I like the guy. But he's not the most talkative."

"He talks to me," Wren said. "And he cares what I think, even off-the-wall stuff like trees having souls, or whether time is linear or stretchy."

"'Stretchy'? You lost me."

Right. The stretchiness of time wasn't for Tessa, and that was okay. The stretchiness of time wasn't for most people, perhaps, and, in fact, time *wasn't* stretchy for Wren except when she was with Charlie.

But with Charlie, she could—and did—talk about anything. Charlie was super smart, and he was reading up on discrete math before starting at Georgia Tech in August. He was doing this for fun. When he came across an idea he thought Wren would appreciate, he shared it with her.

A couple of days ago he'd told her about a math professor who was interested in multiple, coexisting dimensions—beyond the familiar three. This professor tried to explain those overlapping dimensions by making a cube out of paper, then flattening the cube into a cross.

"It's hard to visualize," Charlie said, "but the point was that he'd taken a three-dimensional cube and represented it in two-dimensional space."

"All right," Wren said.

"Then he said, 'Imagine this cube, which now appears to be a flat cross. And imagine I used rubber bands to hold it in that shape, so that it didn't pop back into a cube. Well, now imagine that a mouse crawls onto the cross, and—*bam!* The rubber bands pop, and suddenly the mouse is in a cube. Just think how surprised that mouse would be!'"

Wren had tilted her head. "Was it a two-dimensional mouse? Because if it was a three-dimensional mouse, it would already know about cubes. And if it was a two-dimensional mouse, it wouldn't have snapped the rubber bands."

"I think the math guy was just trying to find a way of helping his students wrap their minds around the concept of assuming the world was one way, and then—*bam*—having those assumptions be forever changed."

"Cool," Wren said. They were lying in their ditch, and Wren leaned on Charlie and ran her finger down his nose. "Meeting you changed my world forever."

Their thighs touched. Wren's breasts grazed Charlie's chest.

"Mine, too," Charlie said in a low voice. Then, even lower, his lips just brushing hers, he whispered, "*Bam.*"

That low voice of his. God. It made her pulse quicken.

Tessa nudged her. She was holding out the lemonade to Wren, and Wren took another sip. She was now truly tipsy, and she closed the bottle and dropped it onto the grass beneath the hammock.

Oh, but she was supposed to be telling Tessa about

Charlie, and how Wren thought he was the most caring person she'd ever met. Wren wanted to help people in theory, but Charlie jumped in and helped Chris and Pamela and Dev—and Wren—without thinking about it or seeing himself as any kind of hero.

Wren sometimes thought that Charlie cared for people in a "realer" way than she did, even though she volunteered at the hospital and even though she'd signed up for Project Unity. Secretly, Wren thought Charlie was realer than she was in general. She didn't want to tell Tessa that part, though.

"He always opens the door for me, if he gets there first," she said.

"Aw," Tessa said. "He's sweet, just like P.G.!"

"And he always makes a point of telling me how beautiful he thinks I am."

"You *are* beautiful. What else?"

"Well, his car? It's a vintage Volvo. He bought it for, like, three thousand dollars, and it's over forty years old, and when he bought it, it didn't run or anything."

"And he restored the engine and fixed up the interior all by himself," Tessa said. "Yeah, yeah, yeah. I heard about it from P.G. But I don't care about Charlie's car. I want the juicy stuff."

"The juicy stuff," Wren said. "Hmm." She gazed at the tree branch that extended over her. "I don't know if this is juicy, but mainly, when I think about Charlie, I just . . ."

"Want to jump his bones?"

Wren smiled. Yes, that. Yes, yes, yes. But there was something different she wanted to share, and it contributed to *why* Wren wanted to jump Charlie's bones, because it had to do with who Charlie was at his very core.

"When I think about Charlie," she tried again, "I think . . . *how*? How did he get to be this brilliant, gentle, amazing guy? He had a crappy childhood. I'm not going to go into details—and I couldn't even if I wanted to, because he doesn't talk about that stuff, so don't you dare go asking him about it. Really, Tessa. Do you swear?"

From her end of the hammock, Tessa made a peace sign. "Girl Scout's honor."

"I mean it, Tessa."

"I do, too."

"I know. Sorry. I guess I get protective of him sometimes." The vodka-lemonade was fuzzing up her thoughts. "He's been through *a lot*, Tessa. I sometimes worry that I'll never understand everything he's been through. Like, he lived in all these different places, and he had lots of different foster parents . . . and some of them were bad."

"But, Wren. Living with your own parents hasn't been a piece of cake."

"Compared to what he's gone through, it has been," Wren said.

"Really? Are you sure you're not doing that good-girl thing you do, where you say everything's fine because you don't want to cause any trouble?"

Wren was startled. Even though she knew she had a tendency to do that, it threw her off balance to hear Tessa point it out.

"Whatever," she said. "But even so, he came out of all that as the sweetest, kindest, most loyal guy ever. He's, like, a miracle. I mean it, that's how I think of him."

"Huh," Tessa said.

Wren felt slightly foolish. "I mean, he's not perfect. I'm not saying he's *perfect*."

"P.G. certainly isn't," Tessa said, and the way she said it made both girls laugh.

Tessa leaned over the side of the hammock and fumbled for the bottle, which still had a little special lemonade in it. "But back to Charlie. What does Charlie do that isn't perfect?"

"He lets me down sometimes," Wren said slowly. "Except, 'lets me down' isn't the right way to put it."

"How?" Tessa said.

"Well . . . his family. He's devoted to them. Especially his little brother."

"His foster brother," Tessa clarified.

"His *brother*," Wren said.

"Okay, his brother. And it's bad that he's devoted to him because . . . ?"

"It's not bad," Wren said. "It's great that he loves Dev so much, and Chris and Pamela. He's never had a real family before, and now he does, and that's *great*. And I tell him it's great."

"Oh," Tessa said. "You're jealous."

"Am I? Ugh, I guess I am, but only when he picks them over me. But that's dumb. I know."

"I didn't say it was dumb," Tessa said. "It's what you feel, and guess what? Feelings are like three-year-olds. They're not rational. They're just there."

"Yes, but I don't want them to be there. That's what I'm saying."

"And I'm saying, too bad."

Wren changed the subject, saying, "Also, someone stuck a note under the windshield wiper of my car. It said *Bitch*."

"Wren. Shit."

"It could just be random, but I think it was Starrla."

"Starrla, Charlie's ex-girlfriend?"

"It was just a note. It was dumb. Childish. And Charlie says Starrla was never his girlfriend, that they just . . . they sort of . . ." She growled. "No, I didn't tell Charlie. What would be the point?"

"Wren. Come on. So he could tell her to back off."

But what if he didn't? Or, more likely, what if he *did*, but in his good and caring Charlie way, and it ended up bringing Charlie and Starrla closer again? What if Starrla still had some sort of hold on him?

"If Charlie told Starrla to back off, all that would do is make her decide *not* to back off," Wren said.

"You don't know that," Tessa said.

"Maybe. But, Tessa?"

"Huh?"

"When it comes to Charlie, those are the only negatives. Well, and my parents. They're a negative because they could be way more supportive of the fact that I finally found this boy I really, really like." Whom you *love*, she admitted to herself. You love him, Wren, and you know it.

"Which do you think bugs your parents more, Guatemala or Charlie?"

Guatemala, Wren started to say. Last night she got onto the family computer to see if any good movies were playing that weekend, and she saw her father's search history. She knew it was his because he'd left his coffee mug behind, a blue glazed mug with elephant ears and a handle that was supposed to look like the elephant's tail. It was a Father's Day gift from when Wren was five.

According to his history, he'd been reading an article called "The Pros and Cons of Taking a Gap Year Before

College." Before that, he'd read "Natural Consequences—Why You Should Let Your Child Crash and Burn," "How Parents Can Help a Teen Get Back on Track," and, worst, "The Bad Parent (Proof That Certain People Just Shouldn't Be Allowed to Procreate)."

Her dad was definitely more bothered by Guatemala.

But before Wren gave Tessa an answer, she thought of her mom, who'd hovered outside Wren's room last weekend until Wren shot off a "gtg" text to Charlie and put down her phone.

"Mom?" she said.

"Oh, hi," her mom said. She hovered in Wren's doorway. "May I . . . ?"

"Mom, yes. Come in."

She did. She sat next to Wren on Wren's bed and said, "So, things with Charlie are going well?"

"Uh-huh," Wren said.

"He's a nice boy. Ann Wilson, who knows him from that cabinet shop he works at, says he got excellent grades. She says he's going far."

"Um, that's nice," Wren said.

"Is he the one who talked you into postponing college and going off with Project Unity?"

"*What?*" Wren said. "Mom, I applied to Project Unity before I even really knew Charlie." She frowned. "Why would you think that?"

"Not going to Emory might keep you two on more of a level playing field," her mom said.

Wren stared at her, not comprehending. Charlie *was* going to college in the fall. He was going to Georgia Tech, which was an excellent school. So what was her mom really alluding to? The fact that Charlie was a foster kid? That Pamela and Chris didn't have fancy jobs?

"I'm not even touching that, Mom," she said. "Charlie supports me. I wish you and Dad could believe in me the way he does."

Her mom had gotten teary. "I just feel like we've lost you already."

Agh, it was all so complicated.

But Tessa's question. Which bugged her parents more, Charlie or Guatemala?

"I'd say it's a tie," Wren finally said to Tessa. "I'd say it's officially a lose-lose situation."

"Hmm," Tessa said. "But you went on the pill for Charlie. Not Guatemala."

"Tessa? That makes no sense."

"I'm just saying," Tessa said smugly.

Wren gestured for the lemonade and finished it off.

Later, Tessa showered, and Wren lay on Tessa's bed, missing Charlie. From the bathroom, Tessa's voice rang out loud and pure. She was belting out a country song, all rolling notes and rollicking guitar chords and a chorus that went, "Girl, you make me smi-i-ile!"

Charlie made Wren smile, and she wanted to see him. She and Tessa hadn't decided what they were going to do that night yet, but if they went out, she wanted Charlie to meet up with them. And at some point, she wanted to sneak off to be with him. Alone.

Wren pointed her toes. Flexed them. She let her fingers trail up and down her body. Tessa was still in the shower—Wren would hear the water turn off when Tessa was done—and Wren was still a little tipsy. She closed her eyes and touched her breasts. She pulled down the collar of her shirt and grazed at the swell of them. She touched herself beneath her bra. Her nipples hardened. She thought of Charlie, and she crossed her feet at her ankles and rolled onto her side.

God, she wanted him.

She groaned, embarrassed and aroused, and pushed herself to a sitting position. Oh, Charlie.

She felt for her phone, remembered she'd taken it out of her pocket, but forgot where she'd put it after doing so. Wow, she was more than tipsy. She rubbed her eyes and glanced around Tessa's room. Oh, right. She'd left it with the big teddy bear that lived on Tessa's floor, propped against the wall and smiling blandly. The teddy bear was almost as big as Tessa, and at one point, Tessa had dubbed it her boyfriend. He had a name . . . what was it?

Lorenzo. Yes. And Lorenzo was holding Wren's phone in his paw.

Wren made her way across the bed on her tummy and inchwormed onto the floor. Hello, carpet. She crawled over to Lorenzo, reclaimed her phone, and tapped Charlie's name from her favorites list. She leaned sideways against Lorenzo, desperate for Charlie to pick up.

Pick up, pick up, pick up, Charlie. Char-lie. Pick up, Charlie-Charlie.

"Baby, hey," Charlie said, and the warmth in his voice sent shivers up and down Wren's body.

"Hi," she said. "I miss you like crazy." Her eyes widened, because as a rule she didn't say things like that. She felt them, and she wanted to say them, but the words often got stuck in her mind. It was harder than she liked to say what she was feeling.

She clutched the phone. "Sorry," she said.

"Sorry for what?" Charlie said. "For missing me?"

"No! I guess I'm just embarrassed."

"Don't ever say you're sorry for missing me. And, Wren, I miss you, too. I miss you whenever I'm not with you. I miss you all the time."

"You do?" she whispered. "Do you . . . think about me? Like, about kissing me? Because I wish I could kiss you right now. Is that bad?"

"Is that bad? Why would that be bad? How could that ever be bad?"

"Oh. Um, good?"

"Wren, I want to spend my whole life kissing you. Don't you know that?"

She did, but it was glorious to hear. She had a feeling she was smiling foolishly.

"Where are you?" he asked.

"At Tessa's. You?"

"The shop. Gotta finish this one order, though for safety's sake I'd better take a short break."

"Safety's sake? Me no understand."

"Power tools. Not good to use when you're . . . distracted."

Distracted. By her. She drew her knees to her chest.

"In that case, you have to take a break," she said. "I don't want you ending up in the hospital."

"The hospital's not so bad," Charlie said. "I've met some awesome people at the hospital."

"You have?"

"And sexy."

"Sexy?"

"The sexiest."

Wren's toes curled. She had never—ever—experienced anything like this. Talking like this. Feeling like this. "But I'm not at the hospital. So if you went now, would you still get an awesome, sexy person? To fix you up?"

"Not a chance, which is why I'm being careful."

"Good. You are a very, *very* good boy, Charlie Parker."

Charlie laughed, and it was beautiful. It was a laugh that said *I like you, Wren. So much. And it's great, isn't it? This. Us.*

"Yes," Wren said aloud.

"Yes?" Charlie repeated. "Yes, what?"

A wildness swirled through her. "Yes, I want to . . . have sex. With you. Or make love to you. With you. Whatever."

He was quiet for a moment, leaving her hanging, and she thought, Oh crap. Oh crap, oh crap. *I want to have sex with you.* Did she really say those words? Maybe she didn't. Maybe she just thought she . . . ?

"I want that, too," he said.

She held still. "You do?"

"Are you kidding?" His voice. God. It was deeper now than before, and she'd done that. Hearing his desire heightened her own.

From the bathroom, Tessa's voice floated over the sound of pounding water. But Charlie was close, even though he was miles away. A private bubble, just the two of them, his voice in her ear and her body yearning toward him.

"I wish I were with you," she said. "I wish I were with you right now."

"Baby, I wish that, too."

She was heady with love, and drunk, and wild. She

thought of something Tessa told her she did, for P.G. She could do that for Charlie. She would do anything for Charlie. "Do you . . . want me to send you a picture?"

She heard Charlie inhale. He stumbled over his words. "You mean of . . . of you?"

"Yeah," she whispered. She unbuttoned her light summer blouse. Blue, like periwinkles. "Can your ghetto phone receive pictures?"

"Yes," he said without hesitation.

She glanced at the door that led to the bathroom. It was closed, and the shower was still on. Tessa loved long showers. Still, Wren's heart beat faster.

"Okay, hold on," Wren said. Charlie said something in reply, but she'd moved the phone from her ear, and she didn't catch it. She felt flushed all over, because of Charlie. Charlie did that to her.

She wedged her phone between her knees and multitasked over to the camera. She toggled to the front-facing camera lens, and there she was on the phone's screen. Oh my God, oh my God. She heard Charlie saying more things, but no, not yet. First this, before she lost her nerve.

She let her blouse fall open. Her bra was one of her prettier ones, and she looked good just as she was. Or, she thought she did. Hoped she did. The fabric was sheer, and her nipples—still hard—were clearly visible. But that was okay . . . wasn't it?

Although maybe . . .

She pulled down the cup of her bra on one side. She cupped her breast with her hand, lifting it higher, and—quick, do it now, or you never will—used her other hand to tap the shutter button on her phone.

There. Done. Charlie's voice was urgent on the other end, and she laughed. She liked his urgency. He wanted her back, and she liked it. "One sec," she said, and she hit SEND, texting him the picture before common sense could return.

"Um, I did it," she said, putting the phone back to her ear. She was beaming. Her pulse raced as she fumbled with her buttons. "Did you get it?"

"—so incredibly sorry, but I'll call as soon as I can, all right?"

His words didn't make sense. "What?"

"It's Pamela. She's saying something about Dev, so bye, baby," he said, fast and agitated. "Call you soon."

"Charlie?" she said. "Charlie?!" She jiggled her phone, then held it out and looked at it. No more Charlie. He'd hung up. The phone had gone back to its home screen, which showed a picture of Wren and Charlie laughing, their faces pressed together.

She felt lost. Then she felt numb. Then she felt hot, but *not* in a good way. She'd taken a naked picture of herself (naked enough) and sent it to Charlie, thinking he'd be thrilled. Wanting him to be thrilled. And he . . . hung up?

Bye, baby. Call you soon?

Mortified, she deleted the picture. She deleted it from her photo folder; she deleted it from the transcript of her texts with Charlie.

The shower turned off, but Tessa kept singing. She sauntered into her bedroom, one towel around her hair and another around her body. Wren shoved her phone under her leg.

"I am revived and fresh as a daisy," Tessa declared. "In fact, I feel like we should go somewhere fun and finish that lemonade. You in?"

"Yes," Wren said. "Please." She wanted anything that would give her a shot at oblivion. "But we finished the lemonade already."

"Not a problem," Tessa said. "We'll make more."

CHAPTER TWELVE

"Whats the emergency?" Charlie said as soon as Starrla opened the door. She wore sweats and an oversize T-shirt, which meant she was truly despondent. Starrla only wore unflattering clothes when she didn't give a damn about life, or didn't think life was worth giving a damn for. But all Charlie gave a damn about was figuring out who'd died or where the fire was. He was only here because his need to protect ran so deep. He wanted to do what he had to do and get back to Wren.

"Thanks for coming," Starrla said sourly. She wasn't using her "I's so bad" way of talking, another indication of her mood. "Where were you? With Wren?"

"No, I was at the shop," Charlie said, looking around. "What's going on?"

"Was she there, too?"

"Who?"

"You know who."

Charlie almost put his hand on her shoulder. "Starrla. You said—"

She narrowed her eyes. "Did you have table sex, or is she too afraid to get dirty?"

Ah, shit. His hand fell to his side. Starrla hated Wren. Starrla didn't know Wren, but she hated her. And, yes, Charlie and *Starrla* had had table sex—or a table fuck; with Starrla it was always "fucking"—in Chris's shop one Saturday afternoon long, long ago. Starrla had been on top. Charlie had gotten a splinter.

Starrla swiped at her eyes, which were smeared with circles of mascara. She gestured into her mom's apartment. "Well, come in if you're going to."

He did, because he didn't know how not to. Starrla's mom was a waitress, and she didn't have time to clean, cook, go grocery shopping, or take care of her eighteen-year-old daughter. "I wish you were never born," Starrla's mom had said to Starrla in front of Charlie, to which Starrla had replied, "You and me both, bitch."

Starrla dropped down onto the ratty sofa in the TV

room. The cushions had lost their plumpness long ago, so Starrla had shoved towels inside the lining to make them hold their shape. Charlie sat down beside her. They'd had sex on this sofa, too. More than once.

"So have you?" Starrla said in a surly tone.

"Have I what?" Charlie said.

"Banged her yet. Your pretty, perfect girlfriend."

Hopelessness stabbed Charlie deep in his gut. Starrla wasn't allowed to talk about Wren like that, and she knew it, just as she knew Charlie wouldn't dignify her question with a response. But Charlie couldn't help feeling bad for Starrla.

And he was here, dammit. If someone was in pain, and he could possibly help, he had no choice but to try. Even if it was Starrla. Even if, again and again, he told himself he was done.

At the same time, being here with Starrla made him miss Wren. Wren had taught Charlie what love was, what love truly was. It was nothing like the twisted back-and-forth of need Charlie had shared with Starrla.

Also, Wren wanted to have sex with him. "Make love" with him. She was so heartbreakingly adorable about it. He had a memory, unexpected but wonderful, of Wren lying next to him in their ditch. She'd reached her arms above her head and stretched, closing her eyes and making a sweet almost-yawn sound. He wanted to be with her *now*.

"My mom got arrested," Starrla said, finally giving up on getting a rise out of him by talking about Wren.

"Ah shit," Charlie said. "What for this time?"

There was a section of the *Atlanta Journal-Constitution* on the coffee table, along with more than a dozen cigarette butts, and Starrla grabbed it and tossed it to him. It was the local crime section, dated with today's date.

Charlie scanned the lists of phoned-in complaints, police calls, and one account of a gas station robbery. Was that it? No. He read a little farther and came to this:

> *A woman described as heavyset and naked except for her shoes was pulled off Northside Drive on Tuesday morning, and while cops and medical personnel were evaluating her, she threw off a blanket that had been wrapped around her, walked up onto the hood of a nearby car that was stalled in traffic, and kicked in the windshield. The owner, Jamaal Farsai, shared the statement he made to his insurance company. "They asked if the car was damaged on the side of a street or in a parking lot," said Farsai. "I told them, 'No, a naked woman just got on my hood and stomped around.'"*

Charlie folded the section of newspaper and tossed it onto the coffee table. "Classy," he said.

"You know what she said? Once she got released and saw the paper? That she was going to sue the fucker who described her as 'heavyset.'" She tugged at the hem of her shirt. "She spent the night in jail. Didn't bother to call me, of course."

"Why'd she do it?" Charlie asked. "Was she high?"

"What the fuck, Charlie?" She threw herself against the back of the sofa. "What. The. Fuck."

"Where is she now? Does she need help?"

"You know what? Her life, her problems. But she disappeared with the car, so how am I supposed to get to work?" Starrla hitched her shoulders. "I told Marcus. He laughed—big surprise."

Charlie didn't know who Marcus was, not specifically. He knew Starrla well enough to know Marcus in general, however. Probably into drugs. Definitely a partier. And after he'd laughed, he'd no doubt *oh, honey*-ed her, gotten her clothes off, and offered a different brand of comfort.

"I'm such a dumb-ass," she said. "Fuck, fuck, *fuck*."

She started to cry, and Charlie felt trapped. He wanted to call Wren, to tell her how beautiful and sexy she was. That picture she'd texted . . .

God, he loved that girl. He wanted to be with her, not Starrla.

Starrla moved closer to him on the sofa. She put her head on his shoulder. His muscles tensed.

"You're the only guy who's ever been good to me," she said. "The only guy, Charlie."

"Starrla . . ."

"You *are*, you dumb-ass." Tears choked her laughter. "You'll always be a dumb-ass, but hell, you're my dumb-ass."

I'm not your dumb-ass, Charlie thought.

She took his arm and put it around her. He smelled her familiar scent. He awkwardly patted her shoulder.

"Do you need a ride to Rite Aid?" he asked.

"I just need to be held," she said. She rubbed against him. "Not by Marcus. By you."

Charlie felt the sinkhole pull that was Starrla.

Ten minutes, he told himself, checking his watch. I'll give Starrla ten minutes. Then I'm going to Wren.

"Things are going to get better," he said.

Starrla snorted.

"If you want them to, they will," he said, and he believed it, because look at himself. "You can change your life, Star."

Starrla snorted. "Oh, fucking Christ. The World According to Wren Gray—is that what this is? 'Oh, Charlie, just think! You could be president one day!'"

Screw you, Starrla, he thought, because dammit, she still had the power to get to him. It wasn't just how Starrla mocked Wren, either. It was the fact that, yes, Wren *did* make him believe in himself. That he didn't have to work in Chris's shop forever. That he was going to do great at Georgia Tech, and that he was smarter than anyone she knew. She'd even suggested, tentatively, that he go to Guatemala with her.

"You'd get accepted to the program in a heartbeat," she said. "You could help build houses! Or you could do computer stuff. I'm sure they need people who are good at computers. You could do anything. You're amazing, Charlie."

No one had ever told Charlie he was amazing.

"I'm sorry," Starrla said. "I'm such a bitch. Forgive me?"

Starrla kissed Charlie's collarbone, the barest flick of lips against skin.

"Star, quit it."

"But you do know she's too good for you, right?" She took his hand and put it under her shirt. Stomach, ribs, breast. No bra. He resisted, but she kept his hand where it was. She put her other hand on his jeans. On his dick.

"I said, quit it," he said, but her touch made him hard.

She laughed. "I'm not saying that to hurt you. I'm saying that to keep you from getting hurt." She stroked him. "When she realizes who you really are—where you really came from—do you think she's going to want you?"

Charlie stood up. Starrla tumbled backward onto the sofa. She laughed again.

"Look at you," she said, jerking her chin at his erection. "You still want me. You'll always want me."

Anger rose in Charlie's chest. Could he help what his body did? How his body responded?

"I'm sorry about your mom," he said curtly. "I'm sorry she took the car. Wash your face, put some nice clothes on, and go to your job. Take the damn bus."

"Won't you take me?" Starrla said. "Or forget Rite Aid. We'll go . . . we'll go anywhere, do anything. Whatever you want."

Charlie walked toward the door.

"*Please*, Charlie!" she cried. "I won't tease you anymore. I'm sorry, and I do want you to give me a ride. Please?"

When everything else failed, she could always get him with a "please." Goddammit. He didn't want to help her. He didn't want to care. He had told himself he was done with all of that, and he tried to act on it, but old habits died hard.

He turned around.

Later, Charlie drove toward Wren's house, but he stopped on a side street before he got there. Hadn't she said she was at Tessa's? He should call her first. He would pick her up, or they could meet at their ditch. Whatever Wren wanted, Charlie wanted. Whatever Wren wanted, Charlie wanted to be the one to give it to her.

He pulled out his flip phone. Thank God it was at least advanced enough to receive pictures, because the one Wren had sent . . .

Again, her beauty took his breath away. Only the lower

half of her face was visible: her lips, the bottom one caught anxiously between her teeth. She had nothing to be anxious about. He hoped she knew that. He would tell her again, when he saw her.

And then . . . her unbuttoned blouse. Her bra, pushed to the side. All breasts were not equal, Charlie thought. He didn't think about Starrla's breast, or his hand on it, because Star wasn't Wren.

Looking at the picture Wren sent, and knowing she had sent it to please him, made him crazy with love and longing. *I miss you*, she'd said. *I want to make love to you*.

He punched in her number. His call went straight to voice mail. "Hi, this is Wren. Um . . . leave a message!"

"Wren. Hey," he said. "Where are you, baby? Call me. I want to see you."

He hung up, puzzled and disappointed. Wren's phone hardly ever went straight to voice mail. Come to think of it, Wren's phone had never gone straight to voice mail when Charlie called her. He racked his brain and couldn't come up with a single instance.

So why now? Was something wrong? Had something happened to her?

Relax, he told himself. She's fine.

He called again. "Hey. I'm not getting through for some reason." He closed his eyes, feeling like an idiot. "I guess you have your phone turned off? I just want to see you, baby. Call me, okay?"

He hit the END button. Do not call again, he told himself.

He could text her, though. Yes. Maybe she was at a movie, or somewhere else where she had to be quiet. But after sending that picture, she'd want to hear from him, wouldn't she?

Hey, baby. You there? he texted.

He drummed his fingers on his thigh. Nothing.

Wren, you all right?

Wren?

He wasn't sure what to do. He could go home. Should he go home? Or he could drive to Tessa's . . .

Half an hour ago he'd felt exhilarated. Now his stomach knotted up. He knew he was overreacting, but he would feel so much better if he just heard from her.

She's busy, that's all, he told himself.

Except she usually answered his texts immediately. She'd set a special text tone just for him, and when she turned the sound off, she set her ringer on vibrate. And the whole straight-to-voice-mail business? Not good.

He texted again.

Did I do somehj wrong? Just let me know yr ok.

He realized the bad spelling too late.

*Something, not somehj. I dont even know what a somehj is.

He hoped that would make her laugh. He hoped it would make him laugh, or lighten his mood, but it did neither. The blank screen of his phone taunted him.

He started the engine. Loitering on this side street wasn't doing him any good. He'd drive to Tessa's house, just to check. Maybe Wren and Tessa were in Tessa's backyard, or listening to Tessa's loud music, or . . . playing Parcheesi, with their phones in another room? He'd driven two blocks when an alert flashed on his screen:

WREN GRAY

TEXT MESSAGE

His heart leaped. He clicked to read her message.

I'm fine dont worry

He felt relieved. Then, within seconds, his confusion returned. Wren usually used perfect grammar when texting, first of all. His own texts, painstakingly tapped out on his crappy ghetto phone, were riddled with misspellings, which amused Wren. She dubbed his errors "thumbles."

But more troubling than her lack of punctuation was the brevity of her message, especially since she hadn't added a smiley face to help him read her mood. Without a smiley face, her text seemed curt.

He pulled over.

Wren, where are you? he typed. You sure everything's all right?

Her response came quickly.

I'm a little mad, but whatever. Don't worry. Just . . . whatever.

He read it twice. A buzzing filled his head. Wren was mad? Why? At him?

He typed quickly, text after text, and now she replied quickly, for the most part. Every so often there would be a pause, and when there was, Charlie could hear how loudly he was breathing.

Mad? Why are you mad?

You really don't know?

I really don't. Are you mad at me?

Well I'm not mad at Tessa.

And I'm not mad at PG

There are a lot of ppl I'm not mad at. I wish I weren't mad at all. So let's just pretend I'm not.

What did I do? Just tell me.

nvm.

I'm worried I let you down somehow. i'm so sorry

Wren?

Oh, and will you delete that pic I sent you? Plz?

Wren, that picture is gorgeous. So sexy. I'm sorry I didn't tell you rigt away.

You are SO sexy, baby. I shld have told you immediately. I hd to go, thats all.

Can you forgive me?

Have you deleted the picture?

Baby . . .

I feel like my heart is being ripped out. I know I let you down and I'm so sorry. YOU ARE THE SEXIEST GIRL IN THE WORLD!

Uh-huh, and that's why you disappeared. You were just . . . gone. Poof.

I told you I had an emergency to deal with, remember?

Oh, ok, it's my fault, then. My bad. Bye.

Wren, I don't understna.

I'm sorry I had to go. Next time I won't.

Wren?

Listen. I suck.

Where are you? I'll come. We'll talk.

If I cld hold you, I'd feel so much better—and maybe you wld too?

Seriously, plz stop txting. We'll talk soon. I guess.

Can I call you? Can we talk over the phone at least?

Um, nah. Bye for real. I'm turning off my phone.

Wren? Wait.

Are you still there?

I feel like my world is falling apart. Can I please please call?

She didn't respond.

Charlie tried to stop panicking, but he couldn't.

When they were talking earlier—when Wren was at Tessa's, right before she sent the picture—he told her he had to go. He'd said that Pamela needed him, because of Dev. Could Wren have found out he lied?

He shouldn't have lied. He was an ass. He was an *idiot*.

But Wren . . .

Refusing to tell him what was really wrong, refusing to talk to him—that wasn't cool, either.

He felt gutted. Long shadows from the trees on the side of the street fell over his car. Everything was wrong. Everything was broken.

He shouldn't have gone to Starrla.

He should have told Wren how beautiful and smart and sexy she was right away, the very second she sent that picture. But Starrla sounded so desperate, so urgent, and it had touched on old needs.

He needed to be needed—but by Wren, not Starrla. He'd messed up.

But why didn't Wren cut him some slack? If she thought he'd gone to Dev—which was wrong and a lie, and he would come clean when he got the chance—why hadn't she cared how Dev was? If it *had* been a Dev emergency . . . It hadn't, but if it had . . .

He was trying to rationalize his behavior, which was

wrong. Everything was wrong. His thoughts circled and spiraled until he felt like he was going crazy. Please text back, he prayed. Wren? Please, just text back.

Ten seconds passed. Thirty. Had she really turned off her phone? "Um, nah," and she was gone?

One minute.

Two minutes.

Ten minutes.

For ten and a half minutes Charlie sat in the deepening gloom. His soul hurt. He shut his phone and drove home.

CHAPTER THIRTEEN

Wren woke up feeling like a three-dimensional girl in a two-dimensional world. Her head pounded. Her lips were chapped, and her tongue was fuzzy. A memory of something bad—something potentially very bad—pressed down hard on top of her, only she couldn't call up the details. They slipped and slid just beyond the reach of her consciousness.

What was it? What was the bad thing? She attempted to sit up, and an ice pick stabbed her brain. Ow. Ow, ow. She gazed at her surroundings through half-shut eyes. Where was she? At Tessa's?

Yes, because there Tessa was, her hair a tangled river on her pillow. She still had on her shirt from last night. Wren looked down at herself. She did, too. Jean shorts, the waistband digging into the skin above her hip. Her summery periwinkle blouse with buttons down the front.

Buttons down the front. Something . . . something about buttons.

She pressed her fingers against her temples. Crap, how much had she had to drink?

She needed to pee. She pushed herself up, squinting even more. She found the floor with her bare feet.

Move, she told herself.

Ow, ow, owwww. Pain shot through her skull. She was surely dying, or might as well be. But she waited, and the pain dulled. She held on to Tessa's bed as she made her way around it. She gripped Tessa's desk chair for balance, and then she used the wall to steady herself. Years later, she reached the bathroom. She didn't turn on the light. She might never turn on a light again. She tugged down her shorts and sat on the toilet, which was cool on the back of her legs. She closed her eyes and leaned forward, resting her arms on her thighs and her head on her forearms.

She peed forever. Afterward, she was sorely tempted to curl up on Tessa's fluffy pink bath mat and take a nap.

But the bed would be softer. There were covers to crawl beneath. And Tessa. She could ask Tessa what the hell they had done last night to make her feel so totally, utterly shitty.

She shuffled from the bathroom to the bed and eased herself onto the mattress. She lay her aching head down.

Did something happen with Charlie? Something bad?

Her blouse, with the buttons.

Oh.

Oh no.

But so much was foggy still.

"Tessa," she croaked. She found Tessa's calf with her toes and nudged her. "Tessa. Wake up."

"No doughnuts on my coffee," Tessa mumbled.

"Wake up, or I'm going to throw up all over you. All over your long, pretty hair."

Tessa moaned. She rolled over, slowly, and peered at Wren with one eye. "That again? Really?"

"What again?"

"My 'long, pretty hair.' Last night, at P.G.'s house. P.G. and I went swimming, and you went on and on about my long, pretty hair."

"We went swimming?" Wren said. Tessa's hair, which usually *was* long and pretty, was matted in places, as if she'd slept on it wet.

"Not you. Just me and P.G.," Tessa said. Her breath was sour. "You sat in a lounge chair. You weren't happy. You were very, very not happy. Can I go back to sleep now?"

Wren frowned. In her mind, she saw the moon, as well

as littler moons that were underwater, their light radiating upward. Pool lights? Yes. They *had* been at a pool—P.G.'s pool—and Tessa, with her long, pretty hair, had resembled a mermaid.

"You swam naked," Wren said.

Tessa sighed. "I did."

"Did P.G.?" Another image came to mind, which she shooed away. "No, forget I asked."

Tessa felt around beneath the covers. Next she patted her T-shirt. "Huh. I must have left my undies there."

"Wait—are you undie-less right now?" Wren asked. She held up her hand. "Again, no. Forget I asked." She paused. "How did we get to P.G.'s? How did we get back? And I didn't skinny-dip . . . did I?"

"P.G. came and picked us up, and later he drove us back to my house. You don't remember?"

"I kind of do," Wren lied.

"Well, you *were* pretty wasted. More wasted than I've ever seen you, to tell the truth. And you were mad at Charlie. Do you remember being mad at Charlie?"

Wren's stomach turned.

Tessa wasn't wearing underwear, and Wren had been mad at Charlie. Was she mad at him still?

She searched her heart. What she (almost) recalled scared her. She stared hard at the ceiling.

"You kept saying your parents were right, that boys

were bad news," Tessa said. "Again and again. You were on auto-repeat. But you wouldn't tell us what Charlie did. What did Charlie do?"

Was that the grand prize question? What did Charlie do? Or was it what did *Wren* do?

Abruptly, Tessa rolled over, got out of bed, and announced, "I've got to piss like a racehorse."

Wren turned away to give bare-bottomed Tessa some privacy. When it seemed as if Tessa had reached the bathroom, she said, "Would you bring me a glass of water?"

Tessa stuck out her arm and gave Wren a thumb's-up. She accidentally whacked her hand on the bathroom doorjamb. "Dammit," she said, but she laughed as she drew her hand to her chest. After a long time, she returned to her bed with a glass of fresh, cold water. Also, she had lounge pants on.

"Hey, don't drink it all at once," Tessa said.

Wren took one last sip and passed the glass to Tessa. She dragged her hand over her face and said, "I don't feel so good."

"No, no, you don't," Tessa agreed. "You don't look so good, either."

"Neither do you."

Tessa gave herself a once-over. "We both look pretty rough, I gotta say."

Cautiously, Wren sat up. Her head still hurt, but she no

longer felt as if she were being stabbed by an ice pick. She propped her pillow against the headboard and leaned back on it.

"This is progress," she said.

Tessa patted Wren's knee. "Absolutely. And you didn't spill water all over yourself." She cocked her head. "Do you remember spilling your Manx Whore all over yourself? Last night at P.G.'s pool?"

"My . . . I'm sorry, what?"

Tessa arched her eyebrows. "Really? We had such a long discussion about Manx Whores. Wow. No more hard liquor for you, my friend."

"What is a Manx Whore? Will you just tell me?"

"P.G. made them for us, but he didn't have one himself, since he knew he'd be driving us home." She considered. "He had a beer or two, though."

"But we had Manx Whores."

"We did."

"And we drank them out of Mason jars. And they tasted like licorice?"

"Because of the sambuca. It's coming back to you!"

Wren covered her ears. "Too loud, too loud. Sambuca? I don't remember that. I don't even know what that is. But I do remember . . ."

She didn't finish. She bit her lip. And then it was happening, her memories mixing with the contents of her stomach, and all of it toxic. She stumbled out of Tessa's bed, and the ice pick was back, but she made it to the bathroom in time. She threw up again and again, but at least she did it in the toilet and not all over Tessa's long, pretty hair.

Tessa's mom was teaching a yoga class, so Tessa and Wren had the house to themselves. After a shower, a piece of toast, and a tall glass of orange juice, Wren felt . . . better. Not good, but better. Able to piece together what had happened the night before without making a mad dash for the bathroom again. Able to tell Tessa she needed a little time to herself, if that was all right, so she could try to sort out her tangled-up feelings.

She was crazy-ashamed of how she'd acted, and crazy-ashamed of sending that sexy picture in the first place, or the trying-to-be-sexy picture that now seemed so foolish. What had she been thinking? Ooh, look at me, I'm so hot?

Only Charlie, without knowing it, had given Wren the courage to think that maybe she *was* hot, at least in his eyes. He told her how beautiful she was all the time, and every time, it made her feel special—which made it hurt even more last night when he didn't.

She felt selfish for wanting Charlie to be there to reassure her instead of helping Dev. She hadn't even asked if Dev was okay.

But she also felt small, and exposed, because in addition

to sending that picture, she'd told Charlie she wanted to have sex with him. She knew in her gut that he wanted that, too, but still. His reply last night had been something along the lines of, "Hey, sorry, but I've got to go. I'll call when I can, all right?"

When Charlie had finally called her back, she was no longer tipsy but drunk. She was at P.G.'s house with Tessa, and drunk and sad, and she watched Charlie's calls come in but didn't answer. He left a series of voice mails, which she listened to and then deleted. She was drunk and sad and *mad*, and because she felt cut off from Charlie, she felt cut off from herself.

Her parents had been right all along, she'd told herself. They'd wanted to help her stay focused on her schoolwork, but they'd also wanted to protect her, even if she hadn't seen it at the time. She wasn't ready for this. She wasn't ready for love. Stupid Charlie with his stupid auburn eyes and stupid gorgeous muscles, his stupid tousled hair and quirky-sweet smile.

Sitting on P.G.'s pool chair with her knees to her chest, drunk and mad and lonely, Wren had come to the obvious conclusion: She couldn't love Charlie, because love hurt too much. Love could be withdrawn. Before Charlie, her world may have been small, but it had been predictable.

Then Charlie had stopped calling and started texting. Her rational mind knew that *he* wasn't withdrawing. *She* was. She couldn't seem to help it. So she didn't respond and she didn't respond, and then, when she finally did, her responses were non-responses. Non-answers. Words strung together that said *I'm afraid that you're leaving me, so I'm leaving you first*.

And then, his last text . . .

Wren's heart ached when she reread it:

I feel like my world is falling apart. Can I please please call?

And her response? *Um, nah.*

That's what she typed back to him. Just *nah*, like what she might say if Tessa offered her some Skittles, or if she was at Starbucks and the barista asked if she wanted her receipt.

Nah. So cold. And she'd *felt* cold, huddled like a ball on P.G.'s chaise lounge while P.G. and Tessa laughed and splashed and skinny-dipped. She'd gazed vacantly at her phone, wanting Charlie to call again, text again, even while knowing that if he did, she was too wounded to reply. She felt as if she were watching her life from afar, willing to let it fall to pieces.

Last night, Wren had felt justified in hurting Charlie, because he had hurt her. This morning, all her justifications fell away like dead butterflies. She did love Charlie. She loved him with all her heart, and that was *why* it hurt so much.

Text him, she told herself, remorse gnawing at her belly.

Make it right. Better yet? Call him. Talking was better than texting; it always was.

But she felt too quivery for an actual conversation, so she opened the text application on her phone and started typing. Once she began, she typed quickly and urgently. Charlie needed to know how sorry she was, and he needed to know *now*, before he called or texted her again.

If he was ever planning to call or text her again, that is.

Fear made her light-headed.

I am so so SO sorry, she typed. About last night. I should have answered when you called. I should have been . . . better . . . when you sent all those texts.

I don't know exactly what was up with me. All I wanted was to see you. Be with you. And I sent that text, I think you know which one, and, Charlie, that was scary for me.

And then you disappeared. You were just *gone*.

I would love to see you today if you want to see me. So call me, or text me, or whatever. I'll be here.

She hesitated, then typed one last message.

I hope Dev's okay.

CHAPTER FOURTEEN

Charlie had a long night. A miserable night. A night of tossing and turning, although he finally crashed as the sun was rising. When he woke up, it was almost noon. Someone was banging on his door.

"Mom wants to know if you're alive," Dev said. He wheeled his chair to Charlie's bed. "Are you?"

"Yeah," Charlie said groggily. He rubbed his eyes, checked the clock on his bedside table, and pushed himself up, swinging his legs over the side of the mattress. "Whoa."

"Whoa what?" Dev said.

"It's late."

"No shit, it's late. That's why Mom sent me to check on you."

"Don't say 'shit.' Pamela doesn't like it."

"Don't call her Pamela. She likes that even less. And Dad needs you in the shop. Something about the chairs for that old lady with the nose ring."

"Agnes," Charlie said. "Right."

Dev wheeled his chair closer and picked up a framed photo of Charlie and Wren. Wren was laughing. Her arm stuck out in that funny way of self-photos, and they were squeezed together to fit in the frame. Wren was looking at the camera; Charlie was looking at Wren.

When Wren had pulled the phone back and they looked at the picture together, Charlie remembered, Wren had groaned and claimed she looked goofy. She didn't. She looked luminous.

"*You* look adorable, though," she had said, and Charlie, as a complete afterthought, glanced at the image of himself. He was startled to see the softness captured in his eyes as he gazed at Wren.

"You look so sweet," she went on. "Like a little boy, almost."

"A little boy?" Charlie said, feeling heat creep up his neck.

"Well, not a little boy, but just . . . sweet, that's all. I bet that's how you looked when you were a kid, playing with your Matchbox cars. Did you play with Matchbox cars, Charlie Parker?"

Charlie had never owned a Matchbox car. There'd been a toolbox in his mother's garage, and during the interminable season he spent there, he'd lined up the hammer, the screwdrivers, and the wrenches in different patterns on the concrete floor, over and over again. He didn't remember much about that time, but he remembered that.

"I did," he said. "Did you?"

"Nope, for me it was stuffed animals all the way."

She had looked at the picture of them one more time before putting her phone in her pocket. She'd wrapped her arms around Charlie's neck and peppered him with tiny kisses. Then she'd grabbed the back of his hair the way she did and kissed him for real.

Two days later, Wren had given him a copy of the photo. She'd printed it at Kmart and put it into a frame for him and everything. These small things. No one had ever treated him like this before.

Dev tapped the image of Wren, pulling Charlie back. "Your girlfriend is *hot*," he said.

"Yeah. Uh-huh. Put down the picture, Dev."

"How many times have you kissed her?" Dev asked. "Five times? Eight? More than a dozen?"

"None of your business," Charlie said.

Dev grinned. Until Wren, Dev had never had much

material to tease his big brother about. But Dev liked Wren, and Wren liked Dev. She knuckled his hair and praised his elaborate LEGO constructions. He'd asked her how to make his crush like him, and she'd said, "Just smile at her and talk to her like a normal person. Dev, you're a catch."

"You're the catch," Dev had said, waggling his eyebrows. "If Charlie doesn't ever treat you right, you know where to find me."

"Thank you, Dev. You're very chivalrous," Wren had said. She looked fondly at Charlie. "But your brother knows how to treat a girl. He takes amazing care of me."

Charlie stood up from his bed and took the framed photo from Dev. He put it back where it had been.

"Is there any breakfast left?" he asked.

"Fat chance," Dev said. "And it was pancakes, so sucks for you."

Charlie pulled on a pair of jeans and a black T-shirt. To Dev, who was blocking the path out of his room, he said, "You gonna move or be moved?"

Dev hiked his chair onto its back wheels and spun to face the door. "There might be one pancake left. Maybe three. Or not."

Charlie's throat tightened. He predicted there'd be a whole stack waiting for him, staying warm in the oven. Even though it was noon.

"Hey. Dev."

Dev glanced over his shoulder. "What?"

"About Pamela. Why I call her that, instead of . . ."

"Mom?" Dev supplied. "It's not a hard word to say. It's only one syllable. Want to know another word with one syllable? Dad."

"Thanks, Dev. Thanks for that English lesson."

"Always happy to help."

Charlie frowned. He didn't have to say any more. He could quit now. But he pushed on, because it was important. "Listen, Pamela and Chris are great. You know that, and you know that I know that. I only call them Pamela and Chris because . . ." He tried again. "The reason I don't call them what you call them . . ."

"Charlie, forget it. It's okay."

"I know," Charlie said. "It's just that sometimes, even when you love somebody—" He broke off. He was hopeless. Hopeless and worthless.

Dev was acutely uncomfortable with the conversation. Charlie could see that, even if he couldn't always see his own emotions clearly.

He found a dark stain on the carpet to focus on and said, "It's nothing they've done wrong or anything. It's just . . . me."

"I know," Dev said.

"But I'm glad you do. Call them that."

Dev nodded.

Charlie nodded back.

The chairs Chris wanted Charlie to work on had legs with tapered tenons, and Chris wanted Charlie to sand the grooves. This sort of detail work was best served by sandpaper, not a sander, which was good, because power tools required attention to the task at hand. Charlie's thoughts were very much elsewhere.

His phone lay on the table by the router, but he resisted flipping it open to check for messages. *If* Wren had called or texted, that would be one thing, assuming her message wasn't *Screw you, I'm done, good riddance.* But if there were no messages, it would kill him all over again.

He was a mess.

He was angry at Wren for doing this to him. For playing with his mind, for treating him like . . .

He didn't want to go there, but maybe he had to step into that dark place if he was to have any chance at figuring out how he felt about last night.

Kneeling on the floor of the shop, he smoothed the swelled cove on the leg of the first chair. Chris had done a nice job. The chair's leg narrowed and widened elegantly, and Charlie thought of Wren. Her hips tapering inward to her waist, her waist stretching into the swell of her breasts.

Dammit. He closed his eyes. He gave himself a moment, then started up again. Work was work.

He sanded the chair leg and tried, for the first time ever, to think about Wren from a distance. He added himself to the mix, too. He added in his past, his present, his unknown future. He added the relationships he'd severed and the relationships he continued to maintain.

Chris, Pamela, Dev. Solid. They'd had their bumps in the road, but what he'd tried to tell Dev was true: Charlie considered Dev and his foster parents his family, and Charlie's inability to say so out loud was his failure alone.

Ammon? Also solid. Ammon was a good and loyal friend. At the same time, Charlie doubted that he and Ammon would keep in close touch when Ammon went to Mercer in the fall. Their friendship was fine for what it was, but it wasn't more than what it was.

And then there was Starrla. A hot mess in miniskirts and fishnets. A sad girl in sweats and oversize T-shirts. For the most part casually cruel, and yet sometimes kind, like last year when she'd picked up on the fact that Charlie was having a shitty day. Starrla skipped class with him and drove him to the mall. She bought him an Orange Julius despite his protests, saying, "Just drink it, asshole."

As for sex. Well. They were fourteen the first time they "fucked," and afterward, Charlie tried to tell her how pretty she was. In his mind, back then, she was. Objectively, she still was, beneath her black eyeliner and vampy outfits. But that first time, tangled together in Starrla's bed, Charlie came fast and hard and then collapsed on top of her.

She laughed and shoved his torso. "You're crushing me," she said. "Get off."

He rolled sideways, dazed and spent and thankful, so thankful. He was also worried that he'd hurt her. "Sorry," he said. "You okay?"

She looked at him as if he were nuts. Then a knowing look altered her features. She smirked and said, "Is this you being tender? In case you haven't noticed, I don't do tender."

He reached for her. She might be hard on the outside, but it was a front. He knew it was. He ran the back of his hand over her cheek. "Starrla . . . that was . . ."

She pushed his hand away and got out of bed. "Shut up and get dressed. My mom'll be back soon."

Sometimes she wouldn't have sex with him unless she'd had a shot or three of whatever cheap liquor was stashed above the fridge. On those occasions, she made a point of telling him that's what it took, given that Charlie was Charlie. "I have to be drunk. No offense, right?"

The chair leg Charlie was working on was sanded to perfection. He wiped the sweat from his forehead, rotated the chair, and started on the next leg. The scratch of sandpaper against wood comforted him. He felt the satisfaction of it in his gums, way back in his mouth. Probably he'd been grinding his teeth without realizing it.

The last time Charlie slept with Starrla was after their eleventh-grade homecoming dance. Someone rented a hotel suite. There was an after-party. Starrla got very, very drunk and complained of being hot, so she fumbled for her zipper and started to take off her short, shiny dress right in front of everyone.

"Starrla, no," Charlie had said. He steered her to the room with the bed while the others hooted and whistled.

"Have fun, kids!" one girl called.

It hadn't been fun. Charlie had taken her to the bedroom for the sake of her privacy, not to have sex with her. But things happened, and he did have sex with her, or she had sex with him. Ten sweaty minutes later, it was over.

"I'm not even your date," Starrla had said, pushing herself up. Her hair was mussed, and one blue high heel dangled from her foot. Her dress was scrunched around her waist.

"I asked you to be my date. You said no," Charlie had said. She'd sobered up slightly, and her eyes had a certain glint in them that Charlie recognized. Anger. Desperation. Defiance.

"I said no because I knew you didn't want me to be. You asked me out of pity. Duh."

"Starrla . . ."

"But you still want me to be your slut, so here I am. Yay. Happy?"

No, and neither was she. They made each other the opposite of happy.

"Starrla. Just tell me what you want from me," Charlie'd said.

Starrla had fixed her dress, jamming her arms back through the sleeves and tugging down the hem. "Nothing, so don't worry, pretty boy. You're doing great."

After that, no more sex. Charlie's decision. Too much wrongness and not enough rightness.

And now. With Wren.

Charlie knew it was right with Wren, or he thought he knew, but last night had changed things.

He wanted to believe that he knew the real Wren, and he wanted desperately to believe that the real Wren was solid and cared about him as much as he cared about her.

He rocked back on his heels and put the sandpaper down.

Did Wren treat me badly? he asked himself.

Yes—but he'd stopped texting with her to run to Starrla, goddammit, and he couldn't help but believe that Wren hadn't *set out* to hurt him. It was an accident, wasn't it? Maybe she'd been in a bad place herself?

Clearly she'd been in a bad place. Still . . .

Once upon a time, Charlie had let Starrla treat him like

shit. Last night, Wren had treated him like shit.

But he wasn't perfect, either. Wren had told him she wanted to have sex with him—and Jesus, he wanted that, too—and yet for reasons he didn't fully understand, or maybe it had been purely a knee-jerk response, he'd run off to check on a girl he knew was beyond his help. God, he was an ass.

Never again, if there was an again.

Charlie's heart told him that Wren was still Wren, that he still loved her, and that he would always love her. If she would have him, he would have her—forever.

CHAPTER FIFTEEN

Wren paced back and forth by her car. Her eyes flew to the park's turn-in. Where was he?

Meet at our ditch? he'd texted, and she'd typed back immediately: Yes!

She'd brushed her teeth, borrowed a clean shirt from Tessa, and dragged a brush through her hair. Then she came here, to the parking lot. She didn't go straight to their ditch, because they always walked there together. Plus, she knew he wasn't waiting for her there, because she'd have seen his car.

Where are you, Charlie? I need you!

He pulled into the lot, and the sight of his ancient Volvo made her feel boneless.

"Charlie!" she cried, running to his car. She stopped when she was maybe three feet away. What would his face tell her? Would it be good or bad? He wouldn't have said to meet at the ditch if it was bad, would he?

He cut the engine and got out of his car. He wasn't smiling.

"Wren," he said. He raked a hand through his hair. "Hey."

"Hey," she said. She took half a step toward him. She extended her hand, her heart beating furiously, and he took it. Oh, thank God, he took it.

"Ditch?" he said.

She nodded. "Ditch."

He led her to his trunk, where he grabbed his blanket. Their blanket. They didn't speak as they cut across the grassy field, and that was okay. He was holding her hand. He was guiding her with his characteristic assurance. He was Charlie, and he was here.

They reached the wooded boundary of the park, and Charlie stepped down the steep incline of the ravine. He braced himself with a wide stance and helped Wren hop-skip to meet him. He spread out the blanket. Charlie sat, and Wren sat beside him. She put her hand on the front of his shirt and, with a question in her heart, gently applied pressure. Do we want to lie down? she was asking him. Do *you* want to lie down?

He did. She lay beside him and placed her head on his chest.

"Charlie. I am so sorry," she said.

"It's okay," he said, though he didn't sound quite like himself. A few seconds passed, and he said, "I'm sorry, too."

Wren's ribs loosened. "Is Dev all right?"

"He's fine."

"Good."

Charlie's chest rose and fell. Wren was in his arms, where she belonged. He was warm and strong and right.

"Sometimes I worry that your problems are bigger than mine," she said softly. "Like with Dev, and your foster parents." She hesitated. "Everything you've gone through. Your job."

"My job?" Charlie said.

"Well, yeah. You work so hard. You put in so many hours."

"You work hard, too," Charlie said. "You sewed me up at Grady, remember?"

Yes, but that was volunteer work, and, while it was important, she could call in sick or take a personal day if she wanted. She got the sense that Charlie really couldn't, because Chris counted on him. Charlie contributed to his family in a non-kid way. Part of her thought it wasn't fair that Chris asked so much of him. She wished Charlie could just enjoy summer and being done with high school and the freedom that came with that. Another part of her admired Charlie's work ethic immensely, along with his loyalty to Chris and Pamela and Dev.

She tried to explain. "I know. You're right. But you have stuff going on in your life that . . . I don't know. It makes my problems seem so silly. And then I feel bad for feeling bad, and I want to rise above it, but—"

"Wren. Your problems aren't silly."

Throwing a tantrum because you didn't text me back after I sent you a sexy picture of myself? she thought. That was pretty silly—and even so, the fact that he hadn't texted her back still hurt.

She *would* rise above it. She burrowed closer and whispered, "I'm just not sure I'm good enough for you."

"Hey," Charlie said. He adjusted his position so that he could look into her eyes. "You are always good enough for me. More than good enough for me. Don't ever say that, Wren."

She gave him a wobbly smile. If he said she was good enough, she should believe him, right? She wanted to be done with the fighting, or the discussing, or whatever they were doing as they tried to get past last night's bump in the road. And that's all it really was, wasn't it? Just a bump in the road, and now that they were past it, wasn't it time for a kiss to make things better?

"You're more than enough, too," she told him, angling her body so that more of her touched more of him.

"Wren, wait," Charlie said.

She brushed her lips over his. "You're perfect. You're kind and you're sweet and you're smart. You also happen to be insanely handsome. You know that, right?"

"Wren. I'm not . . ." He pulled away from her.

She didn't understand. Were they still fighting? She'd messed up last night, which was bad. But he'd messed up at least a little bit, too. They'd both messed up, but just now they'd both accepted each other's apologies, and that meant everything was okay. Was everything not okay?

"Charlie?"

"It wasn't Dev," he said. "Last night—the emergency—it wasn't Dev. It was Starrla."

She didn't get it. "Starrla?"

He nodded. A squirrel scurried up a nearby tree and regarded them. It twitched its tail.

"Starrla," she repeated. "Hold on. I told you I wanted you. I sent you that picture . . ."

"I was thrilled you sent it," Charlie said. "I'm still thrilled."

"And you went to Starrla?" Wren said. Her thoughts were sticky and confused. "Why?"

"I don't know," Charlie said desperately. "Her mom got arrested. She was sad. Scared. She needed me. She needed someone to make her feel . . . safe."

"*I* needed you," Wren said.

"I know."

Charlie sat up. Wren sat up, too. The sun was still shining. Birds called out to one another. The squirrel who'd been spying on them jumped to another branch, and the branch bounced, and the squirrel chittered indignantly. On another day, all that would have made Wren smile. Five minutes ago it would have made Wren smile.

Charlie took her hands. She attempted to free them from his grasp, but he held on tightly.

"I guess it's . . . an old habit," he said. "I guess I fell back into it. But I'm done now."

"What's an old habit? Running to Starrla?"

Charlie hesitated.

Wren pulled away, this time successfully, and clasped her knees.

"Yes," he said. "Going to Starrla. But you're the one I wanted to go to. From now on, you're the only one I will go to."

Wren thought of all the other times Charlie had been called away from her: to help Pamela with Dev, to pick up a delivery for Chris, to take a payment directly to the Atlanta utilities billing office because it hadn't been mailed in time.

And then there were the times he'd texted that he was running late, or whatever, but hadn't been specific about why.

"Wren?" Charlie said. He looked dangerously close to crying.

Wren felt like she was free-falling.

"Wren. Please."

He was begging, just like he'd begged her last night. And, like last night, a scrim was lowering itself over her, isolating her from the rest of the world. She fought it, but it was strong.

Love *isn't* worth it, she thought.

Yes, it is, she argued back. Charlie is.

She swallowed. "Were there other times?"

"Other times? What do you mean?"

"When you ran to Starrla. When you chose her over me."

Charlie looked stricken.

"Were there?"

A muscle twitched along the line of his jaw. Wren had the sense of being trapped in a maze, and again, she didn't know how to get out.

"Once," Charlie confessed. He pressed his lips together. "Twice. Sorry—twice."

"Oh," Wren said.

"But I never *chose* her over you. Please, Wren. You have to believe that."

"Did you sleep with her?"

"When?" he said, which was a horrible answer. "Since you and I have been together? *No*, and not for a long time before that."

Wren hugged her shins. She rested her cheek on her knees and stared at the ravine's incline, then the trees, then the squirrel she'd spotted jumping from branch to branch. He—if he was a boy squirrel—had found a friend, so now there were two squirrels. On any other day, Wren would have pointed them out to Charlie, who would have smiled and wondered out loud if the squirrels were a couple. Charlie, when he was relaxed, could be adorably goofy, and Wren could imagine him naming two love-drunk squirrels. He'd give them goofy names, too. Jerome for the boy and . . . hmm. Ginger for the girl. Jerome and Ginger, Wren decided.

"Wren, Starrla doesn't mean anything to me anymore," Charlie said.

"Well, clearly she means *something*," Wren said.

He tried to meet her eyes. "Wren, I love you. Don't you know that?"

Maybe, but this was the first time he'd said it out loud.

"I only love you," Charlie said, spacing out his words. He gazed at her with such intensity that her eyes could no longer keep skittering away.

She felt dizzy.

He'd said he loved her. That was huge.

He'd said it with Starrla hovering between them. That sucked.

A breeze rustled the leaves of the trees, and shadows played across Charlie's face. The shadows shifted, and a ray of light hit Charlie's auburn eyes, making them look strikingly, dazzlingly clear.

"Starrla was a mistake from the beginning," he told her. "She treated me like shit, and I let her. Then last night, when you . . . when you . . ."

When *she* treated him like shit? She wanted to flee, but Charlie held on to her with his eyes.

"At first, when you sent me that text saying you were mad at me, I just wanted to fix things," he said. "I just wanted to talk to you, because I knew if we talked, we would work everything out. Because we're *us*, Wren. You and me." His eyes stayed locked on hers. "I didn't think love existed until I met you. I thought it was something people made up. I thought people who believed in love were either lying to me or to themselves. But then you came along . . ."

Wren held still.

"What I feel when I'm with you is different from anything I've ever felt before," Charlie said with absolute conviction. His eyes welled with tears. "Last night, I could barely function, and when you shut me out . . ."

Wren wanted to reach out to him, but she was afraid.

"I thought, 'I can't. I can't let her do this to me.'" He blinked. "I knew I'd screwed up, and it killed me, but I also knew that I couldn't be your doormat. It would be wrong for me and wrong for you if I let you walk all over me."

The air left Wren's lungs. She reached for him now out of panic. She gripped his hands, and he was warm and strong, and promises fought to reach the surface. I'll behave! she thought desperately. I'll be better, I promise!

The idea of losing him made her realize how much she wanted him, because *yes*. Love. Charlie and Wren. Their souls colliding. And they were human, and they made mistakes, both of them, but by herself, Wren was alone. With Charlie, she was half of the "us" he talked about, only that didn't come close to expressing what she knew to be true: that together they didn't simply become one. They became greater than one.

Something hot and thick clogged her throat.

"But I can't let you go," he said. "How could I let you go? I searched my heart"—he shrugged—"and I love you."

"I love you, too," she said.

His expression grew almost, but not quite, blank. Not quite, because beneath the blankness, Wren saw a flicker of hope.

"I do," she told him. "I love you so much, Charlie."

He pulled her toward him.

"Last night, that wasn't the real me," she managed.

"I know."

"It was the drunk me."

"I know."

"It was the drunk me, who was also a very, very sad me, because I missed you so much. And I sent that picture, but you never responded, and I felt dumb. *So* dumb. But I know that's no excuse, and I don't ever want to shut you out or walk all over you, and I am so, so sorry."

He hugged her fiercely. "I know. And so am I."

"And I do want to . . . you know. Have sex. Make love. With *you*, Charlie." She pulled back and looked at him. "I want that. Okay?"

"I want that, too," he said in a low voice.

She tried a smile. "You do?"

"Wren." His eyes focused on her for a long, charged moment. "I've always wanted you. I want you now."

She laughed, because she was nervous, even though his words made her toes curl. "Well, you can't have me *now*." Her pulse fluttered. "It'll be a week before I'm safe."

He furrowed his brow.

"I went on the pill."

"You did?"

Wren laughed again, still nervous but not *as* nervous. Also, she was delighted by his stunned-in-a-good-way reaction. "And . . . you need to be tested."

"I do?"

She unfolded her legs and perched on her knees. "I don't want my first time to be with a condom unless we have to," she whispered. "Just you and me—that's what I want."

"Us," Charlie said.

"Us," she agreed.

CHAPTER SIXTEEN

Charlie's test results came back: He was clean, as he'd hoped and assumed he would be. With Starrla, he'd always worn condoms, and Pamela had made sure he had the HPV vaccine along with his other vaccinations.

With Wren, he was happy that their first time—which would be her first time, ever—would also be a first for him, and in more ways than one.

He was determined that their evening be perfect. He had some ideas of his own, but he decided to talk to Tessa, too. Tessa was Wren's best friend, and best friends, when they were girls, talked about things like sex. Charlie had gleaned that much from TV and movies. He knew from experience that guys talked about sex as well, but he had a feeling the content of their conversations was different.

But given Wren's decision to go on the pill (he still marveled that she'd done that, and for him), he suspected that Wren had told Tessa that she expected her first time to happen soon. Charlie didn't know Tessa all that well, but he liked her. Most important, they both loved Wren. So who better to ask about girl sorts of things?

Tessa was delighted to help. She was giddy as she answered his questions, clapping her hands and bouncing on her toes. She gave him unsolicited advice as well, instructing him firmly to take charge when things got "steamy."

"Girls like guys who are strong," she informed him.

"Okay," he said. He hadn't planned on not being strong.

"I'm serious," Tessa said. "When it comes to sex, a girl wants the guy to take charge. Sometimes, I think, guys try to be too sensitive. And there's nothing wrong with sensitive! Sensitive is awesome. But hear me out, all right?"

"Sure," Charlie said. That's what he was there for, even though when it came to that part of it—the physical part—he had a pretty good idea of how to please Wren already. He loved Wren, and so he'd been a quick study when it came to the mysteries of her body. He paid attention. He knew what made her gasp with pleasure.

"Well, it's kind of my mom's theory," Tessa said. "My mom says that girls are told over and over that they can do anything, be anything, have it all. Right?"

"Okay."

"And, of course, we can. Women rock, and in reality, we *are* the stronger sex."

Charlie rubbed the back of his neck. He reminded himself that he'd chosen to approach Tessa, first of all, and it would be rude to raise his eyebrows. He also reminded himself that Tessa was . . . Tessa. "Her bark's bigger than her bite," Wren had said of her friend. "Not that she bites—or barks! But there's more to her than what you might see on the surface. She's actually really smart, and really insightful."

Charlie cleared his throat and said, "Okay."

"But my mom also says that in all this girl-power business, a crucial fact has been glossed over. Wanna hear it?"

"Sure."

Tessa narrowed her eyes. "You don't sound sure."

Charlie was startled. "What do you mean?"

Tessa pressed her fingers to her temples, then dropped her hands. "I'm sorry. I might be the teeniest bit overprotective. Of Wren. I just want everything to go well!"

"I do, too."

Tessa pulled at her hair. "*Aggh*. I'm lecturing you. I'm sorry. I'm such a spaz." She opened her mouth, then closed it, then looked at him hopefully. "It's good, though. It's a *good* lecture. Shall I continue?"

Tessa smiled and wrinkled her nose. Charlie shook his head and said, "By all means, continue."

"Okey-dokey," she said. "Well . . . my biggest point, really, is that girls and guys are different."

"Huh."

Tessa swatted him. "I mean it! And maybe what I'm saying doesn't fit the conventional view of feminism, but I think guys and girls, if they're straight, should celebrate and enjoy their differences."

Charlie wasn't sure how "the conventional view of feminism" came into it, or what "the conventional view of feminism" was.

"It's just my opinion, but a guy should be a guy, and a girl should be a girl, at least when it comes to doing it," Tessa said.

"Doing it?"

"Doing *sex*." She blanched. "Oh my God, did I just say 'doing sex'?"

Charlie laughed.

"Okay, I am so done!" Tessa said, laughing as well. "Wow, I'm kind of an idiot, huh?"

"Nah, you're fine," Charlie said.

"Am I? Aw, thanks, Charlie. And tonight, with Wren—" She clapped her hand over her mouth. When she moved it, she said, "Oh shit. I wasn't supposed to know! And maybe it isn't tonight! Wren kind of thinks it might be, but she did *not* tell me that, and I totally didn't tell *you* that, all right?"

"Tell me what?" he deadpanned. He tried not to show it, but it made him happy that Wren would be guessing and speculating and talking to Tessa about it.

"Right. *Right*. Just, whenever the time comes, take charge."

"Got it."

"Oh!" Tessa cried. "And one more thing."

"Why am I not surprised?"

"Ha-ha—but I'm serious. This is my girl I'm talking about."

My girl, Charlie corrected. But maybe Tessa's girl, too.

No. Tessa's friend; *his* girl.

"I know you're not the kind of guy who gets all glazed-eyes-ish and gropy-hands as things, you know, progress," Tessa said. "And that is extremely good, because when a guy gets like that, it makes the girl feel like she's not even there. That she could be just any girl and it wouldn't matter."

"Wren will never be 'any girl,'" Charlie stated.

Tessa blushed, which surprised Charlie. "I know," she said. "And you know what? I know that *you* know, and I know that you, Charlie, are a really good guy. I'm glad you and Wren found each other."

Charlie started to say, "Okay." He changed it to, "Uh, thanks."

"And I'm going to shut up now, I truly am, except to say that groping hands and glazed eyes aren't what a girl wants. She does, however, want to feel pretty. Pretty, and admired, and . . . seen."

"I'll do my best," Charlie said.

"Make Wren feel special," Tessa said. "That's all."

Wren already is special, Charlie thought. I hope she knows that. I hope I make her feel that way.

"I'm done now," Tessa said.

"Okay," Charlie said. "I mean . . . thanks."

She gave him a spontaneous hug. "You *are* a good guy, Charlie." She stepped back. "What are you going to do when she leaves for Guatemala?"

Charlie's gut tightened.

"Sorry. I shouldn't have brought it up, not tonight." She sighed. "I, personally, wish she wouldn't go, but I think she's pretty set on it. And she's been told no so many times that I guess I'm glad she's standing up for herself. I *am* glad she's standing up for herself."

"She won't be gone forever," Charlie said.

"A year is a long time, Charlie."

He didn't need her telling him that.

"Can I ask you something?" she said.

"Can I say no?"

She pursed her lips. "No?"

He half laughed.

"Why aren't you going with her?" she asked.

"To Guatemala?" he said. He rubbed his face. He'd love to go to Guatemala with Wren, but he couldn't drop everything and follow her. Not that that kind of logic, or any logic, would make sense to Tessa—and maybe it shouldn't make sense to him, either.

He sighed. "Because I'm going to Georgia Tech," he said.

"So?"

So? So that was his plan, just like Project Unity was Wren's plan. It was a big deal that he'd gotten in. Gotten a scholarship. It was a big deal to Chris and Pamela that he was going.

"Never mind," she said. "I just wish one of you could change your plans."

Charlie looked past her at her backyard. What he didn't tell her, and hadn't told Wren, was that, at the end of June, he'd filled out an application to Project Unity. He hadn't heard back yet. He'd also applied for a passport.

The problem was that Charlie couldn't imagine leaving Chris and Pamela and Dev.

Then again, he couldn't imagine being without Wren.

After leaving Tessa's, Charlie went to P.G.'s house. At a stoplight, he flipped open his phone and pulled up the picture Wren sent him on "the bad night," as he thought of it. It *had* been a bad night, but the picture of Wren was wonderful, and he'd never deleted it. How could he?

"My man, good to see you," P.G. said when Charlie arrived, clapping Charlie on the back. He ushered Charlie into his enormous house. "What's up?"

Charlie asked P.G. if he could borrow his iPod dock, and P.G. said, "Hell yeah, buddy, although I've got something better than a dock. I've got a couple of things better than a dock. Follow me."

"Whoa," Charlie said when he stepped into the Barbees' finished basement. He'd never been down here before. The walls of the back room were lined with redwood cabinets, and when Charlie approached them, he discovered that some of them were refrigerated. He heard no refrigeration hum, but he felt the cold radiating from within.

P.G. came up next to him and turned an ornate key that protruded from a lock on one of the cabinet doors. Charlie gathered that the key wasn't to keep P.G., or anyone else, out. It was simply to keep the door latched. When P.G. swung the door open, Charlie whistled.

P.G. grinned proudly. "You came to the right guy, I'm telling you."

"This isn't an iPod dock," Charlie said.

"Nope. But it's for Wren, right?"

Charlie didn't answer.

"Bro, it's me," P.G. said. "I'm in love with Tessa. Tessa is Wren's best friend. You don't think I know?" As they trooped up the basement stairs, he threw more questions over his shoulder. "What else can I help you with? Cheese? Salted caramels? Chocolate-covered figs?"

"How about the iPod dock?" Charlie said. "And, uh . . . maybe your iPod?"

"I've got an old one you can have, my friend. One sec." He jogged upstairs and returned with an iPod, a charger, and a small black speaker, all of which he gave to Charlie. "The speaker's charged. The iPod isn't. I haven't used it in years, and really, I don't want it back. Just go to Settings to activate the Bluetooth connection. Cool?"

"It's great. I'm not keeping it, but thanks."

"You know how to load songs?"

"I think I can manage." With his free hand, he reached for his pocket. "Thanks. Seriously. And, uh, how much for the—"

"Charles," P.G. said, putting his hand on Charlie's forearm. "You insult me."

"Seriously, P.G. Let me pay you."

"Your money's no good here. I'll tell you what you can do, though."

"Sure, name it."

P.G. dropped his slick act and grew earnest. "Treat her well, bro."

Charlie nodded. "Will do."

CHAPTER SEVENTEEN

Tonight Charlie was going to pick Wren up at her house, like a real date. Well, it was a real date. The realest of dates. Wren's stomach held a thousand tiny wings, and she hadn't been able to eat all day. She had managed to paint her toenails and take care of other basic hygiene needs, and she'd taken special care with her hair, drying it with a round brush to accentuate the curls she knew Charlie liked.

She'd bought special lingerie, too. At a real lingerie store, not Victoria's Secret. The bra was made in France and called a "demi cup," which meant that it pushed her breasts up and showed a lot of cleavage, basically. It was sheer for the most part, with a pattern of purple and deep pink leaves scattered ingeniously to barely cover her nipples. The straps of the bra were thin and elegant, and French lace adorned the edges. She chose matching panties to go with it, and both the bra and panties seemed to weigh nothing in the crisp paper bag the saleslady had placed them in. When Wren had carried her purchases from the store, it was as if she were carrying tissue paper and nothing more.

As she was getting dressed, she paused to admire herself in her full-length mirror, wearing nothing but her new lingerie. She turned to one side and then the other. She tried to see herself the way Charlie would see her, and it excited her. She loved being looked at by Charlie. The way his eyes darkened. The way his appreciation—and vulnerability—shone through.

Heat spread up her body. Her nipples hardened, and her breathing changed, and when she imagined not just his eyes on her, but his hands, his mouth, she grew suddenly and undeniably wet.

It embarrassed her, but she didn't want to be embarrassed. Should she be embarrassed? No. She should be . . . she should be excited, which she was, and thrilled, and aroused. Her body's response to the boy she loved was a good thing. It was bodies being bodies.

But it was more than that. It showed the strength of her

connection to Charlie, because she'd never felt this way, or even close, when thinking about any other boy. This—her flushed cheeks, the ache pulsing inside—this was Wren wanting Charlie and knowing that Charlie wanted her.

She was dizzy. Relax, she told herself. Put your clothes on, and go downstairs. Charlie will be here any minute now.

She did, and he arrived right on time. Wren's father opened the door for him—hello, hello, come in—but Wren shot him a secret smile, and he smiled back. It was his reserved-Charlie smile, but it calmed Wren's nerves.

For far too long, Charlie made small talk with her parents. He complimented Wren's mom on the cheese straws she'd made, and he asked Wren's dad questions about certain pieces of furniture her dad had shown Charlie on other occasions.

"Well, we're out of here," Wren said after letting her dad ramble on about an eighteenth-century corner cabinet. "I'll be back by dawn. Don't wait up."

"Wren," her mom scolded.

"Teasing! Mom, I'm teasing."

Charlie smiled uncomfortably. Wren knew that Charlie had a jokey relationship with Dev, but not so much with Chris and Pamela. Though she knew he'd lay down his life for any of them, which sometimes killed her in a small, uncomfortable way she didn't like to dwell on.

"Charlie will have me home by midnight," she assured her parents. "Right, Charlie?"

He cleared his throat. "Yes." He did the man-to-man thing and turned to Wren's dad. "Yes, sir."

Wren went to Charlie and linked her arm through his. "Bye! Love y'all!" Then she dragged Charlie out of the living room and out the front door, which she pulled shut behind her.

"Thank God," she said.

Charlie grinned. He took Wren's hand and started for his car, but Wren stayed put, pulling Charlie toward her. She took two steps backward so that her spine was pressed against the front door. From there, her parents couldn't see them even if they looked out the window.

She placed her hands on Charlie's shoulders and rose onto tiptoe. "First, this," she murmured into his ear before giving him a quick kiss.

She pulled away, watching Charlie's expression go from surprised to pleased.

His eyes darkened, and she shivered. He gave her a longer, fuller kiss, and then he led her to his car.

When they reached the park, the sun was almost fully down. The sky was a purplish blue. Wren unbuckled her seat belt and reached for the handle of the door, but Charlie placed his palm on her thigh.

"Wait," he said.

He got out, walked around the car, and opened her door for her. He extended his hand, and when she took it, he helped her out.

"Such a gentleman," she said.

She expected to go with him to the trunk to get the army blanket. Instead, he walked past his car, over the curb, and onto the open grassy area that led to their ditch.

She went with him but said, "Don't we need . . . ?"

He smiled and squeezed her hand. Her jitters came back. She felt unexpectedly shy, and she didn't speak again until they reached the ditch. At the bottom of the incline, a blanket lay waiting, but it wasn't the scratchy green wool one. It was chocolate brown, thick and plush. A picnic basket held down one corner. A bucket filled with ice held down the corner diagonally across, and jutting from the ice was a bottle of champagne.

"Charlie," she said. Her throat tightened, and she felt as if she might cry. She let go of his hand and slid her arms around him. She pressed up close, her cheek against his chest, and soaked it in: the night, the trees, the chirp of crickets. Charlie's scent. The warmth of his skin through his shirt. His muscles.

A breeze lifted her hair, and Charlie put his arm around her. He felt solid to her in a way that no other person was. Wren understood something then. Not with her mind but with her body. She was meant to be with Charlie—to be with him in all ways and in all meanings of the word—because he made her feel alive. Maybe he brought her to life.

But enough waiting, enough wanting. Wren untangled herself from Charlie and started down the hill. She looked back at him, and when she lost her footing and almost slipped, he lunged forward and steadied her. She laughed, giddy with the glory of this boy, this man, her love.

The picnic basket held cheese, crackers, and sliced peaches that Wren knew came from the tree in Charlie's backyard. Tucked by the peaches were an iPod and a speaker, which Charlie pulled out. He pressed a few buttons, and Harry Connick Jr.'s rendition of "Our Love Is Here to Stay" filled the air.

"Oh, Charlie," Wren said, settling on the blanket and folding her legs beneath her. He sat beside her. She stroked his cheek.

He took two champagne flutes from the basket. "Champagne?" he asked.

"Wow. And yes, please."

He handed the glasses to her and pulled the bottle from the bucket of ice. A drop of water landed on Wren's thigh, below the hem of her soft, clingy sundress, and Charlie ducked and licked the coldness off. Something wonderful and private fluttered inside her.

He pulled the foil from the top and undid the wire

cap, all with great seriousness, then grasped the cork and twisted. He'd worn a soft black T-shirt, which Wren knew he'd chosen because it was her favorite, and the movement of his muscles beneath the fabric was delicious.

There was a muffled *pop*, and Charlie opened his hand to show her the cork, and she nodded happily. She found him amazing. She hoped he knew that. Even such a small thing as opening a bottle of champagne . . . When Charlie did it, it was with grace and confidence. It undid her.

Her jitters were practically gone. She felt a little shy, but that was all right. She and Charlie sipped their champagne and nibbled on peaches and talked about nothing and everything.

"You are *so* gorgeous," Wren said out of nowhere. He'd been telling how he'd been on the chess team when he was younger, which was sweet and adorable, and, without meaning to, she told him how gorgeous he was.

She giggled and said, "Sorry."

"Sorry? Why?" Charlie said.

"Well, because . . . I don't know."

"Don't be." He took her glass and refilled it. She expected him to hand it back to her, but he held it just out of her reach. "You don't need to apologize for telling me what you think, just like I don't need to apologize for telling you what I think, which is that you should take off your dress."

Wren's pulse quickened. "You want me to take off my dress?"

"I do."

She breathed, or tried to. Her body tingled. She rose to her knees, took the bottom of her sundress in her hands, and pulled it over her head. The night air made the hairs on the back of her neck stand up. The night air also made her nipples hard, or maybe it was the way Charlie was looking at her.

"You are beautiful," he said. He brought her champagne glass to her mouth, and she took a sip. Then he moved the glass down her body, charting a course between her breasts and over her tummy.

"Is it cold?" he asked.

She nodded.

He lifted the glass back to her breast, pressing the coldest part to her nipple. He watched her face.

"Yes, cold," she managed. She took the glass from him and placed her other hand along the length of his jaw. "But no more champagne, not for me. Is that okay? It's good. It's *delicious*." She was babbling. *Agh*.

"It's just, I don't want to be—"

"Shh," Charlie said. "It's fine."

"I just want us," she said.

"That's all I want, too," he replied, his voice dropping.

He set his glass on the ground, past the edge of the blanket so that it would be out of harm's way. She put her glass beside his. She had to stretch out on her hands and knees—well, one hand, two knees—to do so.

Charlie fanned his hands over the back of her panties. "God, I love your ass," he murmured.

She was both thrilled and mortified. She was on her knees, and he was behind her, and when she shifted to move back beside him, he didn't let her. Instead, he ran his hands over and under her panties.

"Oh," Wren said. "Um . . ."

Charlie pulled her back to him, and she turned toward him. They were both on their knees, and he put one hand at the base of her neck and kissed her while his other hand skimmed the side of her body and the curve of her hip.

"I think your shirt needs to come off, too," she whispered. Her face flamed, because he'd had his shirt off before, but she'd never been the one to say "take it off."

He leaned back, and she helped pull his shirt over his head. She touched his ribs. His abs. She placed both hands on his chest. He was *so* gorgeous. So warm and hard and real.

He trailed his fingers down the strap of her new French bra. He reached the lace and lightly skimmed it. With both hands, he scooped up her breasts, running his thumbs over the swell of them and making her nipples even harder. They poked visibly through the sheer fabric—Wren glanced down and saw—and Charlie said, "Leaves?"

Wren's mind was foggy. Then she said, "Leaves. Yes. On my bra. Do you like?"

He dipped his fingers under the lace, sliding the fabric of the bra off her breast and anchoring it beneath, so that it pushed her flesh higher. He did the same to the other breast. "I like this better," he murmured, bowing his head and sucking first one nipple and then the other.

Wren couldn't think. It was all sense and touch and heat and shivers. Oh my God, she thought, and she moved beneath his touch, following his hands with her body.

He fiddled with her bra. It took him a moment to work the clasp, and she smiled as she kissed him.

She was wet.

She was scared, but she wanted him inside her.

Her fingers found his jeans. She undid the button and pulled down the zipper, drawing away to check his expression.

"Baby," he murmured.

"Can we . . . ?" She pushed down on the waist of his jeans, not sure how to get them off him. Why had she never gotten his pants off him before? She'd wanted to, but she'd been shy, but now—*aggh*. Why wasn't there a guidebook for this stuff?

He helped, and in the moonlight, she drew in her breath. Boxer briefs. Black and tight. Muscular thighs, so different from her softness.

And in the front. Erect and long beneath his boxers. His dick. Tessa had taught her to call it that, *dick* and not *penis*, because *penis* was a silly word. And this, the solid length of Charlie's dick, of Charlie . . .

She'd wanted to touch him there many times, but she'd been scared. She was still scared. Her heart pounded, and she hooked her thumbs beneath the band at the top of his boxers—but no. They wouldn't . . . they were stuck, caught by the tip of his dick. She bit her lip and used her fingers to pull the waistband up and over him. She tugged them to his knees and didn't know what to do next.

But okay. Wow. She bent and took him in her mouth before she realized what she was doing. And then . . .

Really wow, and really strange. Not bad, but really, really strange.

He moaned, and Wren moved up and down. Her hair swung. She was doing this, and part of her couldn't believe it, but part of her could, especially since he clearly liked it.

"God, baby," Charlie told her, his breath hitching. "But . . . hold on . . ."

He gently pushed her shoulders. When her mouth left his dick, he made a sound. He fumbled with his boxers, less graceful and more urgent than he'd been with his jeans. He got them all the way off, and Wren's eyes widened at the sight of this beautiful boy—her boy, her Charlie—naked and hard in front of her.

He lay her down. He slipped her panties off, and he kissed her toes. He kissed her shins, her knees, her thighs, and when she lifted her hips, he stretched his body over hers and eased his finger, maybe two, inside her. With his thumb, he rubbed other places.

Wren lifted her hips higher. She pressed against him and found his mouth with hers. His dick was hard against her but not yet in her. How was he going to . . . ? Was she supposed to . . . was there something she was supposed to do?

With his knee, he spread her legs. She gasped. She clung to his shoulders, and the night sky was above her and around her. The stars so bright. The *shuush* of the leaves in the trees. Warmth between her legs. Pressure. Slippery, hard, soft—but it didn't go in, or it didn't feel as if it did.

"Charlie? I don't—"

He pushed harder, and she widened her legs. She didn't know what she was doing, but she was willing to try.

Charlie did something with his fingers—she wasn't sure what—and her body acted on its own. She arched her spine and pressed the back of her head into the blanket. She smelled the earth, and she smelled Charlie, who thrust into her. She cried out at a sudden sharp pain, and Charlie stilled.

"Are you okay?" he asked, bearing his weight on his forearms.

"I'm fine," she said, wanting to be. But *ow*. He was sweaty, and she was sweaty, and the pain took her out of the moment, and was it gross that she was all sweaty?

She took him by his hips and pulled him back inside her. Okay, better. Yes. It no longer hurt.

She nudged him out a little with a rock of her own hips. In, out. In, out. It worked, it made sense, it felt really, really—

Their rhythm fell off, and their hips kind of bumped, and again, Wren couldn't get it back. She worried she was letting him down, even though she was fairly sure she wasn't. She worried about the fact that she was worrying, which didn't help, and there was a stick beneath her. *Crap*. She fumbled beneath her.

"What's wrong, baby?" Charlie whispered.

"Nothing, just—" She tried to ignore it. She couldn't. *Crap*. She made a face and said, "There's a stick. Sorry."

He positioned himself on one hip and slipped almost all the way out of her. She missed him. He fished beneath the blanket, tossed something into the woods, and then came back.

She grasped his hips, and he thrust harder. Faster. She moved with him, and oh my God, yes. So silky. Salt from his neck. She nibbled and licked and kissed, and small sounds came from her, and she found that if she twined her legs around his, she could raise her hips even higher.

Charlie groaned.

In and out, together, and she loved this boy. She was doing it. She was having sex with Charlie, making love to Charlie, and everything inside her expanded and connected. Stars. Sky. Leaves. Moon. Two bodies moving together.

More than.

Charlie called out her name, and he stopped thrusting, but he stayed inside her, his muscles taut.

"Oh, baby," he said, panting. He shifted his weight to one elbow so he could pull back and see her. He brushed a strand of hair from her face.

Only, no. Not yet. She moved beneath him, needing more—and more and more. Desire welled inside her. Desire and pleasure, until she felt crazy with it. She grabbed his hips and pulled, and he thrust again and kissed her roughly.

Was this weird? Was she being weird? He moved his mouth to her breast, and she didn't care if she was, because *Jesus*. He circled her nipple with his tongue before sucking and tugging.

"Charlie. God, Charlie . . ."

He switched to her other breast, and everything—

Every nerve, every cell, every particle of air around them—

Her muscles tightened, and she turned her head to the side as she rose one last time to meet him.

Then she let go.

Wonder, followed by a flush of embarrassment, followed by sadness, deep and unexpected.

But why? Why sad?

Charlie pulled out of her, slowly, and lay beside her. They faced each other. She smoothed his damp hair.

He gazed at her, and in his eyes she saw the joy and love and gravity of what they'd shared. Her sadness ebbed, though it didn't completely go away. It was what it was, and maybe sadness was part of the mix?

The joy and love were stronger, and she embraced those truths with all of her heart and sent them back to him. *Yes.*

He gave her the sweetest of smiles. "You are amazing."

You are, too, she silently replied.

She rolled onto her back and stared at the sky. He did the same, then changed his mind and did some rearranging, moving the picnic basket off the blanket, along with the iPod and the speaker. Harry Connick Jr. was no longer singing. The playlist had ended. Wren had no idea when.

Charlie lay back, flipping the other half of the blanket over them to warm their sweat-cooled bodies. They linked hands and listened to the shadowed scuttlings around them. Cicadas sang, and tree frogs called to one another in their funny, rasping chirps.

"I don't want this night to end," Wren said. She kept her focus on the moon. "You're still here, but I miss you already."

"We'll see each other tomorrow," he said. He squeezed her hand. "And I *am* still here, and so are you. You're right where you belong."

"I know," she said, and maybe a little of her sadness slipped out, because Charlie pulled her to him.

"Hey," he said. "Come here." He wrapped his arm around her and kissed the top of her head. "I love you, Wren."

"I love you, too. Forever." She looped her arms around his waist and put her head on his chest. She could hear the thrum of his heart, strong and constant.

CHAPTER EIGHTEEN

The rest of July was hot and sweaty, and so were Charlie and Wren. They were together every chance they got. They had sex every chance they got. But while the sex was exhilarating—he couldn't get enough; he wanted her all the time—what was even better was the closeness that came with it.

Actually, Charlie thought, it was the closeness that made the rest of it possible.

"We're like bunnies," Wren said to him after making love in P.G.'s pool house. They'd done it on an enormous pool float shaped like a dolphin, which Wren was still lying on. She laughed. "Can I be your bunny, honey?"

"Absolutely," Charlie said, tossing Wren her bikini top and scanning the floor for his swim trunks. He found them and tugged them on. "But I think you're more like that dolphin: slippery when wet."

"Charlie!" Wren exclaimed. Her cheeks turned pink, but Charlie knew she wasn't truly offended. "Come here," she said.

He lay beside her on the dolphin float, and she put her head on his chest. Skin to skin, soul to soul.

"This feels so right," she said, softer.

"Because it is," he said.

The next time they made love was two days later. It was in the middle of the day, so no ditch—too hot, too bright, too many kids on the nearby playground—and Tessa and P.G. were off doing their own thing, so no pool house. But they craved each other and couldn't keep their hands off each other, so Charlie drove them out of the city and halfway to South Carolina before finding a remote dirt road that hairpinned lazily into the dense forest. They parked, and Wren put her seat down as far as it would go. She draped herself over it, hugging the headrest, and Charlie took her from behind.

"God, you make me feel good," she told him afterward.

"Baby, you are the sexiest woman in the world," he replied. "You know that, right?"

"And you're the sexiest man," she said with a giggle. She stopped giggling and regarded him with half-lidded eyes, drowsy and content but oddly solemn. Her seat was still reclined, and she rolled onto her side and tucked her hands beneath her head. Her shirt was half-unbuttoned, exposing her bra. It was black today. So were her panties.

"You know what?" she said as the humid summer air blanketed them in his Volvo.

"What?" he said. He'd climbed back into the driver's seat. The gearshift made it nearly impossible for the two of them to snuggle. Plus, it was so hot. But he reached for her and took her hand. Their interlocked fingers rested on his thigh.

She bit her lip, then said, "I know you're kidding about . . . you know. Me being the sexiest woman in the world."

"I'm not kidding. What are you talking about?"

"Well," she hedged, because sometimes she still had a difficult time accepting his compliments. "But—and don't laugh—you make me feel like I *am* a woman, if that makes sense."

She said it like a confession. As if he might actually laugh, as if she didn't quite believe she was a woman despite the abundant evidence to the contrary.

But he thought he understood what she was trying to express.

"You make me feel like a man," he told her, and it felt

like a confession to him, too. It felt scary.

A boy and a girl having sex in a car? That was a thrill ride, the excitement of a summer fling.

But a man and a woman making love to each other again and again, sometimes fast and sometimes slow, from the front, from the side, from behind, sometimes rough, but always tender . . .

He looked at her, and she held his gaze, and he knew her well enough to recognize the mix of hope and uncertainty in her eyes.

Her fingers tightened around his, and he responded with a strong squeeze. By telling him he made her feel like a woman, Wren wasn't just making conversation; she was putting out a question. Not *Do you love me?*—because she knew he did. He told her so all the time, and she answered with the same.

What, then? What was she asking?

Charlie weighed as best he could Wren's loaded, expectant energy. He turned it over in his mind. He didn't rush, because he took Wren's thoughts and feelings seriously. He took Wren seriously.

He concluded that Wren's question assumed love was a given but nudged timidly at something deeper.

Is this real? she wanted to know. *How real* is *real? How real are we?*

Wren was waiting for Charlie to say something, and the

pressure to not screw up was almost unbearable.

Charlie's thoughts went to Starrla, who once upon a time had claimed that Charlie told her "I love you" too often. Starrla never said it back, and one time she had said, "Jesus, Charlie. I'm going to fuck you anyway," which made him feel foolish.

But sometimes Starrla had clung to him and said he was the only good thing in her world. Other times, she smirked at him and told him he was an idiot, that no one liked him, that everyone laughed at him behind his back.

I hate you; don't leave me. That had been Starrla's creed, and it had messed with Charlie's mind.

With Wren, he had discovered what real love was—and, yes, what he and Wren had *was* real. He just didn't know how to tell her without bringing up Starrla, because bringing up Starrla was never, ever a good idea.

Last week, as Wren lay snuggled against Charlie's chest, she had asked him if sex with her was better than sex with Starrla. Charlie was boggled, because in his mind there was no comparison. How could Wren not know that? Then again, since it was Charlie's mind and not hers, how could she?

Wren interpreted his hesitation as a need to think the question over, and she pulled away from him. Not to the degree she did on the bad night—the night of the sexy picture, the night of their first and only fight—but she grew distant, even when Charlie told her over and over that sex with her was amazing and real and genuine. Intimate in a way that it never was with Starrla.

Finally Wren said, "I just don't like thinking of you having sex with anyone else, period. Even if it was . . . you know."

So bringing up Starrla was a nonstarter, not only because of the lingering reality of Charlie and Starrla's past, but also because someone—surely it was Starrla—was still leaving notes under the wipers of Wren's car. *Bitch. Slut. Fucking whore.* Wren hadn't told Charlie about the notes. Tessa did. When Charlie went to Wren about them, she pulled away from him again.

"Please don't do anything," she'd said. "That just gives her power. Anyway, confronting her would mean talking to her, and you said you didn't anymore. Or do you?"

No, he didn't, not even when Ammon came to him and told him that Starrla had a new boyfriend who was big and mean.

"She's hanging with a rough crowd, man," Ammon had said.

"Not my problem," Charlie'd said. He didn't mention that to Wren, either.

In the hot car, with her shirt unbuttoned, Wren was still waiting for his answer. *Is this real? Are we real?*

Bringing up Starrla was out.

His other option was to bring up Chris, Pamela, and Dev, and maybe he'd have to, because as he held Wren's hand, he realized what else Wren was asking: *And if we* are *real . . . why won't you come to Guatemala with me?*

If a man loved a woman, he should find a way to be with her. That's what Wren seemed to believe, though she never said so directly. Maybe she didn't say it because she also believed—and this she did say directly—that Charlie was doing the best he could.

Was he? He was trying, but he felt like a shit for disappointing her. He knew that, deep down, she wanted him to come anyway. With her. To Guatemala.

Charlie felt like he was in a bind. He also couldn't help but wonder: If a woman loved a man, couldn't she find a way to be with that man? Instead of Charlie going to Guatemala to be with Wren, couldn't Wren stay in Atlanta to be with him?

Wren sighed and broke off eye contact. Charlie knew he needed to catch her now, before she slipped away from him.

"Wren, I love you to infinity and back. You're the love of my life. You know that, right?"

Wren sighed again.

"And you do make me feel like a man," he said. "No one makes me feel like you do."

"I'm glad," she said.

"I am, too," he said.

"But, Charlie, you *are* a man." She turned her head and looked at him. "I'm glad I make you feel that way, but it's not me. It's you. You *are* a man, and not just a man, but my man. I need you."

"I need you, too, baby," he said, worried that she didn't fully grasp the truth of that.

"And also, I just plain *want* you," she said. "Don't you want me? Don't you want to be with me?"

"Of course I want you. Of course I want to be with you."

"Well, okay. But I'm leaving in three weeks, so why . . . ?"

And there it was: *If you want me, why don't you put me first?*

Or, closer yet: *Why don't you want me enough to* want *to put me first?*

Because in three weeks, Wren would get on a plane and fly to a strange new land, while Charlie would stay in Atlanta, swallowed by the hole she'd leave in his life.

It tried to swallow him now. He resisted, because she hadn't left yet. They shouldn't waste what time they had. He ran a finger along her hairline, tracing the side of her face and down the line of her jaw. She had beautiful lips, full and generous.

"Do you remember that day at the hospital?" he said. "When I came in, and you fixed me?"

She smiled. Of course she did, and he knew it, just as he

knew that she loved the way he'd turned the hospital visit into part of their personal mythology. She loved the idea that she had "fixed" him, even though she always denied it.

"I didn't fix you," she said. "You didn't need fixing."

"I did," he said, unwaveringly sincere. "I did, and you did."

She pulled down his hand, which was still cupping her face. She kissed his fingers, each one in turn, and Charlie thought, Good. Yes. She's back.

He didn't want to mess that up, but he didn't want to avoid her question, either. Avoiding her question, even if she hadn't put it into words, would be the coward's way out.

"Do you remember how we talked about Dev that day?" he asked.

She drew her eyebrows together. Then her brow cleared. "Oh—now I do. You were telling me about how you'd been to the ER before. And that Dev . . ." She drummed her fingers on her leg. "That Dev had been burned. Is that right?"

"Yeah. Only, I let you think it was an accident."

She let go of his hand and pulled the lever that brought her seat upright. She crossed her legs beneath her. They made a skin-sucking sound when she moved them, but neither she nor Charlie laughed as they might have if the topic of their conversation was something lighter.

"It wasn't an accident?" Wren asked.

"No."

"Then what happened? Why didn't you tell me?"

Because he didn't know her then. Because it was too private.

She studied him. "Will you tell me now?"

Charlie went away for a moment. Thinking about it brought back an acrid smell. "It was two guys who go to Dev's middle school. Two eighth graders."

"Two boys burned Dev? On purpose?"

"With a cigarette lighter. Dev wouldn't tell us who, so I figured it out on my own."

"Charlie," Wren said. "Jesus."

Charlie had driven to the middle school in the mornings and in the afternoons. He'd tutored there for his senior community service hours, plus he'd gone there himself when he was Dev's age, so he knew the schedule.

He noticed who was nice to Dev and who laughed behind Dev's back. He paid particular attention when the buses came, knowing that buses were a bully's anything-goes zone. He saw the asshole who rammed into Dev's wheelchair—sorry, dude, my bad—and he saw the second asshole who high-fived the first. He spotted asshole number two's cigarette lighter, because asshole number two pulled it out and flicked it to life, let the flame die, then reignited it.

Flick, flick, flick, right in front of Dev, who blinked and pretended not to be bothered.

Dev's hand had gone to his leg, though, where it tapped a jittery dance on the exact spot where Pamela had applied a fresh bandage that morning.

"What did you do?" Wren asked. "Did you turn them in?"

"No, Dev didn't want me to."

"So? I mean, I understand that Dev didn't want to be a tattletale, but I'm sure you didn't just . . ." Wren let her sentence trickle off. Her face fell. "Charlie, I am so sorry."

"I know. It's okay."

"No, it's not."

"I know."

She hesitated. "So what did you do?"

Charlie looked at her face. How much of this did he feel comfortable revealing? It was in the past. In some ways, he'd been a different person, because he hadn't yet met her. But would he do the same thing now?

Yes, because he loved Dev, and when he loved someone, he protected that person. He loved Wren, and if he needed to, he would fight to protect her, too.

"I followed the two guys to a gaming café, and I, uh, stole their computers."

"You did?"

Charlie nodded. While the two eighth graders were

ordering their drinks, Charlie casually cruised by their table and swiped their laptops. He left the café and drove to the deserted middle school parking lot, where he worked quickly, dousing both laptops with kerosene and laying them on the concrete. Then—he wished he had that kid's own lighter—he lit a match.

"I burned them," he told Wren.

"You *burned* them?"

"Yeah. Where they would find them."

When Charlie watched the plastic cases melt, he'd envisioned the clocks in a Dalí painting he'd learned about in his junior year classics class. Time was relative; maybe that was what Dalí had been trying to represent. Pain was relative, too, Charlie thought. Dev might not have felt the cigarette lighter's flame eating through his jeans, but those kids had given him a third-degree burn, and Dev would have a scar for life.

"That's pretty intense," Wren said.

"Should I not have told you?"

"No. I asked. I wanted to know. And, Charlie, you can share anything with me. I love you."

"I love you, too," he said.

"You're a good big brother."

"I have to be. It's my job."

"To take care of him?"

He shrugged. "Yeah."

"Is that why you have to stay?"

He didn't answer, because he knew, again, what she was really saying. She was saying, *Why Dev and not me? Don't you want to / need to / have to take care of me?*

She looked away from him. "It's all right."

Charlie was aware of everything about her: the warmth radiating from her skin and the citrusy smell of her hair. Her bare thighs. Her curves.

"I'm not choosing Dev over you," he said.

"I know."

"I just . . . I've never had a family before. I've had other foster parents, but none like Chris and Pamela."

Wren faced him, and the look on her face almost killed him. He wanted *her*, not her pity. "Can we not talk about it?" he said.

"Okay. But . . . I'm so sorry. I never meant—"

"Don't," Charlie said curtly.

Wren blushed. She returned to staring out the window, and he let go of her hand and started the car. She buttoned her shirt as they pulled out of the secluded nook they'd found. They didn't talk, which was fine, as the ride was loud on the bumpy dirt road.

When they reached the highway, Charlie rolled up his window and turned on the air-conditioning. Wren glanced at him, then rolled up her window as well.

"Charlie?" she said.

He pretended everything was normal. "Yeah?"

"Do you remember that day in my car? After the ditch?"

"I remember many days in your car after the ditch. Sometimes your car, sometimes mine." He saw her naked in his mind, and his voice changed. "Sometimes, as I recall, we even went back to the ditch."

Wren blushed. "Ha-ha. That was only once."

"Twice."

"Twice. Fine." She whacked him, and he smiled, feeling more like himself. He steered with one hand and rubbed Wren's neck with the other.

She scooched closer. She put her hand on his leg. They were connected again, the way they were meant to be.

"On the day *I'm* talking about, we talked about how a home was more than a house, more than a place, and you were, like, 'Okay.'" She paused. "You might not remember, and that's all right."

"I remember."

"Well, I heard a song recently, and I kind of love it. It's about a guy and a girl who are in love. The guy tells the girl that she's the apple of his eye, and the girl tells the guy that he's her best friend."

He kept rubbing her neck. "You'll have to play it for me."

"Uh-huh, I will. But the part I love most is the chorus, which the guy and the girl sing together. It goes, 'Home is wherever I'm with you.'"

Her voice, as she sang, was a patter of rain on a dusty road.

She leaned over—it was awkward with the gearshift between them, but doable—and rested her head on his shoulder. He moved his hand from her neck and slipped his arm around her.

"Anyway, that's what it's like for me," she said. Her voice dropped to a whisper. "You're my home, Charlie. Thanks for finding me."

Charlie stroked her hair. He was the one who'd been lost, but now he was found.

CHAPTER NINETEEN

August came way too fast. And hot. August in Atlanta was almost unbearably hot. Wren knew it would be hot in Guatemala, too—hotter, possibly—but she didn't want to think about that.

She drifted nowhere in P.G.'s pool on a ridiculously comfortable, extra-thick float. Tessa, on her own float, was a few feet away. They didn't even have to be inflated, these pool floats. They were made of foam and molded into the shape of chairs. They had armrests. They had drink holders. In the drink holders were fancy plastic cups of lemonade, and if the girls got hungry, they could paddle themselves over to a floating foam square with several indentions carved into it. The indentions held bowls, and the bowls held a variety of snacks: cashews, grapes, pretzels. Oreos.

P.G. had fixed them up with everything they needed, and then he'd left to play golf with his buddies. Not Charlie, because Charlie had to work, and anyway, he didn't play golf.

Wren couldn't imagine Charlie playing golf. She could imagine him doing other things, though. She could imagine him kissing her, laughing with her, getting on a plane with her.

Except he wouldn't, not that last one. She was wrong to want him to, and selfish, and yet she *did* want him to, because she wanted *him*. She wanted to be with him, always.

"Ugh," she said to Tessa. "Why is love so hard?"

"Huh?" Tessa said.

Wren groaned, not wanting to voice her thoughts.

But this was Tessa, she reminded herself. Tessa wouldn't judge her—or if she did, she'd tell Wren why, and ultimately Wren would feel better. She came clean, saying, "Ugh! I am having *feelings*, bad feelings, and I don't like them!"

"Bad feelings about what? Love? Charlie?"

"Why won't he go with me?"

"To Guatemala?"

"Yes, to Guatemala. Duh!"

Tessa's head lolled toward Wren. "Did you just say 'duh'?"

"Maybe."

"And you're how old? Eighteen?"

Wren splashed her. "*Duh*."

"Well, that's embarrassing. Maybe that's why he doesn't want to go—because you say 'duh.'"

"Oh, please."

Tessa tilted her face to the sun and didn't reply.

"What?" Wren said. "Am I being selfish? I'm being self-ish, aren't I?"

"Probably."

Wren sighed. "I love Charlie for being so loyal to his family. I do. I just don't love the fact that he's choosing them over me."

"That's what he said?" Tessa said. "'I pick them over you'?"

"No, never." Wren hit her float with her fist. "And I *know* I'm not being fair. Charlie helps Chris with the shop, and he helps with Dev, and he loves them all, and *they're a good family*. God, maybe I want that. Maybe I want that with Charlie? I do want that with Charlie!"

"Well, here's a crazy idea: Instead of wishing Charlie would go with you, why don't you stay here?"

Hopelessness welled within Wren, because what seemed so simple in words didn't feel so simple in action. "Because I can't, Tessa. I already said yes. I already sent in my forms."

"And that stopped you from withdrawing from Emory, too, huh?"

"Forget it," Wren said.

"No, tell me."

"Ugh. Withdrawing from Emory was different from withdrawing from Project Unity because . . . because . . . I don't *know*. Because of my parents, because of Atlanta, because of everything! I don't know!"

She fought back tears. Why in the world was she fighting back tears?

"Hey," Tessa said gently. "Wren. Shhh."

"Everything sucks," Wren said.

"No, it doesn't."

"Yes, it does, and I'm such a jerk. I'm such a selfish jerk."

Tessa propped herself up on her forearm. She gave Wren a hard look. "Wren. Stop beating yourself up. I didn't mean to make you flip out, and I'm glad you're taking care of your own needs for once. I just . . ." She exhaled. "It's not as complicated as you think, that's all."

"It *is*," Wren said.

Tessa was quiet. She flopped back onto her float.

Wren looked at the tops of the trees bordering P.G.'s

yard. Atlanta was a city within a forest; there was green everywhere. When she was younger, her parents had taken her to Aspen one winter break, and on the drive from the airport to the ski lodge, Wren was struck by the lack of trees. She felt unhinged, as if she, her parents, and the rental car could fly off the road at any moment, sucked into the vast gray sky.

She wondered what Guatemala would be like. She'd seen pictures of the youth hostel and spoken to the regional director on the phone. The hostel looked an awful lot like the YMCA here in Atlanta. She'd have Internet access, which was good. She'd have hot water. She'd be sharing a room with three other girls, and she'd be sharing a communal living area and kitchen with about a dozen other kids, guys and girls. It seemed real and not real at the same time.

Then again, the cotton-candy world of P.G.'s backyard seemed real and not real, too. Lazy pool days. Foam lounge chairs and floating snack tables stocked with Oreos.

"Starrla threw a naked Barbie onto my lawn," she told the clouds.

"O-o-o-okay, that's creepy and stalkerish," Tessa said. She paused. "Why naked, d'you suppose?"

Wren trailed her fingers in the water. She had no clue, although, in her experience, most Barbies ended up naked over time. She didn't want one of Starrla's old Barbies in her yard, that's all.

"Do you want me to tell her to knock it off?" Tessa asked. "Do you want me to wave my new gun around and be scary?"

"You're not capable of being scary, and you don't have a new gun," Wren said.

"I might."

"You don't."

"But P.G.'s taken me shooting five times so far. I'm getting really good."

"You almost hit the target?"

"I almost hit the target! Yes! And P.G.'s cousin is twenty-one, which means he could legally buy that cute pink Glock. Remember that cute pink Glock? He could give it as a gift to P.G.—you can *own* a gun when you're eighteen, but you have to be twenty-one to *buy* one—and P.G. could give it as a gift to me. I could wave it in Starrla's face and say, 'Hey! You! Enough with the naked Barbies, you!'"

"You're not taking this seriously," Wren said.

"Well, neither are you," Tessa pointed out. "Unless—did you tell Charlie this time?"

"No."

"Why not?"

"Why would I?"

"God, you're hopeless."

"I know."

"And Starrla is a nutcase. She is a loose cannon just waiting to go off."

"I know, which is why Charlie should say *Adios, amigo* and come with me." Wren said it without any conviction, knowing she was going down a dead end but stuck nonetheless with her melancholy. "He'd be rid of her forever. Just kidding—I know it'll never happen."

"Which brings me again to my brilliant idea," Tessa said. "Which is—just brainstorming—*you stay here*."

Wren closed her eyes.

"Wren, tell me one thing," Tessa said.

"What?"

"Did you ever say to Charlie, using real words, 'I feel like you're choosing your family over me, and it makes me really sad'?"

"No. I would never."

"Well, Charlie isn't a mind reader, you know."

"I know." Hopeless, hopeless. It was totally hopeless.

She lifted her hand from the pool, sprinkling water onto her tummy. She did it again, sprinkling water on her chest, and she made a conscious effort to think about the good things she had with Charlie.

Cool water. Warm skin. The time Charlie pressed the chilled champagne flute to her breasts.

Keeping her movements slight, she bent one knee to allow her legs to splay open. She skimmed her hand through the pool. She closed her eyes and let droplets fall from her fingers onto the tender stretch of her thigh. Charlie, Charlie, Charlie.

Often, after making love with Charlie, she could smell his scent on her skin. And there was a particular spot on the innermost part of her leg—soft and pale—for Charlie only. He stroked that spot with a downward motion, and the pleasure drew heat to the most private parts of her. When her breathing quickened, he noticed, because he always noticed.

"I love it when you squirm," he would murmur, perhaps putting his mouth to her breast. Sucking. Nibbling. Tugging.

There had been times, afterward, when she felt embarrassed by how she twisted and turned, how she arched her spine, imploring him wordlessly to have his way with her because there was nothing she wanted more.

On the pool float, she shifted positions, curling her toes. You are at P.G.'s house, she reminded herself. You are outside! In the open air!

She felt better, though. And being outside in the open air hadn't stopped her before. Not when she was with Charlie.

"Hey, I *am* sorry you're sad," Tessa said.

"I'm all right," Wren said. "But thanks."

"Well, if it helps, P.G. doesn't do everything I want him to, either."

"Tessa, I do not want Charlie to do everything I want him to. God." She gazed at her friend. "What does P.G. not do?"

"He hasn't bought me that sweet pink Glock, for one."

"Ha."

"He went to play golf with his buds instead of hanging with us. He's claiming he's not going to go through Rush. And he refuses to unfriend Colleen even though I've told him specifically that it makes me sad. He really should unfriend her, right?"

"Yes," Wren said. "Absolutely." Colleen was a girl P.G. had slept with multiple times before he and Tessa became a couple. P.G. insisted that he and Colleen had never "dated," that Colleen meant nothing to him, and that it didn't feel right to him to unfriend her out of the blue for no good reason.

"Whatever," Tessa said. "But do you know what I think we should do?"

"Wait a sec," Wren said. "You're up to something, aren't you?"

Tessa smiled. "My mom's going to Santa Fe this weekend. She's going to a yoga retreat and won't be back till late Sunday night, which means . . . drumroll, please . . . I'll have the house to myself."

"And?"

"And I think we should have a dinner party." She paddled to Wren and reached over awkwardly, taking Wren's hand

and linking their floats together. "It'll cheer us up. It'll be awesome. It can be a farewell party for you!"

"I don't want a farewell party," Wren said.

"Then we won't call it that," Tessa said, squeezing Wren's hand. "Guest list of four: you, me, P.G., and Charlie. You and I will make a wonderful meal, and maybe we'll have wine, maybe a little bubbly. Ooh, we could watch *Wizard of Oz*!"

"*The Wizard of Oz*?"

"Well, yeah, because there's no place like home, silly. But we don't *have* to. We could just talk and laugh and just . . . not worry about what happens next."

"That sounds nice," Wren admitted.

"And since my mom will be gone"—Tessa waggled her eyebrows—"the guys could sleep over. P.G. and I would sleep in my room, and you and Charlie could have one of my brothers' rooms since they're both out of town. We deserve a night like that, don't you think?"

A dinner party did sound fun. A whole night with Charlie sounded even more fun. And a whole night that ended with the two of them in a bed together, followed by a morning when they'd wake up—assuming they got any sleep—and *still* be in bed together?

They'd be like . . . well, they would be like a husband and wife, as dumb as that sounded.

"You can lie there like a lump, or you can say, 'Yes, Tessa, let's throw a dinner party,'" Tessa said. "Your call."

Wren rolled off her pool float and into the cool water, which felt marvelous on her sunbaked skin. With cupped hands and strong legs, she swam the length of the pool and back. She emerged mermaid-style, tilting her face toward the sky so that her wet hair hung heavily down her back.

She only had four days before she left for her new life. She should enjoy the time she had left.

She rested her arms on Tessa's float and said, "Yes, Tessa, let's throw a dinner party."

"Hmm," Tessa said, tapping her nose. "I am intrigued by your ideas and would like to subscribe to your newsletter." She grinned and tapped Wren's nose. "I'm in."

CHAPTER TWENTY

Tessa's house was smaller than Wren's. That was the first thing Charlie noticed when he arrived for the "verrrrrry fancy, grown-up-style dinner party," as Wren had put it. She'd winked to detract from the implied formality, but Charlie could tell that the evening, with all the planning Wren and Tessa had put into it, meant something to Wren.

It meant something to him, too. She was leaving in two days, which he hated. He would take every minute with her he could.

He greeted Tessa, who'd opened the front door to let

him in, and handed her a bouquet of orange tulips. "Hey," he said. "Thanks for having me over."

"Oh, Charlie, what a gentleman," Tessa exclaimed. "I can't believe you brought flowers!"

Charlie shrugged self-consciously. He'd looked up "dinner party etiquette" online.

"Come on in," Tessa said, and Charlie stepped inside. He knew from Wren that Tessa's mom taught yoga. "A bit floofy-doofy, but she's nice," Wren had said. The "floofy-doofy" explained the dream catchers hanging in the windows, the folk art, the butterfly wind chime. On the mantel behind Tessa, Charlie spotted a collection of black Santa Clauses. Huh. Christmas in August?

Christmas seemed far away, while August was relentlessly upon them. Two days, two days. The minutes, hours, and days ticked by too fast.

"Wren, Charlie's here!" Tessa called.

"He is?" Wren said, her voice coming from upstairs. She appeared at the top of the steps. "Charlie! Hi!"

Charlie's heart turned over. She was wearing what he supposed might be called a cocktail dress. It was pale blue and clung to her curves. There were straps instead of sleeves. The skirt, which was fuller than the top, swayed against her thighs as she hurried down the stairs. She came to him, placed her hands on his shoulders, and rose to her toes. She rubbed her cheek against his.

"You're stubbly," she whispered, her breath warm on his ear. "You look hot with a little stubble."

"And you look beautiful, baby," Charlie said, slipping his arm around her. He'd refrained from shaving on purpose, knowing she liked him this way, and he knew from a quick peek down her dress that she was wearing her sexiest bra, the one with the sheer, leaf-patterned lace. He knew she wore it on purpose, wanting to please him.

"Why, thank you," she said. "Can I offer you some champagne?"

"Yes." He cleared his throat. "Yes, please."

"Well, right this way," she said, leading him farther into the house.

As soon as they were out of Tessa's line of sight, Charlie said, "Hey. There's something I need to do."

Wren stopped. "There is?"

He touched her lower lip, then lowered his hand and cupped her breast. She gasped, and Charlie ran his thumb over her nipple. She pressed against him, and when she closed her eyes, he kissed her long and hard.

"God, Charlie," she murmured. Her cheeks were flushed, and she put her hands on his chest. He felt very tender toward her. Her protector, her man. He took her chin and gazed at her, and she smiled up at him.

"I'm glad you're here," she said.

∞

P.G. was late, and Tessa lit into him the minute he walked in the door, but then she noticed the box he held. It was large enough to hold a soccer ball, or a puppy. The box wasn't wrapped, but it didn't need to be, because it was coated with gold dust and topped off with a huge gold bow.

"A present? For me?" Tessa said, giving a quick series of claps. "Oh yay! Can I open it? What is it?" Her eyes widened, and the volume of her voice shot up. "Oh my God, is it what I think it is?!"

"It better not be," Wren said.

Charlie glanced at her and saw that she looked alarmed.

"P.G.?" Wren said. "It's not, is it? It's, like, a coffeemaker for her dorm room. Right?"

Charlie was lost.

Tessa hopped up from the kitchen table where she, Wren, and Charlie had been enjoying champagne and cheese straws. She bounded toward P.G., who lifted the box high.

"Not yet," he said. He placed the gold box on the kitchen counter. "You have to wait. If you don't, you won't get it."

"P.G.!"

Tessa lunged for P.G., and P.G. took her in his arms and spoke in a low voice. Charlie couldn't make out what he said, but Tessa rolled her eyes. She whispered into P.G.'s ear, covering her mouth with her hand, and P.G. grinned.

"Definitely," he said.

Charlie found Wren's knee under the table. He ran his hand under her dress and up her leg, making her press her lips together, as well as her thighs. She shot him a look. He shrugged and grinned, too.

Tessa suggested that they eat. "I made lasagna, and it is marvelous," she said. "Wren made the salad, and it's okay, too."

"Ha-ha," Wren said. "*I* made the lasagna, and brownies for dessert. Tessa made the salad."

"Details, details," Tessa said.

As Tessa loaded up everyone's plates, Charlie's hand traveled higher between Wren's thighs. Tessa sat down, and everyone dug in, chatting and laughing. Charlie stayed in the conversation, but his real interest lay elsewhere. With his hand that was under the table, he reached the lace bordering Wren's panties. Wren dropped her piece of bread. She tried to act as if nothing unusual was going on, but her hand joined his under the table. She clutched his forearm. Her fingernails dug into his skin.

"I'm sorry, what?" she said to P.G., and P.G. repeated a plot detail of the story he was telling.

Charlie's fingers went to the strip of silk stretched over Wren's crotch. Wren's grip on him tightened. He looped his thumb under the top edge of Wren's panties and tugged the fabric upward, and finally Wren couldn't take it anymore. She gripped Charlie's wrist and moved his hand forcibly away, relocating it to his own thigh and pressing down on it for several seconds to ensure that he'd stay put.

"Jesus," she said under her breath, but the look she gave him thrilled him.

"I want you," he mouthed.

She laughed.

"What's so funny?" Tessa said.

"Blame Charlie; it's his fault," Wren said.

"It always is," Charlie said.

"I blame you, Charlie," Tessa said. "Are you going to let us in on the joke?"

"Leave the poor kids alone," P.G. said. "They're young and in love. What more do you need to know?"

The minute everyone finished eating, Tessa shoved back her chair and said, "Well, that was delicious, and now I think P.G. should give me my present. Wren, do you agree? Charlie?"

"No," Wren said.

"Sure," Charlie said, and Wren lightly slapped his leg. "I mean, no, this is a terrible time. Sorry, Tessa." In his pocket, his phone vibrated. The ringer was off, for Wren's sake. It vibrated again. He'd check it when he could.

P.G. rose from the table. He went to the refrigerator and pulled out a second bottle of champagne. He topped off Tessa's glass and asked Wren if she would like a refill.

"I'm good," Wren said, covering her glass. She moved

her other hand higher on Charlie's leg, and heat spread through him. She smelled sweet, and her body was soft, and she had no idea what she did to him. She might think she did, but she didn't.

He swallowed and whispered, "You're so gorgeous."

"I am?"

He had a dead-on view of her breasts, which threatened to spill from her see-through bra. Damn, it was hard not to touch her. "You are."

"We can hear you, you know!" Tessa called from across the table. She was a little drunk—they were all a little drunk—but it was okay. All four of them were spending the night there, which meant no driving.

P.G. poured champagne into Charlie's glass and his own, then proposed they adjourn to the den.

"To open my present?" Tessa said.

"To open your present," P.G. said. "Although it's not a coffeemaker, just to warn you."

"Oh God," Wren said. She stood up. "I'll get the brownies."

"I am not doing the dishes," Tessa said. "Not yet, possibly not ever." She, too, rose from the table. P.G. grabbed the gold box, and the two of them headed for the den.

"Do you need help?" Charlie asked Wren.

She smiled and said, "Nah, I've got it. You go on. I'll be right there."

His phone vibrated again. He paused in the hallway and pulled it out.

Two voice mails, both from Ammon. That wasn't what he'd expected. He felt a pang of guilt, because he hadn't been much of a friend to Ammon these last two months. Ammon had asked Charlie if he wanted to hang out tonight, but Charlie had begged off. Ammon gave him hell until Charlie told him that it was a special dinner set up by Wren and Tessa.

"You know how girls get about these things," Charlie had said.

"No, unfortunately, I don't," Ammon had said.

Charlie explained that there'd be no parents and no curfew, and that Wren was leaving for Guatemala on Monday. Only then did Ammon lay off.

Charlie pressed PLAY and raised the phone. "Charlie, call me," Ammon said, sounding tense. "I'm at Piedmont Park. There's a bunch of us here, including Starrla, and I messed up, dude. She asked me where you were. I didn't tell her, I swear, but she kept hounding me and asking, 'Well, is he is at this place or that place? Huh?' And she mentioned Tessa, and—" Charlie heard loud voices in the background. A guy yelled, "Shit! No fucking way! No fucking way, dude!"

Ammon spoke again. "Sorry. Crazy scene. But Starrla's on a tear, and the guys she's with, they're not from Southview. I get the feeling—"

The voice mail cut off. Charlie was about to punch PLAY to hear the second message, but Wren swished out of the kitchen in her sexy blue dress, carrying a plate of brownies in front of her.

She smiled at him. "You waited for me. You are so sweet."

"That's me," he said, slipping his phone into his pocket and striding to her. He placed his hands on her waist. He slid his hands to her lower back and then to her perfect ass, pulling her closer.

He thought of Starrla and whatever trouble she was getting into.

No. He would not think of Starrla or whatever assholes she chose to get wasted with. Only Wren.

Wren spun out of his grip. "Come along, young Charlie. I will corrupt you with my delicious brownies."

"Be right there," he said. He tugged at his jeans. "Except I might have a hard time walking for a minute."

She looked slightly shocked, and then pleased. She winked and swished off, and his dick, which had begun to soften, grew stiff again. It was mind-blowing how easily, and often, she aroused him.

He shook his head. He needed to listen to Ammon's second message, whether he wanted to or not.

"Get a new phone, bro," played Ammon's recorded voice. "And I strongly suggest that you and Wren get out of there. Get out of Tessa's house, and tell Tessa to maybe—"

Charlie had a hard time hearing Ammon over whatever was going on in Tessa's den. He pressed the phone closer and hunched over.

"—over there." Charlie heard Ammon sigh. "Just watch yourself. And call me when you can."

Charlie closed his phone. What the hell was Ammon talking about, and why tonight? Starrla's craziness, that was real. Assholes getting drunk and belligerent? Of course. But Ammon telling Charlie to get the four of them out of Tessa's house seemed extreme. Unless Starrla wanted to stage a face-off with Wren, or with Charlie . . . ?

"Hey, Charlie!" Tessa called from the den. "What's the hold up, dude?"

Wren, laughing, called, "Yeah, I need you. Get in here!"

He raked a hand through his hair, put on a grin, and followed the voices to the den. He didn't want Wren thinking his attention had been elsewhere.

"Can I open it now?" Tessa said. "Please?"

The gold box was on the coffee table. Tessa pressed her palms together and made puppy-dog eyes at P.G.

"Wait," Charlie said. He rubbed the back of his neck. "I, um, got a call from Ammon. I think we should head out."

"Huh?" Wren said.

Charlie heard the hum of a distant motor. Headlight beams washed through the windows, and Tessa shielded her eyes.

"Whoa, not cool," she said. She raised her voice. "Hey, people! Don't use my driveway to turn around in!"

"We have to go," Charlie said. "We have to go. Now."

"Charlie, why?" Wren said. "What's going on?"

Charlie strode to the window. It was too dark for him to recognize the driver. Without looking at Wren, he said, "P.G., I think we might have some visitors."

P.G. appeared by his side. "Dude, what are you talking about?"

A car door opened. Then another. Voices spilled into the night, raucous and crude.

Tessa got to her feet and joined Charlie and P.G. "What the . . . ? Shit. Is that Starrla Pettit?"

Wren went to the window. She looked small, and Charlie wanted to stop her. Freeze her in time. Keep her safe. She put her hands on either side of her face and peered out the glass, and a sour taste rose in Charlie's throat.

She stepped back, and her retreat made their visitors hoot.

"Come back, sweet thing!" one of them said. They were out of the car and almost to Tessa's front door.

The door. P.G. had been the last to arrive. Had he locked the door behind him?

The knob rotated. Charlie strode forward, but it was too late. The door opened, and a guy the size of a bouncer jammed his foot into the crack before Charlie could slam it shut. The bouncer shouldered his way in, and Starrla and two other guys followed on his heels.

"Not cool," P.G. said.

"Charlie, *hiiiii!*" Starrla exclaimed, and Charlie heard how drunk she was.

"You need to leave," he said.

"Or not," she said, scanning the room. She spotted Wren and whistled, or tried to, but failed because she was also laughing. She tottered on her high heels. "Whoa. I mean, *whoa*."

Charlie's hands formed fists. "Starrla, stop."

"But, Charlie." She grabbed her bouncer friend for balance. She mock-whispered, "I knew she was stacked, but whoa. Get that dress off her, and we's talking porno."

The bouncer laughed, and Charlie swung, throwing a cross punch straight to the bouncer's jaw. It was a solid punch and should have taken him out, but the bouncer only crinkled his wide brow. Then his forehead smoothed.

"Oh buddy," he said. "Bad idea."

He swung at Charlie, but he broadcast the punch the way a four-year-old might, and Charlie dodged the blow. The bouncer's friends circled in, and so did P.G.

"You guys need to leave," P.G. said.

"Or I could shove your head up your ass," the bouncer said.

"Or you could leave. Tessa, call the police."

Charlie glanced from Starrla's friends to Starrla. Her expression was careful, but her eyes burned as if she had a fever. She started across the room.

Pain skyrocketed through him. One of the bouncer's friends had thrown a solid uppercut to his solar plexus. He couldn't breathe, which meant he couldn't warn Wren, except Starrla wasn't going for Wren. Not yet. She made a beeline for the coffee table, for the oversize gold box.

"Hey, no!" Tessa cried.

"Aw, a pwesent," Starrla slurred. "For me?"

"Charlie, help," Wren whispered.

Starrla opened the box.

CHAPTER TWENTY-ONE

It was a snow globe. Not a gun, but an ornate snow globe, and inside the globe was a farmhouse with a picket fence. From *The Wizard of Oz*, Wren thought disjointedly. Because there's no place like home.

Starrla lifted the snow globe and looked at Wren. Her eyes glittered. She couldn't seem to focus quite right. "Is this from Charlie?" she said. "A happy, happy house for the two of you to live in?"

Wren had nothing. No words, no thoughts, no . . . nothing. She was hollow inside, and when Starrla raised the snow globe, she did nothing.

Glass flew everywhere, and water, and snowflakes, and everyone jumped.

Starrla stepped on Dorothy's miniature farmhouse, grinding it against the floor with the toe of her shoe, and Tessa cried, "What is *wrong* with you?"

Starrla swayed but righted herself. She held Wren's gaze. "There. Now it's broken, just like Charlie."

Wren turned to Charlie, who was pale. She wanted to go to him, but *she* was broken. A bird with no wings. Her words stayed broken, too—broken boys, broken birds, broken words—but she forced them out, using sheer willpower.

"No," she said. "He's not broken. You're not broken, Charlie. Stop looking like that."

"Oh, but he is," Starrla said. She veered toward Charlie in her awful high heels and baby-doll socks. "Want me to tell her, baby? Want me to tell her how broken you is? But it's okay. I'm broken, too."

"Starrla," Charlie said. "Please."

Wren didn't understand. "Please"? "Baby"?

The guy Starrla had come with, the one in the leather jacket, took a step, glass crunching beneath his motorcycle boot.

"Hey, Star—"

"Tyson, shut up," Starrla said, and Tyson held his hands out, palms forward.

There was something not right with Starrla, and it wasn't just her eyes. Everyone saw it, and the energy in the room grew charged in a different way than before.

"Baby," she said again. "I need you, baby. That's why I'm here. I need you, and you need me!"

"No," Charlie said. His throat worked. "You need to leave."

"You're kicking me out?" Starrla said, her voice rising. "That's how you treat a damn dog, Charlie. Toss it in the garage and throw away the key. That's what your junkie mom did, right? Locked you in the garage like a mutt from the pound?"

Charlie went pale. Wren's stomach dropped out.

"Starrla—" he tried.

"What, Charlie?" Starrla demanded. She gestured at Wren. "You like her tits better than mine? Okay. Do you suck them like you sucked mine? Okay, that's super. That's great. Have fun. But do you cry on her shoulder first, *boo hoo hoo*, and tell her all about your poor sad childhood?"

Wren started to cry.

Starrla graced her with her skit-around gaze. "Oh, you didn't know?" She barked a laugh. "Guess there's a lot you don't know, bitch. Oops."

"Star, c'mon," Tyson said.

Starrla reached for Charlie, but he stood frozen. Suddenly she sank to the floor. "Charlie," she whispered. Wren was no longer visible, it seemed. Tyson was invisible, too. Starrla could only see Charlie. "Honey, baby, please. You loved me once, you can love me again. We're alike. Nobody else understands us. Nobody but you. Please?"

Charlie shook his head again, and something left Starrla's eyes. Wren saw it.

"Fuck you," Starrla said, and she took a slice of glass from the floor and slashed it across her neck.

It cut deep. Blood spurted onto Starrla's skin, her dress, the floor.

Then Charlie moved.

"Starrla!" he cried, dashing toward her and catching her crumpling body. Tyson, too, was instantly at her side. He knelt beside her as Charlie pressed the heel of his palm against her wound.

"Did you call the police?" P.G. asked Tessa.

Tessa nodded. "I did. I did. I called 911! They said they were coming. They said they'd—"

Sirens blared. Lights flashed through the windows of Tessa's front rooms for the second time that night. One ambulance, two police cars.

One EMT bandaged Starrla's neck and took her stats.

Another asked questions. Starrla was unconscious, so Tyson answered some and Charlie answered others. He ran his hand down his jeans, and it left a red trail.

Wren pressed herself against the wall. She went from

hot to cold to hot. Sweaty-hot. She wrapped her arms around her ribs.

"All right," the EMT said. To her colleague, she said, "We'll need the gurney."

"Hey, what?" Tyson said. "Why? What do you need a gurney for?"

"Standard procedure," the EMT said.

"What do you mean, standard procedure?" Tyson said. "She's fine. She's hardly bleeding, see?"

Hardly bleeding? Her bandage was soaked through.

"Suicide watch," the EMT said curtly. "Someone who tries to kill herself isn't 'fine.'"

She strapped Starrla to the gurney. Starrla's skirt rode too high, and Wren, ridiculously, wanted to fix it for her. She didn't know how to fix things, though. She didn't know how to fix anything.

Tyson shadowed the EMT. "Will she have to stay overnight? Will she be all right? She'll be all right, right?"

Tyson cared about Starrla, Wren saw from afar. And so did Charlie, who stepped forward and said tightly, "I'm her cousin. I'll ride with her."

Wren sank into herself, and Charlie looked at her over his shoulder, and everything *was* broken. Baby. Please. No.

"How long they keep her will depend on her evaluation," the EMT said. To Charlie, she said, "If you're coming, let's go. Everyone else, out of the way."

"Wren, I'll be back," Charlie said.

She might have shrugged, or maybe not. And then he left.

With Starrla.

The rest of the night was a blur. One of the police cars trailed after the ambulance; the remaining officer stayed and took statements. Tessa's mom was called. The broken snow globe still needed to be cleaned up, but at some point Tessa had whisked away the champagne flutes, and nobody ratted anyone out. The drama with Starrla had sobered everyone up, so the officer just gave them a lecture on responsible behavior and keeping themselves and their friends safe.

"Understood?" he said.

"Understood," everyone said, except for P.G., who nodded maturely and said, "Yes, sir."

Tyson and the other two guys took that as their cue to leave. After scribbling a few more lines in his notepad, the officer followed suit.

"What the fuck?" Tessa said when she, Wren, and P.G. were the only ones left.

P.G. rolled his shoulders and rotated his neck. "It's my fault," he said, unusually subdued. "I didn't lock the door."

"What?" Tessa said. "No. You didn't barge into my house uninvited. You didn't shatter my snow globe. You didn't . . ."

She dropped onto the sofa. "*Jesus*. What just happened here? Did that really just happen?"

P.G. sat beside her and pulled her close.

"Jesus," Tessa said again. And then, "Wren. Come sit."

"No thanks," Wren said. She was inside herself and outside of herself at the same time, and all she knew was that she had to leave this place, this world, this unwanted dimension of honey-baby-please. She didn't like Starrla, and yet she felt horrible for her. So, so sad for her, and for Charlie . . . *Toss it in the garage and throw away the key.*

Wren shivered. Feeling sad for herself, on top of everything that had just happened, was so wrong.

"I think I'll . . . I'm just . . . I'm going home."

Tessa raised her head from P.G's shoulder. "Wren. Stay."

Everything buzzed. "Sorry," she said. "I can't."

"Is this because of Charlie? Because he . . . ?"

Wren walked to the kitchen, grabbed her keys and overnight bag, and headed back through the den. "Sorry about your snow globe," she told Tessa.

She left, because Charlie was already gone.

For Wren, that was it. The cold set in. She knew she was wrong to refuse Charlie's calls and ignore his texts, but she couldn't figure out how else to be, because she despaired of ever crossing the chasm between them.

Starrla knew Charlie better than she did. She knew

about his past, all the terrible things he'd never told Wren because he thought Wren wouldn't understand.

She'd been so sheltered growing up.

She was trying to change that. She was trying to live more, experience more, be more, but it all felt hopeless. She would never catch up with him. She would never understand all he had been through. She would never be able to absorb his pain, to make things better, to fix him. He didn't need fixing, not in Wren's mind, but if *he* thought he did, and yet he couldn't come to her, or thought he couldn't . . .

How could she be his everything if she, herself, wasn't enough?

Anyway, what was the point? She was leaving for Guatemala on Monday. It felt unreal, and she'd long ago forgotten why Project Unity had seemed like a good idea, but there it was. She had her ticket. She had people waiting for her, eager to meet her and put her to work. She'd have a purpose. At least she'd be useful to someone in some small way.

Was it good of Charlie, and right, to ride with Starrla to the hospital?

Of course. Charlie helped Starrla even though Starrla was Starrla, even though she tried to hurt him. He didn't say, "Look at me, I'm off to save the world!" He just did what needed doing, even when the world was so unfair.

(Charlie, as a boy, locked in a garage. Her heart broke.)

He was more of a hero than Wren would ever be. He was good and noble. Wren loved him for it, but she hated herself for being so small.

I didn't choose Starrla over you, he texted late Saturday night. You know that, right?

Yes, she knew that. It killed her that he felt the need to say so.

She's going to be fine, and she says she's sorry, he texted on Sunday morning.

That's good, Wren thought. Her heart still hurt and hurt.

I love you, Wren. So much. Plz don't shut me out again.

Can I come over?

Can we talk?

Plz?

On Sunday, after a painful lunch with her parents, she curled up in the fetal position on her bed. 14 TEXT MESSAGES, 4 MISSED CALLS, her phone said. She was such a baby.

Her dad rapped on her door. She knew the sound of his knuckles hitting wood. She'd know it anywhere.

"Wren?" he said.

She shut her eyes and pushed hard on her eyelids. She didn't want to; she didn't want to.

She had to, or there'd be more questions. More fuss. More worry, especially after she hadn't been appropriately appreciative of her parents' gift during lunch. They'd given her a tote bag packed with textbooks recommended by one of the Emory professors Wren's mom worked with. They'd said that if she was going to go through with her Project Unity plan, then she could at least get a head start on her college curriculum in her downtime.

Her dad knocked again, and Wren sat up. "Come in."

He came, holding something behind his back. Another book? "Wren, are you all right?" he asked.

"Um, yeah. I guess." She made herself smile. "Yeah, I'm fine."

"Is it the flight? Are you worried about flying? You always get worried about flying."

"Dad, I'm fine with flying."

"You're being very brave. I thought, maybe because it's an international flight . . ." He cleared his throat. "You've got your passport? You know how to fill out the customs form?"

She nodded.

Her dad exhaled. "Is this about your mother and me?"

"What? No."

"I think it is. I think we—I—owe you an apology."

What? she thought. Her father, offering her an apology?

"You will *always* be my little girl," he told her. "I will *always* be proud of you. I'm sorry if I—"

He choked up.

"Dad, it's okay," she said.

He straightened his shoulders. He handed her the book from behind his back and said, "Well. All right. I dug this out for you. I thought maybe the kids would like it."

Tears sprang to her eyes. It was the picture book she loved, the one he used to read to her in a funny singsong voice. *Charlie Parker Played Be Bop*.

"You used to like it," he said gruffly. "You asked me to read it over and over. Do you remember?"

"I do," she whispered.

"Charlie Parker," he said. "That's funny, isn't it? Your Charlie has the same last name."

Her Charlie. God, it hurt. She smiled painfully.

"Well, don't forget to pack toothpaste," her dad said.

"I won't."

"And fingernail clippers."

"Got 'em."

"Do you have a good English/Spanish translation guide? Because Rick Steves has a handbook that's ranked highest on Amazon. That's the one you want."

She had a translation app called Babylon. "Okay," she said.

He planted his hands on his thighs and pushed himself up. At her doorway, he turned around. "We love you, Wren," he said, looking puzzled.

"I know," she said. "I love you, too."

∞

Her flight was scheduled to depart late Monday afternoon. On Monday morning, as she was packing her shampoo and hairbrush and other last-minute items, P.G. sent her a text saying that Charlie was in bad shape. He didn't want to interfere, but couldn't she cut the guy a break?

No, not if she couldn't cut herself a break.

It was going to happen regardless, she told herself. We were going to break up by default. It'll be easier for him this way, because he can decide you're not worth it, which you aren't. And why should you get to see him one last time? You don't deserve to.

She kept packing.

Five hours before her flight, she thought, Oh crap. What if Charlie comes over? What if he comes over and wants to see me? How will I turn him away?

If she saw him in person, her soul would fly to him like a honeybee to nectar, and that would be the end of her.

So she grabbed her keys, told her parents where she was going, and drove to Tessa's house to say good-bye. She was supposed to, anyway. She'd told Tessa she would.

She intended on sliding by with small talk and false cheer, but Tessa wouldn't let her get away with it.

"Will you please actually talk to me?" Tessa said as they sat side by side on her bed. "Not about Guatemala. Not about UGA. I want you to tell me what's going on with you and Charlie." She took Wren's hands. "*Please*."

The fake Wren answered. The real Wren, small and cold, stayed trapped in ice. "Well . . . I guess I just realized how hopeless it all was," she heard herself say. "Love. Relationships. Being with Charlie."

"Being with Charlie is hopeless?" Tessa said. "Why?"

"It was hopeless from the beginning," Wren said. "I just convinced myself it wasn't. I convinced myself that because we loved each other, we should be together, when really, what *is* love? It's not something you can prove, is it?"

"Oh, okay," Tessa said, cocking her head. "Is this because of Starrla? Because of what she said about Charlie?"

Yes, thought Wren. Because he told her, but he didn't tell me. Because he was afraid to tell me, because he knew it would upset me. Because it *has* upset me.

"I'm not good enough for him," she whispered. "His problems are always going to be bigger than mine."

"So, what, you're cutting him off like . . . like a tag on a piece of clothing? Something you can just throw away?"

Wren shrugged. It was easier not feeling things. "There's no room for me."

"Wren. You're being ridiculous."

"I know."

"You're hurting him, and you're hurting yourself."

"Yep." I'm in the killing jar, she thought, flashing on a gruesome memory from her biology class. They'd caught butterflies and needed to kill them in order to study them. Their teacher told them that the easiest way was to saturate cotton balls with ethyl acetate, drop them into a glass jar with a butterfly, and watch it slowly die.

For a startling moment, Wren both knew and felt the truth: She was killing the one true part of herself.

Maybe Tessa knew it, too, because she said, "Wren. Who are you punishing here?"

"No," Wren said doggedly. "No, because I have to learn to not need people. To not need Charlie."

"Why? That's nuts."

"Is it? If he doesn't need me, all of me, then I shouldn't need him, right?"

"He doesn't need you? He's dying without you."

"No."

"Yes."

Wren scrunched her shoulders, and Tessa sighed. She sat with Wren, quietly holding Wren's hands.

"Sometimes, when a relationship is real . . . God, it hurts," Tessa finally said. "Because it's so raw. Everything. Right?"

A lump formed in Wren's throat.

"And if you shut yourself off, you don't have to deal with it," Tessa went on. She was being Gentle Tessa. Wise Tessa. Wren hated it, even as she tightened her fingers around Tessa's and held on. "I get that."

Long seconds passed.

"But just because it's easier, is it better?" Tessa said. "Because, Wren . . . Charlie loves you."

A tear sploshed onto Wren's leg, fat enough to leave a wet spot.

Tessa squeezed her hands. "He does. And I *know* it's hard, Wren. I do. But you love him, too. Don't you?"

More tears, hot and salty. *(I do. I do!)*

"So I guess you have to ask yourself, is he worth it?"

Wren sniffed. "What do you mean?"

"Well, you said love is hopeless. That love doesn't exist. But, Wren, you've also said there's no such thing as a tesseract, haven't you?"

Wren let out a sob-laugh. "There *is* no such thing as a tesseract."

Tessa smiled. "And yet here I am, and I'm solid and real, and so is Charlie."

Wren cried harder.

"So, you know, I'm thinking that you can either keep yourself safe and not feel anything, or you can take the risk of just loving him and letting him love you." She paused. "Is Charlie worth the risk? And if he's not, what is? What are you willing to take a risk for, Wren?"

Charlie! her soul cried. *I'm willing to risk everything for Charlie. Yes. It's just scary. But yes and yes and yes.*

An infinity of yes.

An infinity of Charlie.

She sobbed, and Tessa held her, and when Wren's tears ran out, she continued to hold her.

"I miss him," Wren confessed. She swiped the back of her hand under her eyes.

"Of course you do," Tessa said.

Wren took a shuddering breath. "Maybe . . . I could call him?"

Tessa let out a small laugh, which made Wren cry all over again, but that was okay.

"You can't leave without making up with him, Wren. He thinks you hate him."

"I could never hate him! I love him!"

Tessa nodded.

"I'm just afraid, maybe, that I love him more than he loves me."

"No," Tessa said simply. "Call him. Tell him you're coming over. Hug him and kiss him, and then kiss him again. All right?"

Wren almost fell apart again, but she knew there wasn't time.

"And you guys can Skype," Tessa said. "They have Internet access in Guatemala, right?"

"Yes, they have Internet access in Guatemala."

"And you're going to come home for holidays. And surely he could go visit you at least once."

"Yes, and more than once, if he can swing it. He's been saving his money."

"If anyone can make a long-distance relationship work, it's you two," Tessa said. "So *go*. Go to him. Now!"

"Okay," Wren said with a tremulous smile. She felt a swell of gratitude for her friend, who was indeed solid and real.

She rose from Tessa's bed. She was halfway across the room when Tessa cried, "Wait!"

Tessa ran to Wren and gave her a huge, rib-breaking hug. She kissed one of Wren's cheeks and then the other.

When she let Wren go, Wren felt better. Lighter. She walked to her car. She thought about Charlie, about touching him and being in his arms, and her cells rearranged themselves. She let herself consider the craziest idea ever, which had been lurking within her all this time but which she hadn't found the courage to set free.

It wasn't a new idea, and maybe it wasn't crazy. But . . . what if she decided not to go to Guatemala? Was it possible that it wouldn't make her weak, but strong?

She'd have to figure out how to handle her parents. She didn't want to slip right back into being their little girl and nothing but their little girl. She'd also have to figure out a way to give back to the world here in Atlanta, because giving back was a true need inside her.

As for Emory? Maybe yes, maybe no. She didn't have

to work out all the details this very second, and she could still change her mind if she wanted to. But maybe with Emory, just as with Project Unity, she could be open to compromise? Even if she didn't yet know what that would look like.

It felt enormous to say yes to such uncertainty. It felt terrifying, too. Could she really trust the world—and herself—enough to take such a leap?

She missed Charlie so much.

She wasn't happy without him.

She loved him, and the proof of their love was inside her.

You're my home, Charlie, she'd told him once. Was he still?

Hope filled her chest as she pulled out her phone. She clicked on Charlie's name. She hit CALL. She raised the phone to her ear and prayed for the right words, whispering, "Please."

CHAPTER TWENTY-TWO

Ever since Charlie could remember, the adults in his life had told him one of two things. The ones who hurt him told him that he was born a failure and would die a failure; the ones who wanted to help him told him to follow his dreams, that he could do anything.

For years, Charlie had rejected both perspectives, believing life was a crapshoot. There was no "good" or "bad." No grand scheme. You were born alone, and you died alone, and if you got lucky, maybe you'd have some decent moments along the way. Or not.

Then he was placed with Pamela and Chris. They fell

into the "if you can dream it, you can do it" camp, but unlike the rah-rah foster parents who liked to show off Charlie as their example of Christian charity, Pamela and Chris seemed to mean it.

When they brought Dev into their lives, they told him the same thing.

"Screw your wheelchair," was how Chris put it. "Screw your handicap, or your 'challenge,' or whatevah the hell you want to call it. Listen, buddy, there are things you can change and things you can't, and when it comes to the ones you can't, screw 'em."

He rapped his head. "Take me. You think I choose to mix up my sixes and nines like a damn five-year-old? I'm serious here. You think I choose that?"

"No?" Dev replied.

"Hell no," Chris said, making Dev giggle. Dev was eight at the time, and such a sweet kid, always wanting to show Charlie stuff or offering him dirty, beat-up sticks of gum.

"Now, let's take a look at your brother, Chahlie," Chris continued. From the day Dev joined the family, Chris and Pamela referred to them as brothers. "Poor guy's so ugly, he can't even throw a boomerang. Know why?"

"Why?"

"Because it'll nevah come back. Ha! Whatcha think of that, huh?"

Dev giggled and glanced at Charlie.

"I ain't lying," Chris said, holding up his right hand as if he were in court. "Am I lying, Charlie, or am I lying?"

"He's lying," Charlie told Dev. "He's jealous because I'm better-looking than he is."

"Ah, you got me, son," Chris said, clapping Charlie on the back. "Other than Dev here, you're the handsomest guy around."

Partner, buddy, son—that's what Chris called Dev and Charlie. Pamela called them "her boys," or sweetheart, or darling, and before Dev joined the household, Charlie had felt like a phony. How could he be good enough to be Chris's son? Pamela's sweetheart?

After Dev came, Charlie started to get used to it. He saw that Chris and Pamela weren't playing games, because he saw for himself how great Dev was. Any parent would be proud to have Dev for a son, just as any guy worth knowing would feel lucky to claim him as a brother.

If it was true for Dev, might it be true for Charlie?

After Dev came, Charlie also started praying, despite remaining unconvinced of God's existence. *Thank you*, he said silently. Nothing more.

Then he fell in love with Wren, and he wondered if maybe there *was* a God.

Maybe.

But if so, He was cruel.

Wren hadn't spoken to him since the night Starrla

showed up at Tessa's. When he called, she didn't pick up. When he went to her house, she wouldn't come to the door. Did she view him differently now because of what Starrla said? Did she not want him anymore? Was she repulsed by him, see him as trash? Charlie was sick from missing her. From worrying what she was thinking about him. Aching for her voice, aching for her touch. Frantic to make things better, but not knowing how.

She was getting on a plane in four hours, and Charlie was beside himself with longing for her. He paced back and forth. Should he go to her? Try to catch her before her flight?

What more could he say?

Would she listen?

He knew from experience that when Wren fell into a funk, she fell hard. Given her refusal to talk to him, it seemed she'd decided to cross him out of her life. End of story.

Charlie couldn't accept that. Wren wasn't Starrla. She wasn't shutting him out to hurt him or make him feel ashamed. He couldn't believe that of her. But it seemed Wren no longer believed in *them*. He could help her believe again, but he didn't know how to get to her. Dammit. He didn't know what to do.

Dev butted the door to Charlie's room, ramming his wheelchair into it repeatedly until Charlie crossed the worn carpet and yanked it open.

"Dude," Charlie said.

"Dude yourself," Dev said. He wheeled past Charlie and circled around behind him. He butted the backs of Charlie's knees, saying, "Move your butt. Family conference. Walk."

"What? No. I'm busy." He dragged his hand down his face. "What?"

"Mom and Dad want to talk to us in the kitchen."

"They do? Is something wrong?"

"Less talking, more walking," Dev said. "Move your butt."

"Hey. *Ouch*. Okay, but—"

"Nope," Dev said, blocking Charlie from getting to his desk. "You don't need your phone. You've been checking that damn thing like it's going out of style, but you can live without it for ten minutes." He reversed and rammed Charlie again. "Go, fool."

Charlie went to the kitchen, nerves jangling, and found Pamela and Chris waiting for him at the table. Dev joined them and jerked his chin at Charlie's chair.

"Sit, my brother," he said.

Charlie sat. Pamela and Chris wore matching expressions, and their concern alarmed him. What was going on—and could it wait? Wren's flight. Four hours. Less than. His brain hurt.

"What's going on?" he said.

Chris flipped something over to him. His passport. Charlie felt the blood drain from his face.

"Going somewhere, Chahlie?" Chris said. "Anything, ya know, ya want to tell us?"

Charlie glanced at Pamela, whose blue eyes were big and round.

He looked at Dev, who said, "I found the letter from that program. The one in Guatemala."

Charlie struggled for words. "Uh . . . I, ah . . ."

"Project Unity," Pamela said. "You got accepted. That's great, Charlie."

"It is?"

"I wish you would have told us, but yes. They're lucky to have you."

"If you're going," Dev said. "Are you?"

"No," Charlie said sharply.

"Hey," Pamela said. "Charlie."

He wondered if he was going to be reprimanded. "What?"

She found his hand. "Do you remember when you were a little older than Dev, and you found me crying in the kitchen?"

"Um. Yeah . . . ?"

"You were my age once?" Dev said to Charlie. "Ha." He turned to Pamela. "Mom, why were you crying?"

"I don't remember," Pamela said. "What I do remember

was how worried your brother was." She turned from Dev to Charlie. "I always wondered if maybe that was the first time you realized I was just a person, with problems of my own. Do you think?"

Charlie remembered being scared that he'd done something to make her unhappy. When Pamela assured him he wasn't responsible, he wanted to find out what was and make it go away.

"We're all just people," Pamela said, squeezing his fingers. Her manner was so mild that it took Charlie a moment to realize she understood more than she'd first revealed. "Okay, Charlie? We all have things we deal with, but it's all right. We always muddle through."

"*Yeah*, Charlie," Dev said.

"Yeah, Dev," Charlie said. "You don't even know what she's talking about."

"I do so."

"I don't think so."

"*Boys*," Pamela said.

Chris put his fingers to his mouth and whistled.

Charlie and Dev stopped arguing.

"Charlie, isn't Project Unity the program Wren applied to?" Pamela asked.

"Yep," Dev said.

Heat rushed to Charlie's face. He'd told no one about his application, not even Wren.

“We think you should go,” Pamela said gently.

“What?”

“Hell yeah, if you want to,” Chris said. “For once in your stinkin’ life, we want you to do what *you* want to do.”

Charlie took a shallow breath. He’d thought that Pamela would be hurt and that Chris would be pissed. Pamela did look concerned, but not hurt, and if Chris was pissed, it wasn’t for the reason Charlie had assumed.

Why had Charlie thought they wouldn’t support him? His biological mother, long ago, had treated him like garbage to be disposed of. Other foster parents had pushed him this way and that. But what had Chris and Pamela ever done to make him feel anything other than loved?

“Mom and Dad said we can visit you,” Dev said. “There’s an active volcano in Guatemala. Did you know that? I totally want to see a volcano.”

“But I already told you. I said no to Project Unity.”

“Dude,” Dev said. “Why?”

“Because . . .” Charlie blinked. Was it because he was scared his family would fall apart without him, or was he scared that he’d fall apart without them?

“If you don’t know, then call them or whatever and tell them yes,” Dev said. “Tell them you changed your mind.”

“What about Georgia Tech?” he said, feeling slow. “In a week, I’m starting at Tech.”

"I called the dean of admissions," Pamela said. "They're happy to let you defer."

"But Wren said that Emory . . ." He stopped. Wren said that Emory was happy to let her defer, too, just that they couldn't guarantee a spot. But since when did life offer guarantees?

"Um, what about you?" Charlie said, his heart pounding.

"Who?" Chris said. He looked around, then held up his palms. "Us? Me and Pammie and Dev here? What'd ya think, Chahlie, that I was going to make you work at the shop till you were sixty-five?"

"We would never want to hold you back," Pamela said. "We'll miss you, but we'll be fine."

"Yeah," Dev said. "Anyway, I can help Dad. I've got this."

Chris slid a piece of paper in front of him, a document of some sort. "Listen," he said. "Do what ya want, but sign this for me first, would ya?"

The words on the document blurred, but Charlie had seen a version of a similar document once before. This one was different mainly because of the word *adult* in front of some of the other words. Adult adoptee—that would be Charlie. Adoptive parents? Chris and Pamela. The first time, Charlie had said no, because he was afraid to get attached. But who was he kidding? He already was attached.

Dev bounced in his wheelchair like he needed to pee.

"We want to adopt a bouncing baby eighteen-year-old!" he said. He cracked up. "Meaning you! You're the bouncing baby!"

"Your brother is not a baby," Pamela told Dev, "but yes. It's time. Don't you think, Charlie?"

"It's been time for a *long* time," Dev said

"We shoulda brought it up earlier," Chris said. "But after that first time we asked, we didn't want to pressure you. Or, hell, maybe we were gun-shy. So shoot us." Chris laughed awkwardly and clapped Charlie's shoulder. "Sign the fucking paper, Chahlie. Do it for your mothah."

Charlie's throat tightened. He picked up the pen and scribbled his name, and Dev thrust both arms into the air.

"Yes!" he crowed. "Welcome to the family, dumb-ass."

"Dev," Pamela scolded.

"How about 'welcome to the family, dumb-shit'?" Dev tried. "Can I call him dumb-shit?"

"You can call him Charlie," Pamela said. "And he was already part of the family. Now it's just official."

Chris pushed back his chair and gave Charlie a noogie. "Welcome to the family, dumb-shit."

After that, everyone moved fast. Pamela called the airline and reserved a ticket for him, to be paid for and picked up at the airport. Chris found a duffel bag and threw in clothes and a toothbrush. Dev wheeled himself to their neighbor's house, who was a frequent traveler, and came back with a stick of gum and a converter for his electronics.

"Ms. Sheldon said you could keep it," Dev said. "She says 'good luck' and 'have fun.' And don't eat street food."

"Thanks," Charlie said, humbled by all they'd done for him.

At the airport, in the passenger drop-off lane, Chris turned around from the front seat of the car and pressed ten twenties into Charlie's hand. That, plus the cash Charlie had saved up, would just pay for his ticket and short-term living expenses.

"Consider it a bonus for that big chair order ya did such a bang-up job on," he said gruffly. He dug again in his wallet and handed Charlie a prepaid phone card. "And listen. Call us when you get there."

Charlie, who was halfway out of the van, stopped and said, "My phone. Crap."

"You don't have your phone?"

"I don't have my phone."

"Does Wren know you're coming?" Pamela asked. "Have you let her know?"

"No. I guess I'll—" He looked at the airport. There were so many people. Was Wren already through security? More important, would she listen to what he had to say?

Well, he'd have the entire flight to get her back. He'd either succeed or die trying.

"Charlie," Dev said from the back of the van. He held up Charlie's battered Nokia and wiggled it. "See how smart I am?" He grinned and tossed it to Charlie. "Told you, I've got this."

And then there was one more round of hugs and goodbyes, and when Chris finally drove off, it was 3:43. Wren's flight—*their* flight—left at six, which meant Charlie didn't have any time to waste.

But before he mad-dashed through the crowd, he had to talk to Wren. Or try. He needed to hear her voice, even if all she said was, "Hi, this is Wren. Leave a message!"

He flipped open his phone. He tapped the power button, and the screen lit up. Across the top was an alert that made his heart skip a beat.

WREN GRAY

MISSED CALL

She'd called him?

He went to his home screen. She'd not only called him but left four messages and a string of texts as well. His pulse raced, and all of his insecurities came flooding back.

No, he told himself. Breathe. Find out what she has to say and then decide what you want to do.

Except he couldn't wait that long.

Instead of listening to her message, he hit RETURN CALL and raised the phone to his ear. Something good and certain filled him up, because he knew, suddenly and absolutely, that all would be well.

"Charlie?" Wren said, answering halfway through the first ring.

"Wren," he said, letting go.

It wasn't the end of their story. It was the beginning.

ACKNOWLEDGMENTS

Again and again, I am humbled by the outpouring of help that comes my way when I set about to write a book. It would be absolutely impossible to go at it on my own; I am inordinately grateful that I don't have to.

Thanks to Emily Lockhart, Sarah Mlynowski, Alan Gratz, and Ruth White for being first readers of this one. I gladly took every single one of y'all's suggestions and put them into place as best I could. Thanks to Sterling Backus for talking to me about guns, because I knew nothing. Thanks to the faculty and students at Vermont College writers' retreat, spring of 2013, for infusing me with hope.

I was in a down spot, and y'all lifted me up. Thanks to Andrea Vuleta, bookseller extraordinaire, for early words of encouragement. Andrea, to answer your question, I've decided that I don't mind kicking the hornet's nest if it's for the sake of a good story. And huge fuzzy thanks to Bob, for being Bob.

Thanks to my amazing agent, Barry Goldblatt, for adoring *Say Anything*. I do, too! Thanks to Tricia Ready, his assistant, for—omigod—writing me rap songs about Wren and Charlie. You are so adorable. Thanks to everyone at Abrams for saying to me, "Yes, you are family; yes, you matter; yes, we like your books," and especially to Morgan Dubin, Laura Mihalick, Jeff Yamaguchi, Chris Blank, Jen Graham, Erica Finkel, Elisa Garcia, Mary Wowk, Alison Gervais, Chad Beckerman, Tamar Brazis, Maria Middleton, Jason Wells, and Michael Jacobs.

Thanks to my editor, Susan Van Metre, who never stops caring, never stops pushing, never stops—ahem—passing the manuscript back to me and saying, in her sweet and innocent-sounding way, "Well, but I wonder if you could [fill in the blank, and by tomorrow, please, and if it involves rewriting the whole frickin' thing, then so be it!]." ☺ My books would be nothing without Susan. I, as a writer, would be nothing without Susan.

Thanks to Al Myracle-Martin and Alei Throckmorton for reminding me, every day, how magical first love is . . .

. . . and thanks to Randy Bartels for showing me, every day, that the magic lives on.

ABOUT THE AUTHOR

Lauren Myracle is the author of the *New York Times*–bestselling Internet Girls series (*ttyl*, *ttfn*, and *l8r, g8r*), *Shine*, *Rhymes with Witches*, *Bliss*, and the Flower Power series, among many other books for teens and young people. She lives with her family in Fort Collins, Colorado. Visit her online at laurenmyracle.com.